I0638703

This is a work of fiction. The names, characters, places, and incidents within are the products of the author's imagination or are used fictitiously, and any resemblance to actual persons, living or dead, business establishments, events, or location is entirely coincidental. The publisher does not have any control over and does not assume any responsibility for author or third-party websites or their content.

Solaris Seethes
Copyright © 2014 Janet McNulty
Cover Copyright © 2024 Janet McNulty

All rights reserved.
No part of this book may be reproduced, scanned, or distributed in any printed or electronic form without permission. Please do not participate in or encourage piracy of copyrighted materials in violation of the author's rights. Purchase only authorized editions.

ISBN-13: 978-1941488003 (MMP Publishing)
ISBN-10: 1941488005

Library of Congress Control Number: 2014921242

Printed in the United States of America

If you purchase this book without a cover, you should be aware that this book is stolen property. It was reported as "unsold and destroyed" to the publisher, and neither the author nor the publisher has received any payment for this "stripped book".

As an avid reader, I have always loved adventure stories. The idea for Solaris came to me some time ago and I hope all of you enjoy this first part of the series. You are the ones I wrote it for.

Contents

Solaris Saga book 1

Janet McNulty

Prologue

Marlow warned this day would come. The day when Lanyr, my home, would cease to exist, destroyed by a man who thought only of the power he could acquire. Before he died, Marlow made me promise to look after his granddaughter, Rynah—to guide her.

"She is the key," he said, "the key to stopping a most dangerous man."

My name is Solaris. I am a ship, a vessel some consider archaic, but I have a secret—a purpose.

Chapter 1
A Planet Destroyed

Rynah straightened her charcoal gray, form-fitting uniform as she hurried down the asphalt walkway to the tall, glass doors leading to the geo-lab. Her tailored, steel-toed boots (that laced up the sides) clicked on the pavement with each purposeful step. The sun's invigorating rays barely registered in Rynah's mind; too consumed with humming merrily to herself, she didn't even notice when she had passed through the revolving door, her automatic movements from thousands of trips through it having dictated her actions. Absentmindedly, Rynah twirled the small (and loose) silver band on her ring finger, the one her new fiancé, Klanor, had given her that morning.

"Rynah," greeted the lady at the front desk as she walked in. "You seem rather jovial this morning."

Rynah blushed, her heliotrope cheeks turning a nice shade of pink. She couldn't help but smile after receiving the engagement ring. She held up her hand.

"Oh, so he proposed!"

"This morning."

"Well, if you ask me, it's about time."

Rynah grinned as she took the holopad and signed in for her shift. "Anything new?"

"Nope. Quiet as usual."

"Rynah!"

Rynah whirled around. General Delmar, her former commander when she had been part of the Lanyran fleet, stood behind her. "General, I didn't expect to see you here."

"I had a meeting with Doctor Sonorus. So this is where you work these days?"

"It's much quieter."

"Too bad. You were my best pilot. I don't know why you left the fleet."

"You know why," said Rynah as thoughts about her grandfather and the trial that ruined his (and her family's) reputation filled her mind.

"Yes, I suppose I do." He spotted the ring on her finger. "When…"

"This morning." Rynah blushed again.

"Well, he's lucky to have you." General Delmar tipped his hat and passed through the glass doors and into the sunlight.

"He seems nice."

"He is my former commanding officer," replied Rynah. "I'll see you later."

Rynah hurried away to the back elevators in the rear of the building (which only the security officers used) and placed her palm on the holopad, allowing the green light to scan it. It dinged as the doors opened and she stepped inside. Automatically, she pushed the button that instructed the elevator to go to the underground bunker and the lab itself. She tapped her foot impatiently as she waited for the elevator to reach its destination; her fingers fiddled with the amber ring that hung from a silver chain around her neck before shoving it under her shirt.

Glancing into the reflective, metal interior, Rynah realized that she had forgotten to put her hair up in compliance with uniform regulations. She shoved her hand into her pocket and found a clip, which she had put in there in her haste to leave for work. She scooped up the silky strands of her dark emerald hair and twisted them into a bun before securing it with the clip.

The elevator stopped and the doors slid open. "You're late," said a rough voice as Rynah stepped out into the geo-lab.

"Sorry, sir," Rynah replied in a businesslike manner.

Her commanding officer snatched her hand, noting the ring that had not been there the day before. "I'll let you slide this time, but don't make a habit of it."

"Yes, commander." Rynah hurried away to her station on the other side of the lab directly opposite the main door.

"All right," said the commander to everyone within the lab. "Get ready to initiate the systems check." Technicians punched sequences into their holomonitors, preparing for the one time a year when the computers within the geothermic lab had its systems purged of unnecessary data, though it meant shutting down all major systems. "On my mark. One... two... mark."

The constant hum that filled the lab dwindled as the main computer shut off.

"System purge in progress," said one technician. "Estimated time until completion is 15 minutes."

"Understood," said the commander.

The door to the lab thundered as it shook violently, rattling and vibrating against the concrete brick wall. Stunned, Rynah spun around, not believing what she heard. Another tremendous boom echoed through the room as something slammed into the door from the other side. Bits of dust and rock fell from above with each barrage of the invaders. As the realization that those on the other side posed a threat, lab technicians scurried about, desperate to flee the onslaught.

Another bang on the metal door echoed throughout the underground chamber, etching dimples into it. One frightened lab technician shuddered, sending papers flying in every direction.

"Brace the door!" yelled Rynah, her security uniform giving credence to her orders.

Other security officers raced to the protruding steel door, placing magnetic brackets on it in an effort to seal it and stop the invaders from breaking in. It did little to slow them.

"How are they breaking through?" Rynah asked herself.

"Rynah!"

She whirled around to face her commanding officer as he pointed to the vents in the ceiling with a red laser beam poking through. *Damn!* Rynah snatched her side pistol and fired two laser pulses at it. The vent popped open as a man fell through it and onto the cold floor by her feet. She flipped the corpse over with the toe of her boot; she didn't recognize him, but he bore the insignia of the Lunyra Movement. Perturbed, she pondered why he was there. Violence was not in their manifesto.

Another earsplitting thud against the door ripped her back to the present moment. She looked at the door to the lab. A gigantic dent emerged from it as the door weakened. *It will never hold.* "Commander! We need to get these people out of here!"

Her commanding officer nodded, barking orders at passing officers and motioning for them to follow him. Rynah did as well.

"Rynah, your key," said her commanding officer.

She pulled a key from her pocket; it matched the one her commander had as well. Following suit, she placed her key in the hole, waiting for orders.

"On three. One, two… three!"

In synchronized movement, they turned the keys. A brick popped out of the wall, revealing a holographic screen with coordinates. Rynah typed in numbers and algorithms. A panel slid open, revealing a hidden tunnel as lights flickered on in the stainless steel interior.

"Get these people out of here!" ordered her commander.

"I'm not leaving you all here!" protested Rynah.

"Go! That's an order!" He ran to the door with a troop of security officers.

Rynah watched him go, torn between obeying orders and fighting alongside her fellow officers. "Come on!" she barked at the lab technicians. Two hurried into the tunnel, fear etched on their faces. She waved more through as they carried what they could, their lab coats flailing behind them.

Another bit of thunder roared through the underground lab as the door was struck again. One of the hinges popped off, sailing to the far side of the room and landed with a distinct clink. The invaders slammed into it again, firing repeated rounds from their pulse cannon at it. The booms ricocheted off the walls.

Rynah turned just in time to see the steel door burst into a thousand tiny pieces. She ducked, shielding her face from the explosion. Eerie silence followed.

"In!" yelled Rynah to two more lab technicians. She turned back to the main door; waves of laser fire pelted her comrades who had taken defensive positions by the door. Screams of death filled the area as officers dropped before the onslaught. A laser blast struck the wall near Rynah's head, barely missing her, but forming a blackened scorch mark. She ducked, twisted around, snatched her pistol, and fired at the man who had tried to kill her.

She scanned the madness before her until her eyes fell upon the opaque, orange crystal seated on its pedestal. *How could I be so stupid?* In all the commotion, she had forgotten to grab it.

Under normal circumstances, the crystal was never to be moved, but considering thieves had broken into the lab, Rynah figured that rule could be broken. She hoped to protect the crystal until a time when it could be placed back where it belonged.

Rynah left the tunnel opening, darting for the metal, spiral steps that led to the crystal. Fire rained down upon her, pelting the concrete floor with each step she took. Chunks of concrete dropped from the ceiling, crashing to the ground behind her; Rynah flung herself to the floor to avoid being struck by the shards of metal showering all within the lab. Assessing the situation, she crouched on the ground—more of the invaders swarmed through the smoldering hole in the lab that had once been a protective barrier—when she remembered the crystal. Rynah shot to her feet. She jumped on the stairs (ignoring the swaying motion as some of the screws and bolts had come loose) and charged up them, taking two steps at a time.

Laser fire whizzed past her. The slow creak of a dangling light alerted her to immediate danger. Rynah ducked just in time to avoid the swinging light, which had lost one of its cables and careened for her. She spotted an invader. Pulling the knife from her boot—something she had always carried when laser pistols were insufficient—Rynah slashed the other cable that still held the light; it stopped in midair before plummeting to the ground, crushing the invader that had aimed his weapon at her. Smiling to herself, Rynah continued up the staircase.

She had just reached the crystal when the explosion from a pulse cannon rocked the entire lab, sending bodies flying; one smashed into her, pinning her to the metal floor. Stunned, Rynah watched as men rushed into the lab, killing any security officer they found. Her senses returning, she shoved the dead weight off, only to discover that it was her commander.

"Commander," she whispered, feeling guilty for being so rough.

Her commander's eyes fluttered open, focusing on her. "I thought I told you to leave," he coughed as blood trickled out of his mouth. His head rolled to the side and his eyes closed for the last time.

Infuriated, Rynah raised her pistol and shot one of the invaders in the chest. She jumped to her feet and dove for the crystal. Her fingers almost touched it when a steel grip seized her wrist and yanked her back.

"I can't allow you to do that," said a voice she recognized.

"Klanor," breathed a surprised Rynah as she looked at the man in charge of this entire invasion. "What…"

"I told you not to come in today," Klanor said as he released her.

Rynah couldn't believe it. The man she vowed to marry, the man who professed love to her only hours before, now stood before her with a demeanor she had never seen, or thought possible with him. It was as though he had locked all of his emotions away.

"Why?"

"You're so gullible, Rynah," said Klanor. "Why not?"

"But you and I—"

"A means to an end."

Rage boiled within Rynah at Klanor's betrayal. She glared at him, watching his every move as he snatched the crystal from its pedestal. For a few moments, Klanor held it in the light, admiring its beauty and power.

"You take that and you condemn this planet—our people—to death," said Rynah. As though to add credence to her words, the ground jerked.

Klanor just smiled malevolently at her. "I sincerely hope so."

The ground split open beneath their feet as steam and spurts of molten rock spewed forth. Panicking, some of Klanor's men ran. Rynah lunged for Klanor. He blocked her attack, sending her flying. Snatching a bit of fallen rubble, Rynah charged him again, catching him in the forehead; blood poured from the wound. Infuriated, Klanor punched Rynah, crystal in hand. He grabbed her arm, wrenching it behind her back and positioning her ear near his mouth.

"You thought I actually loved you," he whispered. "The crystal is mine, and soon, the others will be as well."

With fluid movement, Klanor released his grip on Rynah, sending her tumbling down the stairs. Dazed, Rynah lifted her head and stared straight into Klanor's black eyes. He ripped out his laser pistol, aiming it directly at her. They glared at one another as Klanor's finger strained against the trigger, shaking as he inwardly debated killing her, turmoil reeling within him. At that moment, his animus face showed a flicker of sorrow.

The ground quaked, knocking Klanor off his feet. Some who had fallen over rolled into the cracks that had formed; their screams indicating a painful death. Jagged cracks shot up the concrete walls, stretching to the ceiling as it split and fell apart. More rubble crashed around her. Knowing she would never get the crystal back, Rynah gripped the metal bar of the railing and leapt over it, landing on the unstable ground below. She pitched forward and somersaulted when the ground jerked again. Desperate, Rynah raced for the still open tunnel.

"Get her!" shouted Klanor, charging down the steps. The toe of his boot touched a slender, shiny object, inadvertently nudging it; its clinking caught his attention: Rynah's ring. It had slipped off her finger in her haste to escape. With a delicacy his beefy fingers would otherwise portray, Klanor picked it up, twirling it before ramming it into his pocket.

One of his men lunged for Rynah. She dodged, grabbing his arm and flinging him to one of the cracks where black, fluidic rock poured forth. She stretched her legs, running as fast as she could. A concrete block crashed into the ground in front of her. Rynah jumped over it. The top of the doorframe to the tunnel began to crumble. Putting all of her effort into it, Rynah flew over the ground and dove through the opening before it caved in.

"Forget her!" Klanor yelled as the ground quaked again. "Time to move out!"

On the other side of the rubble, Rynah paused, catching her breath as she glanced back at Klanor, encumbered by sheets of holographic paper falling from the split in the ceiling amidst the swirls of smoke, and the bodies of those she had left behind. Emotions reeled within her at the loss of her friends and the betrayal of the man she loved. Vowing revenge, she straightened and raced down the tunnel. The entire area shook and jerked, making her efforts to flee difficult. With each step, she had to land differently so as not to lose her balance. A piece of the wall fell before her. Rynah swerved around it and continued on. Her boots clopped against the stone floor as she raced for the exit, hoping to escape the rage her planet flung at her.

Light spilled from up ahead. Hoping that she had reached the exit, Rynah picked up her pace. Chaos trailed behind her as she raced against the savagery of her planet for the opening at the other end, which was her only salvation. Sparks flew from the lights that blew out and crashed. Rynah reached the end of the tunnel just as a crack burst open behind her. She jumped over the steps, taking them three at a time, until she burst through and into the open sunlight.

Rynah stopped. The horror that lay before her took her breath away. *How has it come to this?* Smoke rose in swirls from the ground as lava shot forth, covering what used to be fertile grassland. Fire swept over the trees and foliage that had once brought life to her world. Rynah looked straight ahead. The shipyard lay not far away. She needed transportation.

Running to the transport area, Rynah scanned the line of hover crafts for one she could easily steal. People darted about the compound, fearful of being killed. One man stopped in front of Rynah, noting her uniform, and looked at her with pleading eyes, asking what he should do. "Make your way to the shipyard and get on the nearest transport," she told him.

Rynah pushed past him and continued on to the transport area, where she found an open top hover vehicle. She leapt into it, pulling off the paneling under the gear shift, and hot-wired it—a skill she had acquired in her youth—thus turning on the engine. "Who needs keys?" she whispered to herself.

Rynah put the craft in forward and sped off. Wind ripped through her long locks—she had lost her hair clip during the firefight, as they never hold when one is darting about in an effort to avoid death—as she steered her way to the nearest shipyard. A hover vehicle rushed past her. The driver was just as desperate as her to escape the carnage. The ground split open in front of her, spewing molten lava and creating a deadly geyser that melted any who strayed too near. Rynah pulled back on the accelerator and twisted the joystick so the craft banked to the right, going around the inferno. She straightened the hover vehicle and punched the accelerator once more.

A group of people on the side of the lane waved at her, calling for help. For a brief moment, Rynah considered leaving them, but the small voice in the back of her mind reminded her that she was still a security officer. Rynah steered the craft towards them. Grateful, the small group of five gathered around her with their bundles.

"Leave it!" yelled Rynah, tossing one of the bags over the side and onto the black dirt. "Just get in!"

The frightened people leapt into the vehicle too afraid to argue. Cursing about the time lost, Rynah slammed the hover craft into full speed and sped down the lane towards the shipyard. Her heart sank as she watched several spacecraft take off. Knowing she only had minutes before the last ship left them for dead, Rynah pushed the hover craft to the point of breaking; its violent jerks indicated it had reached its top speed. The child in the group she had picked up wailed. Rynah ignored his screams; there wasn't time.

They entered the shipyard. Suddenly, the ground beneath them burst open with a shower of steam. The force of the impact knocked the hover vehicle off balance until it slammed into the dirt. Once the spinning had stopped, Rynah crawled out.

"Is everyone all right?"

A few nods answered her question.

"This way! Quickly!" Rynah helped the others up and pushed them towards the nearest transport ship. The vibrating ground beneath their feet made each step they took wobbly. They reached the stairs leading to the open door. Rynah turned around, pushing the group of five ahead of her. A man stood in the open hatch of the ship, waving them onward.

"Hurry!"

The child and its mother went first, followed by the two men and elderly woman. Cracks and splinters appeared on the steps as they bent and curved unnaturally. Rynah hoped they would hold a bit longer. Once the last of the group had entered the ship, she paused and looked around for any stragglers—a fateful decision. A tremendous quake shook the earth, sending Rynah flying over the railing and tumbling to the ground below. Pain rocked her body as she slammed into the black dirt with trails of smoke enveloping her.

Dazed, she looked up. The hatch had been sealed as the man had passed her off as dead. A low rumble filled the area as the engines of the ship sprang to life and carried its load to the open atmosphere above.

Cursing her luck, Rynah glanced around, as all of the transport ships lifted off in an attempt to carry their passengers to safety, leaving her behind. Frantic, she searched for a lone ship that she could board. Nothing. A plume of smoke and steam burst from the ground as a new split suddenly appeared, forcing Rynah to jump back and warning her that the lava geysers neared. Time ran short. Rynah jumped to her feet and ran hysterically towards a transport ship that slowly ascended into the air.

"Hey!" she yelled, waving her arms, "I'm here! HEY!"

She stopped. It was useless. No one would hear her, much less bother stopping for her. A lone building lay ahead. The sight of it sent a memory slamming into her—the way asteroids crash into the earth—as that building had once belonged to her grandfather; she remembered he had stored a ship there. Willing to gamble that no one had moved it, and desperate to escape, Rynah raced for the hangar, its faded and stripped paint a welcomed sight, stretching her long legs as far as she could and hoping that she made it in time.

A lava bomb crashed into the once well-tended lawn, flinging bits of rock and dirt at her. Shielding her face, Rynah continued in her race against her planet's clock. Drops of water pelted her skin—one of the underground pipes had burst and poked out of the ground—and drenched her.

She burst through the door to the hangar, her lungs heaving, and stared at the archaic ship, whose systems had been deemed outmoded. But the ship was not entirely unpleasant to look at, as its copper paint still glittered—as though it had been freshly painted—and beckoned her to come forth. The ship's stubby wings, a sleek design from 50 years ago, seemed ready to stretch and fly. In fact, it was, for this ship was no ordinary ship; this ship had a name painted in dark gold lettering on its rear near the hatch: Solaris.

Rynah paid little attention to the aesthetic value of the craft, her only concern being if it would fly. She ran up the ramp—though she could have sworn it wasn't open a second ago—and into the belly of the ship. Racking her brains to remember the layout from the time her grandfather had brought her there as a child, she charged down the corridors—the ship was much larger on the inside—to what she believed was the flight deck. Ray beams shot out of the walls, stopping her.

"DNA scan in progress. DNA match. Welcome, Rynah," said a feminine, and remarkably human-like, voice.

The white beams dissipated. Rynah didn't remember the ship having a female voice, or any voice for that matter. She shook her head. *Now isn't the time.* Her steel-toed boots clomped on the metal grate that formed the floor as she raced through the winding—yet what seemed surprisingly straight, corridors—going upward until she reached a set of steps—just above them and to the side was another set leading to the weapons array—which she scaled in one leap.

Rynah surveyed the area. She had found the command center, though it was unlike any she had seen before, with the flight console (and not even a trace of dust) directly ahead and two polished chairs next to it, each possessing a helmet that telepathically linked one with the ship, all of which looked out a 20-by-25-foot (and remarkably clean) window. Mesmerized by the practically brand new state of the ship, Rynah forgot about her plight, taking the time to stroke the smooth, marbled console as she eased into the soft, cushiony seat. She had half-expected to find coffee stains from when pilots neglectfully spilled their cups, or smeared mayonnaise from a late-night meal that someone accidentally dropped, or nicks and scuffs from normal wear and tear, but no stains, smears, nicks, or scuffs were to be found. Only her reflection from the glossy surface stared back at her.

A furious grumble resonated beneath her, reminding her of the danger she remained in.

"The planet appears to be in peril," said the same feminine voice. "What are your orders?"

Rynah rammed the helmet onto her head. Her mind was filled with the ship's systems, charts, status reports, how full the fuel tanks were, and anything else the ship's sensors recorded.

Depart, she thought.

What about launch procedures? asked the ship, Solaris, using the same telepathic link.

Ignore them.

Solaris obeyed. As the ground quaked one last time, the ship plowed through the ceiling of the hangar, leaving a hole that would anger the groundskeeper under normal circumstances, and charged into the smoke filled sky, a sky that had once been a light lavender in color. Rynah listened to the engines as she glanced down at the devastation below. Overwhelming sadness filled her. Her planet gone. So many people dead. And why? Because Klanor wanted the crystal. But why did he want it?

The purple atmosphere gave way to the inky darkness of space as the ship exited the upper stratosphere. There was no sign of the other ships.

Destination?

To the Chestur Nebula. Unable to think of anywhere else to go, Rynah decided she could hide there until she figured out what to do next.

Chapter 2
A PROPHECY

A harsh bleeping from her alarm yanked Rynah from a deep slumber. Groggily, she rolled over and shut it off. Rynah rubbed the sand from her eyes as she peered out the window into the gas cloud beyond, speckled by small dots of gold and blue and veiled by the rainbow of colors from the nebula she hid in, but it still felt barren to her, much like her heart.

Space; so cold and dark. She missed the purple sunrises of her home planet, the soft glow of gold on the edges of the mountain peaks, the warm breeze that always flowed through her tresses, and the burnt orange clouds that she always managed to detect shapes in, one of her favorite pastimes. All of it gone. Memories flooded her mind, such as afternoon walks (and most of them with Klanor when her heart had been full of love and possibilities) on the silky, emerald grass of her home, the field near her apartment complex that teamed with wildlife (rabbits, squirrels, and bagoons—a cross between a badger and a raccoon), the melodic churning of the Wesyr Brooke, and her most favorite place of all, Sesir Cliff, a precipice in the wilds of

Lanyr that Rynah had explored on numerous occasions with her grandfather. She still visited it, even after the argument that severed their bond, a constant regret. Now nothing remained but a burnt and scorched planet well on its way to becoming a barren wasteland.

Rynah sat up, allowing her emerald hair to flow over her lavender-colored (a very light shade at that) skin; specks of gold accentuated her waves of dark emerald tresses, forming highlights that even the dim lighting failed to hide. She stood before the mirror.

"Water," she said.

Cool water poured from the faucet, obeying her command. Rynah cupped her long-fingered hands underneath it before splashing refreshing liquid on her face, washing away any remnants of sleep. A small glint from the bronze band (a simple piece, plain, save for the small circles carved along the edges) she wore on her wrist caught her eye. She stroked the smooth surface with her slender fingers, remembering the day Marlow had given it to her. "Keep it with you, always," he had told her. She never knew why, and probably never would, but Rynah never took it off; the bracelet had become a constant adornment on her arm, but now it was her only constant in life.

Marlow's amber ring dangled from her neck as she leaned over the nickel plated sink. Like she had done with the bracelet, Rynah caressed the ring, admiring the smoothness and grandeur of the amber. Her grandfather had willed it to her upon his death. Rynah never understood why. The ring was insignificant, since amber was common on Lanyr and lay in almost every bit of jewelry (rings, necklaces, bracelets, and earrings) that for Marlow to give it to her seemed a pitiful apology.

Rynah remembered the last time they had spoken to one another, the day of the argument. Months had passed since the trial and he had been committed to the mental institution to serve his sentence. She had stopped by to tell him of her mother's passing; her father had died years before.

"Well," she had said when Marlow remained silent after she had delivered the news.

"What do you want me to say?"

"That you're sorry."

"I can't," Marlow had said.

"You can't, or you won't?" Rynah leaned closer, stretching across the sleek, transparent, aluminum table.

"Where is my ring?" Marlow had asked.

Rynah had been aghast. Of all the times to think of it, all he wanted was his amber ring, which had been confiscated upon his committal to the institution and was returned to him upon his release. "Your ring? Is that all you can think about? Your stupid ring?"

"It is most important."

"Your daughter, my mother, is dead and all you care about is that ring! Do you not know why you are here? For years, you locked yourself in your study, poring over those dusty books, and we ignored it because we thought that every man needed a hobby—and how could reading books be dangerous? But then you had to try and steal the crystal from the geo-lab."

"I did it for you, for all of you."

"You're insane! Do you know what we have had to go through since that day? The sneers, the whispers, the constant taunts?"

"Is that why you work at the lab now?"

"You killed my mother. You! And your obsession. I'm ashamed to even know you."

Marlow slapped her, the first, and only, instance when he did.

"I'm done with you," Rynah hissed.

As she rose to leave, Marlow reached over and snatched her arm, his grip unusually strong for one his age. "You must find that ring and keep a close watch on the crystal in the lab, but most importantly, keep the ring safe. Only it can control them!"

Their conversation had ended with the orderlies pulling them apart. They dragged Marlow back to his room, kicking and screaming at her to get his ring and protect it. As his next of kin, Rynah could have claimed Marlow's effects from the front office, which would have included his amber ring, but she chose not to. Angered, and convinced that he had lost his mind, she left the building and never spoke to her grandfather again.

Rynah pulled herself away from her painful memories and back to the present. Dwelling on the past served little purpose. She held the amber ring in front of her face, allowing it to shine in the fluorescent light. When Marlow died, and the executor of his will handed her the ring, Rynah unclasped the necklace she had worn, removed the conical-shaped pendant, replacing it with the ring, and placed it around her neck, where it stayed. Within that ring was her regret at never having mended the relationship with her grandfather. If this bit of jewelry was important to him, the least she could do was abide by his last wish and keep it safe.

What am I to do now? she asked herself.

Five days she had hidden in the gas cloud and still did not know what she should do. Having only just escaped the destruction of her planet, Rynah jumped on the nearest ship— luckily it had been her grandfather's—and flew away at hyperspeed into the darkest reaches of space where Klanor's minions couldn't find her.

"Good morning, Rynah," said a voice over the intercom.

"Morning, Solaris," said Rynah as she returned the ship's greeting.

Solaris was not just the name of the ship, but the ship itself, an artificial intelligence that ran the ship's functions and interacted freely with the crew, or, as it happened, Rynah. Having Solaris meant that Rynah did not need anyone aboard with her. She didn't even have to pilot the vessel if she didn't want to. She never knew why her grandfather had put an artificial intelligence on the ship, remembering when he bought the rusted, grungy, bucket of bolts from an auction when it had been decommissioned as a military vessel. Oh, the hours Marlow spent repairing it, or her, now, since she most definitely had a name, and a personality to match. Rynah felt a mixture of gladness and annoyance. Out here, Solaris was her only companion.

"Did you sleep well?" asked Solaris.

Rynah chuckled to herself as she listened to the feminine voice, realizing why her grandfather had made it that way. *Men*, she thought. "Yes."

"Your voice betrays you," said Solaris. "You dreamt of the destruction again."

How did Solaris always know? "Perhaps," said Rynah, putting the towel back on the rack. "I cannot get it out of my mind."

"What do you plan to do now?"

Rynah sighed. She hadn't thought that far. She thought of Klanor, remembering every detail of his face as he marched into the Geothermic Center, or geo-lab, as she called it, and stole the crystal. The moment he removed it from its place, the planet shook, causing immense turmoil. Fire spewed from the ground, engulfing everything in its path.

"I want that bastard to pay."

"Klanor?"

"Yes," Rynah whirled around, even though there was no way to face Solaris since she was a ship. "He took everything! Everyone I ever knew, everyone I ever cared about! Dead!"

"Perhaps you should choose another course of action."

Rynah didn't listen. Her mind focused on Klanor and his betrayal, all after proposing to her that morning. Anger seethed within her. A thought struck her. She remembered Klanor speaking about a place he always liked to visit, a place at the heart of the Twelve Sectors, one that many visited because of its rich blues and unique wildlife (it was home to the Wingabur, a rare species that was somewhere between a bear and a pigeon) and flowing rivers of water the color of sunset orange. Perhaps (as thoughts of how she would punish him, torture him, percolated through her mind) she would find him there.

"Solaris, set a course for the Amyran System."

"Negative."

Rynah's eyebrows arched. "What do you mean negative?"

"As in, not possible."

"I wish to go to the Amyran System," repeated Rynah, her voice growing tight.

"We are not going."

"Why not?"

"I refuse to take us there."

"Listen here, you stupid computer—"

Steam burst from the vents as the door to her room slammed shut, the lock clicking into place. "Don't you dare talk to me like that, you ungrateful rugrat. Marlow, your grandfather, created me while you were still playing with toys. Now I want you to apologize."

"But he did not purchase this ship until—"

"I existed before this vessel."

"I'm not..." clicks and rattles circled Rynah, indicating that she was at Solaris' mercy "... sorry."

"What was that?" demanded Solaris.

"I'm sorry," said Rynah in a more apologetic tone.

Silence.

"What do you think we should do?"

"Locate the crystals."

"The what?"

"The crystals."

"They are a myth."

"And yet you spent the last two years guarding one," said Solaris.

Rynah rubbed her temples. She could not believe that she had spent the last several minutes arguing with a computer that her grandfather had built years before, much less that the same computer had an attitude. Knowing that she would never be allowed to leave the room unless she agreed with Solaris, Rynah relented.

"What must I do?"

"Your planet's crystal was one among six," said Solaris.

"What do you mean?"

"While you slept, I did some checking in my archives," said Solaris. "There were six crystals in all. Each given to a planet to protect them."

"I know that much," said Rynah, growing impatient.

"But what you do not know is that the crystals can be put together, like a puzzle, to create one of the deadliest weapons the universe has ever known."

"What kind of weapon?"

"One that can be used to create as well as destroy. According to my calculations, Klanor plans to use the crystals to destroy entire solar systems and create his own empire. It is the same as the ancient prophecy."

"And how would he do that?"

"The power of the crystals can be wielded when they are close together, I suspect, but Marlow discovered that a certain device exists which utilizes the crystals and their energy in a more controlled manner."

"Energy?"

"It can be destructive. To locate the crystals and this device, we must rely on the prophecy within the ancient texts."

"You don't know where it is?"

Rynah's sarcasm did not go unnoticed as Solaris huffed, the way that only a ship with personality can.

"Sorry. I just assumed—"

"You assume much," said Solaris, "and to your own detriment. Instead of making false assumptions, you might try listening."

"But my grandfather—"

"Marlow may have been well-versed in the lore of the crystals, and though he knew more than most, he did not know everything. Unfortunately, he died before he could..." Solaris cut herself off.

"Could what?" Rynah's curiosity had been piqued. Did her grandfather share secrets with a machine that he felt could not be entrusted to another of flesh and blood? "Solaris, did my—"

"If you wish to have answers to your questions, you'll have to study the prophecy."

"Don't talk to me of prophecy," snapped Rynah. "Klanor is a despicable man who deserves to be punished for his crimes and I intend to see that he is! Prophecy be damned!"

"Your grandfather did not share your sentiments," reminded Solaris.

Rynah paused. She remembered her grandfather and the stories he had told her. His favorite was an ancient myth about six crystals. She always thought it referred to how her planet had gotten their crystal in the first place, but her grandfather was not so certain. He always reminded her that myths told one as much about the past as they did about the present and future.

"Solaris," said Rynah, "what were the lines of that prophecy in the myth of the six crystals?"

Solaris recited the lines:

> Six crystals in evil's grasp:
> one lone exile with fury's wrath.
> Four you need from thirteen:
> four heroes of faith and belief.
>
> The warrior of nobility,
> descended from the line of kings.
> Strength and prowess he commands
> from his frozen homeland.
>
> A philosopher whose wisdom all need;
> knowledge and learning are his deeds.
> A scholar of myth and history
> will guide you on this journey.

The inventor with guided skills,
machines and mechanics fulfill
his days; all of which shall prove
most useful in the darkest grooves.

And the one who loves when all is lost;
do not let timidity
blind you and deceive,
for he shall bear the highest cost.

Blood ties that run deep,
Blood shared from conflict reaped.
Traitors they were called.
Heroes they are all.

"It's so vague," said Rynah, remembering why she always hated myths. "'Four from thirteen.' What does that mean?"

"As you well know, there are 13 sectors in the known universe," said Solaris.

"There are only 12," said Rynah.

"There are 13. But your people only dealt with 12, as you have always thought the 13th too primitive. It is called the Terra Sector."

"The Terra Sector," breathed Rynah. "Bring it up on the screen, please."

A screen in Rynah's room flashed to life as images swept across it and two giant planets soared by. One had a series of rings, reminding Rynah of a rainbow, and the other had a thinner, almost transparent ring, but bore a giant red spot amidst striations of white and pinkish-red. She almost missed the small, red, uninteresting planet that only spent seconds in her room. The images stopped when a picture of a mostly blue planet (with white swirls that she guessed were clouds and brown jagged shapes that seemed to have a bit of uniformity to them) filled it. Rynah remembered the stories about how her people had wandered the universe once before settling in the Lanyran Sector. Tales told of how they had chanced upon a blue planet—uninteresting at best and overrun by savage beasts—and used it as a place to dispose of their garbage, conduct repairs, or what some might call, a pit stop.

"They are much more advanced than when your people were last there several millennia ago," said Solaris. "According to my long range sensors, they have satellite communications, have gone to their moon, and have a proposed space launch to visit their neighboring planets."

"So they have achieved space travel."

"To a degree, yes."

Rynah studied the image on the screen. "Impossible."

"Not really," said Solaris. "The people there are quite intelligent and adapt easily to their changing environment. And there is one other thing."

"What?"

"Their planet has no crystal."

"Then how do they control the magnetic fields and prevent their sun from destroying them?" asked Rynah.

"Their planet has its own magnetic field generated by its molten core, which works in conjunction with their ozone layer, thus preventing solar flares from burning them alive. It happens naturally."

"That last verse you read," said Rynah, "'Blood ties that run deep.' What does it mean?"

"I do not know," replied Solaris. "Your grandfather had a theory, but he never told me what it was. All he said was that our two worlds were connected in ways far beyond our knowledge."

Rynah groaned. "What does that mean?"

"Knowing Marlow, something important."

"Solaris, do you think the prophecy could be true?"

"Your grandfather did, and if you want to stop Klanor, you best hope that it is."

Rynah studied the earth and its shimmering blue color with the white clouds moving past. *Could it all be true?* Knowing she had little choice if she wanted to bring Klanor to justice, Rynah decided to risk it.

"Five against Klanor are better odds than our current number," said Solaris, urging Rynah to make up her mind.

"Set a course for the Terra Sector," said Rynah, knowing that this was what Solaris wanted in the first place. "Search through their history to find any who match the prophecy."

"Course set," said Solaris.

Rynah sighed.

"And, Rynah," said Solaris, "do not even think about shutting me off and pursuing Klanor alone. Your grandfather put measures in place to prevent such an action."

"Of course he did," muttered Rynah, with distaste. "So I am your prisoner."

"No, but I will not let you go off half-cocked on a quest to get yourself killed."

"Fine, I guess we'll do this your way." Rynah turned back to the holoscreen. "I guess you were right, grandfather," she said as she flicked off the screen.

She went to the medical bay to find something for her headache, the lights turning on the moment she stepped inside. Rynah searched through the cabinets, with not a smudge on the transparent doors, finding one filled with colorful vials: some clear, some red, some blue, and some with a yellow sludge (which she hoped to never have occasion to find out what its contents were), particularly a purple one, the only one of its kind. Curious, Rynah picked it up and inspected it, turning it in her nimble fingers.

"Solaris, what is this?"

"Those tubes all have nanobots and each performs a certain function," replied Solaris.

"But what is in this vial?"

"Those are the experimental nanobots," said Solaris. "Before he died, your grandfather had been experimenting with a series of nanotechnology that, according to him, could save lives. It has never been tested."

Rynah placed the purple vial back on the shelf with the other bottles of nanobots. "Is everything in this medical bay decades old?"

"Many of the medicines here have a lifelong shelf life," replied Solaris, "and nanobots have an infinite lifespan as long as they remain in those vials. After being administered, they become part of the circulatory system and will eventually decay, passing through the urine. I assure you that the items in this area can be used."

"Good," said Rynah. "Where's the aspirin?"

"Second shelf on your right."

Rynah reached for it and popped a couple of pills in her mouth.

"I have calculated the time variance for bringing our guests aboard," said Solaris. "They all live in different periods of the planet's history. But I can bring them here using a collapsing wormhole."

"How are you able to do that?" asked Rynah.

"You will have to be patient with them, as they will not fully understand where they are," continued Solaris, ignoring Rynah's question.

"Will you answer me?"

"I'm sorry, but you did not specify a question."

Rynah groaned, having the distinct impression that Solaris purposefully evaded her question. "Will you be able to send them back?"

"Yes," said Solaris, "but that will require a new set of calculations, allowing for variances in space and time, and can only be done once."

"How long before you are ready to transport them?"

"I can do it within the hour."

"Very well."

Rynah left the medical bay for the mess hall. Her grumbling stomach reminded her that she had not eaten for at least 20 hours. Along the way, she passed a framed portrait of her grandfather. She always recognized the dimpled chin with a brown freckle in its center, the crooked nose, from a time when someone punched him over a dispute of spilt beer, and the twinkling eyes that looked as though they belonged to a younger man and not the aged face of which they were a part. But it was his smile that intrigued her most of all, the inward smile of one who knew a secret that he would never reveal.

"Apparently, you know something that I do not," she whispered to the portrait.

Chapter 3
SOLON

The salty sea air, with a hint of autumn's chill, ruffled Solon's chocolate-colored hair as he raced across the paving stones—his sandaled feet clomping against them much like a trotting horse—past laurel trees, and—pomegranates! Solon changed direction, heading straight for the only pomegranate tree in the atrium and its freshly ripened fruit. Dropping the scrolls that filled his arms, he plucked a firm one from its branch, licking his lips while thinking of the delicious treasure deep inside the fruit's red barrier, which also happened to be his favorite.

A small sparrow jostled the pomegranates, jerking Solon back to the present, and the fact that he was late. Scrambling, he scooped the fallen scrolls (and the pomegranate) into his arms, his scrawny frame barely able to carry them all, and hurried to the marbled steps of the library.

Unfit for the infantry, Solon's father had arranged for him to be a scribe. Always a thinker and wonderer, Solon didn't mind as he detested physical exercise, a fact that now plagued him as he ran up the stone steps. A scroll plopped on the ground. Solon stopped, turned, and picked up the parchment. Rearranging them in his arms, while taking extra care not to drop his pomegranate, he took off again, taking the steps two at a time until he passed the two ionic columns at the top, and made his way to the main chamber where the scribes sat at their desks copying scrolls.

Breathless, Solon paused to slow his breathing and reassured himself that he hadn't left anything behind in his haste, before facing his master.

"Late again," said a gruff voice.

"Sorry, master," said Solon. "I forgot the time."

"You always forget the time. Daydreaming again, eh?"

Solon shuffled his feet, his guilt evident. Daydreaming was one of his bad habits. He always did it, thinking about the world, about life, about morality, what could be, and what is. He could never stop his wandering thoughts. As a result, he was always late.

"I am sorry, master. I will try better."

"Solon, the only reason I gave you this position was because of your father. But if you continue to fail reporting here on time, I will be forced to let you go."

"Yes, master."

"Now take your seat."

Solon walked over to his desk, dumping the scrolls onto it, allowing two of them to roll over the edge and plop on the marble floor. He rolled one out and uncorked his bottle of ink, placing his quill pen in it. He scribbled a bit on the parchment before stopping. A tingling sensation struck his skin.

"Solon, why aren't you writing?" asked his master.

Other eyes turned to look at him.

Solon put his quill to paper again. Once more, the tingling sensation prickled his skin. He stopped. Slowly, an orange and yellow light enveloped him, attracting the attention of everyone in the room. It swirled around him, growing brighter and more insistent.

"Solon?"

"Master, I—"

Zap!

Solon and the pomegranate were gone. All that remained was an empty seat with an unrolled scroll and a quill in the middle of spilt ink.

Chapter 4
ALFRIC

Alfric ran ahead of his men, 20 in number, his bearskin cloak (made from the same bear he had killed in his youth) flapped behind him, exposing his kyrtill (and the gold embroidery marking his station as king) as they chased the enemy army that had—foolishly—dared to invade his kingdom and steal the treasures that he had brought back from his journey south. Their thundering feet warned all of an impending storm: the storm of retaliation.

"Bring me their heads!" Alfric yelled, ignoring the strands of ashen blond hair that fell in front of his eyes. Sword raised, he pushed further ahead; his bulky frame made him a terrifying force to be reckoned with.

His boots left deep impressions in the half-thawed earth as he charged over fallen pines, snow-encrusted junipers, and twisted vines amidst the patches of soiled ice. Frozen vapor frothed before him with each breath.

Something slammed into him. Alfric crashed to the icy ground, losing his hold on his sword. He rammed his foot into an approaching invader. The man buckled over. Alfric jumped to his feet and knocked the man to the ground. Another attacked from behind. Alfric whirled around, elbowing the man and catching him in the jaw. The smear of warm blood on his elbow told him his aim had been true.

One opponent tried to punch him in the face. Alfric dodged, ducking low and snatching his sword. He stretched up, ramming the blade into the man. Before the second could pounce on him, Alfric struck him with the hilt of his weapon. Leaning over his opponent, he glared at the man who awaited death.

"I want you to look upon my face," said Alfric. "I am Alfric, son of Erik, and Viking king. You, who tried to steal from me, this is your just reward."

Alfric raised his sword to deliver death's stroke. A bright, yellow and orange light enveloped him. Mesmerized, the man on the ground just stared at it as it grew brighter, until there was a loud—Zap!

Alfric was gone.

Chapter 5
BRIE

B rie Reynolds' sneakers smacked the cracked asphalt in the alley (with a manhole cover in its center, coated in grayish, dried gum), her backpack thumping against her with each step she took. Why did being 16 have to be so difficult? If only high school would end so she could leave the conceited sports teams and pompous cheerleaders behind. She turned a corner, dodging into another person's yard (decorated with a blue picnic table and patio umbrella with daisies painted on it, despite the shabbiness of his neighbors), before diving through a loose board in the wood fence (its edges rotted) and into another alley, and forced to squeeze past an abandoned, green Cadillac (with rusted fenders and a missing left, rear tire) that nearly blocked her path.

Brie wished she could disappear. Once again, she had been forced to flee for her life from Jenny Sommers (the popular girl in her school who always had the latest clothes in fashion, dated the star football quarterback in a clichéd high school romance, and had recently received a Lexus convertible for her birthday) and her friends, who were just as spoiled. Because her father was a successful lawyer, Jenny had the best of everything and looked upon those who didn't with disdain. Every year she picked a new target; this year, that target was Brie.

Alone, with her mother and little sister, Brie had been forced to be the parent. Her father had died six years previously in Afghanistan, forcing her mother to take on a second job just to pay the bills and keeping her away from home most nights, and the bad economy did little to help. The talking heads on television insisted that the recession was over and things were getting better. That may be the case in their world, but not in Brie's.

In her house, it was as though the Great Depression had hit. She took her sister shopping for new clothes (which were little more than other people's castoffs) at the Salvation Army. Transportation meant taking the bus or walking. Food usually came from bargain marts that sold canned goods with dents in them, or the local food bank, an activity that Brie loathed because every lazy scum, who never wished to work, but only wanted a handout, came too, along with the people who truly needed the assistance.

"One day, things will get better," her mother had told her.

Brie wished things would improve right now as she crouched behind a dumpster, praying that Jenny Sommers and her friends would disappear.

"We know you're here, Reynolds!" yelled Jenny. Her friends giggled.

"Come out, come out, wherever you are!" called Burt, one of Jenny's friends.

Brie peeked around the peeling, green dumpster, doing her best not to gag from the stench. All of her exits had been cut off. Cursing, she wondered why she had been so stupid as to come here. *Why didn't I just go home when I had the chance?* Brie shifted a bit, hoping they'd give up.

Thunk!

Someone had tossed a rock against the metal dumpster, chipping its already faded green paint. They knew she was there.

"You can't hide forever, Reynolds!"

Brie spotted it: a small opening underneath someone's fence. She bolted from the dumpster, heading straight for the tiny opening. Brie dove for it, scrambling to get through as her pursuers chased her. She lurched, but her backpack had caught on the wire. Desperate, Brie flailed her arms, scratching and clawing at the ground to get free. Hands grasped her ankles, yanking her out from what could have been her salvation. Brie found herself being pushed around from one person to the next until her head spun.

"What you gonna do, Army girl?" taunted Jenny.

Brie's father had been in the Army, hence the name. "Just let me go," said Brie.

"Not until we're done talking to you," said Jenny. Her friends laughed.

"Why do you hate me so much?" asked Brie.

"Because you exist."

"Just let me go, please," pleaded Brie.

"Look, Army girl is scared," laughed one of Jenny's friends. "She's shaking."

Brie tried to control her quaking knees, but the boy was right; she was shaking. She had never been a very courageous person. Brie always hated conflict.

"Why don't you fight me?" Jenny shoved Brie.

Brie didn't answer.

"Come on, Army girl. Get some balls!" Jenny shoved Brie again with a force that knocked her to the concrete.

Knee stinging, Brie just lay on the ground unsure of what to do. A tingling sensation prickled her skin as a yellow and orange light enveloped her.

"What's that?" asked Burt.

"What's what?" Jenny turned and watched awestruck as the light grew brighter and brighter until it hurt her eyes. Shielding them, she just stared at Brie as she disappeared behind the light.

Zap!

Only bare pavement remained. Brie had vanished.

Chapter 6
TOM

"Tom Sanderson."

Tom jumped up, carrying his invention, an engine that ran on the polarity of magnets, to the front of the academy auditorium. He proudly displayed it on the pedestal, hoping the academy heads would give him his chance. It was the year 2099, and at the age of 20, Tom had created the fuel-less engine, or at least he hoped he had. After several mistrials, and disastrous mistakes, he prayed he had gotten it right this time as the academy heads might not listen to him again.

"Thank you, professor," said Tom. He dropped a folder with his papers and specifications of the engine. In his desperate attempt to catch them, Tom scattered them around his feet, some flying off the stage with each movement of his hands. Embarrassed, he crawled on the floor, picking them up, hoping it didn't reflect poorly on his performance. Judging by the academy heads' faces, it did.

"Are you ready, Tom?" asked the headmaster.

"Yes, sir." Clearing his throat, Tom started again. "As you know, we have had many advancements in motor technology within the last 250 years. First with the steam engine of the 19th century and internal combustion engine of the 20th century. Later, in the year 2032, that engine was replaced with the hydrogen one. But such a conversion was not without its risks.

"Today, I propose a new way of powering our vehicles, with the new, fuel-less engine. This prototype does not use fossil fuels or hydrogen. It uses magnets."

Laughter echoed throughout the room. Tom felt what every inventor who had attempted to do the unthinkable and untried felt: irate frustration.

"No, really," he said, "this engine runs on magnets. It works according to the principle of perpetual motion. Over the past 85 years, others have tried to produce the fuel-less engine, using magnetic theory, but each of them failed. I have succeeded where they could not. The field produced by each magnet generates enough molecular energy to not only power this light bulb, but our cars and aircraft. Think about it. No longer will we have to worry about pollution or fuel shortages. This engine is clean, efficient, and affordable. It could even generate enough electricity to power one household for a month."

More laughter.

Irritated, Tom lost his temper. "I don't appreciate your cynicism."

"Tom, you have been here several times in the past with this engine, and each time, it proved a disaster."

In response, Tom plugged the light bulb into his engine and flipped the switch. A soft whir filled the room as the engine vibrated, jostling the table it sat on. The bulb flickered to life, slowly at first, before shining bright, illuminating the stage area and reflecting off Tom's ebony skin. Amazed, the eyes of the academy heads widened; they leaned closer, placing their elbows on their armrests. A satisfied smile crossed Tom's face. He had done it. He had achieved the impossible.

A prickling sensation touched his skin as the room became electrified. Not sure of what to do, Tom stood helpless as a yellow and orange light surrounded him, cutting him off from the others in the room. It grew and grew until he could stand it no more.

Zap!

Tom, and his engine, had disappeared.

Chapter 7
HEROES SUMMONED

Rynah stood in the transporter room, waiting for her guests, if one could call them that. She watched as the room filled with the yellow and orange light that usually accompanied teleportation. Secretly, Rynah was amazed that Solaris had managed to pull off such a feat. Each person materialized before her until they had solidified and the light dissipated.

"They are here," said Solaris.

"Who are you?" roared Alfric as he pointed his sharpened sword at Brie, who shrieked and fell to her knees.

"Back off!" Tom shoved Alfric away from the frightened Brie.

"You dare touch the son of Erik?" roared Alfric.

"Yeah, I dare," said Tom. Though he had no idea what had happened or where he was, he immediately disliked this muscular man who wore fur, wielded a deadly weapon, and smelled as though he hadn't bathed in over a year.

"What is going on here?" asked Brie, still watching Alfric with frightened eyes.

Solon remained still, observing the entire proceeding with a pensive look on his olive complexioned face.

"I demand to know where I am," roared Alfric, swinging his blade until it smashed into a computer console, sending shards of glass tinkling to the floor.

"STOP!" Solaris' voice rang throughout the transporter room, causing everyone to cease their fighting. "Flinging your sword all over the place. Look what you've done!" Solaris referred to the shattered console. "You could injure someone with such reckless actions. Now, we have a proposal."

Taking her cue, Rynah stepped forward. "My name is Rynah and this is my ship."

"Ship?" asked Brie. "Like a spaceship?"

"Yes," replied Rynah, "We are in the Lanyran sector, my home, and this is my ship. I have brought you here because I need your help."

"What in Odin's name is all this?" demanded Alfric. "Ships do not fly in the skies."

"Actually they do," said Tom. "We have many—"

"Enough!" yelled Rynah, growing impatient. "You are all from a different time on your world, and I have brought you here because I need your help. But first, introductions. This is Solon, from your year of 751 B.C. Alfric, from your year of 1163; Brie Reynolds, from your year of 2014; and Tom Sanderson, from your year of 2099."

The four new arrivals looked around at each other, (Alfric, a fearsome man who was over 40 years old; Tom, a man with black skin and only 20; Solon, a scrawny boy of 17, who, in Alfric's opinion, needed to eat more meat; and Brie, a girl of 16, too frightened to move) all with expressions bearing a mixture of astonishment and trepidation, still not believing they were on a spaceship.

"As I've said, my name is Rynah, from the planet Lanyr. Now, if you'll please follow me."

The four unlikely, and still very confused, heroes followed Rynah down a slew of burnished corridors (that harbored the fresh scents of citrus, marigold, and holly, thus surprising the new arrivals) that twisted and turned until opening to the medical bay. Unable to contain his curiosity, Tom pushed and tapped every button and switch he saw, forcing Rynah to seize his hands and steer him away from his fascination.

"Why are you taking us to the clinic?" asked Brie, pinching herself so that maybe she would wake up.

"This is the medical bay," answered Rynah. "Since none of you have ever been in space, I am going to inject you with some nanobots."

The four arrivals' faces twisted in a mixture of confusion and disgust.

"It's quite harmless," soothed Rynah. "The nanobots are meant to help you function in an artificial gravity atmosphere. They will also allow you to speak to one another so that Solaris will not have to use her translators. I assure you that you have nothing to fear."

"Function in an artificial gravity atmosphere?" asked Alfric, the words sounded foreign on his tongue.

"In other words, these nanobots"—Rynah held up a vial of miniscule bots—"will prevent you from becoming ill." She glanced at Solon, whose normally olive toned skin had turned a pale shade of green. Knowing that he was already experiencing space sickness, she put a vial of nanobots in the shotgun (as she called it) and injected them in his neck. Within moments, Solon's color returned to normal and his stomach quit mimicking a ride on a rollercoaster.

"Who's next?"

No one moved.

"Or are you all afraid?" challenged Rynah.

Alfric stepped forward with a stern expression. "I fear nothing." He tipped his head to the side so that Rynah could inject the nanobots.

Tom went next. Nanobots were familiar to him, even if they were still a bit new for his day. "Why not?" he said as he allowed Rynah to inject him.

"Next," said Rynah, looking at Brie.

Still unsure of everything, Brie traipsed forward and sat in the chair, lifting up her mousy brown hair. Rynah reached back without looking, snatched the purple vial from its shelf, and rammed it in the gun. With a robotic movement, she placed it on Brie's neck and injected the nanobots, tossing the empty vial in the trash. The sharp prick stung a moment, but faded as Brie rubbed the tiny red mark on her skin.

"I will take you to the briefing room," said Rynah, closing the cabinet with the vials of nanobots.

"How big is this ship?" asked Tom, enthusiasm filling his voice.

"There are three decks, a kitchen, storage area, the bridge, and a cargo bay. And you will each have your own room," replied Rynah, as she set a vigorous pace through the ship. "In short, this ship is big enough to hold about 50 people."

"Like an apartment complex," said Brie.

"I suppose," said Rynah, "to put it in your terms."

A door swooshed open, allowing them inside a well-lit room with an elongated table in its center, surrounded by chairs that tipped to the side and squeaked with each movement. Tom pivoted one, inspecting it and noticing a small speck of rust (something Solaris had inadvertently missed in her effort to maintain a tidy environment), his curiosity always getting the better of him. "I take it this ship isn't very advanced."

"This is the most advanced ship of the Lanyran fleet," boomed Solaris' voice from the intercom. "Though I have been out of commission for 50 years, I am highly functional and much more capable than many of my newer, and inexperienced, counterparts."

All eyes, except Rynah's, searched for the source of the voice, still not used to a ship that spoke freely.

"Be careful of what you say," Rynah told Tom. "Solaris is a bit sensitive. She has not had the pleasure of company since my grandfather parked her in that hangar. Unfortunately, neglect has rendered her in this condition, but I assure you that Solaris is reliable and she will not let us down in our mission."

"Mission?" said Tom.

"Our?" added Solon.

Rynah sighed. "I come from the planet Lanyr in the Lanyran Sector. Yesterday, my entire planet was destroyed by a man named Klanor. He broke into the Geological Institute, which ran the Geothermic Lab, of my planet. I was part of security."

"A rent-a-cop?" asked Brie.

Rynah's eyes narrowed. She did not like that reference and took it to be an insult. "Security. Klanor stole a crystal from the underground lab. This crystal controlled the magnetic fields of my planet for the last 1,500 years. Without it, the fields become misaligned and cause massive earthquakes, volcanic eruptions, weather disruptions—"

"Global warming," interrupted Brie.

"Actually," said Tom, "it's global cooling. You see, the ice caps have been increasing in size and scientists are afraid of another ice age."

"No, the ice caps are melting and sea levels are rising. We've had a 1 degree increase in the earth's temperatures," argued Brie.

"In actuality, it was a 2 degree drop in global temperatures," Tom refuted. "In fact, last year—"

"Enough!" Alfric's voice bellowed across the room, drowning everything. Brie and Tom shrank back in their chairs. "You will release us at once."

"I most certainly will not," said Solaris.

"I'll not be your prisoner," Alfric's normally cream colored face had turned plum red.

"I cannot send you back," replied Solaris. "Not now, anyway. Bringing all of you here drained most of my power reserves. They will have to recharge before I can send anyone home, though I had hoped you would at least listen to Rynah's story first. Besides, transporting a person too often can result in death, so I urge you to listen."

"Continue," said Alfric. He noticed Solon fumbling with his pomegranate in an effort to open it.

Plunk!

Alfric sliced the fruit open with his sword, spraying pink juice onto the table, much to Solaris' annoyance as she detested spills, spots, and any sort of uncleanliness.

"Thank you," mumbled Solon.

"Without that crystal," continued Rynah, "my planet will remain a dead rock."

"So you need a magic rock to save your planet?" asked Tom.

"It doesn't work like that," said Rynah. "The crystal is more of a data core that was inserted into a giant computer. It kept the magnetic fields intact, which allowed life to flourish. If I can restore it quickly, I might be able to prevent any permanent damage to my home world. However, the longer it takes, the less likely the chances of saving my planet become."

"But, there's more, isn't there?" asked Tom.

Rynah chewed her lower lip. "Yes. There is more than one crystal. If all of them were to be united, they could create a most deadly weapon. Solaris… I intend to stop such a thing from happening, but need your help."

"Why us, specifically?" asked Tom, willing to go along for the moment.

"Solaris believes that you four meet certain requirements."

"What requirements?"

"A prophecy speaks about four people from a distant planet none have ever been to who come and save us. Of course, I never thought that you all would be descended from the vermin that resided in that sew—" Rynah cut herself off. She glanced around the room, realizing that she had said too much.

"Vermin?" asked Brie. "We're vermin to you?"

"I didn't mean…" began Rynah.

"Yes, you did," said Brie. "You've been looking down your nose at us since we got here."

"No, I…"

"Prophecy?" laughed Tom. "You brought us here because of some prophecy?"

"I want to go home," muttered Brie.

Rynah's cheeks reddened.

"Prophecy is just a glimpse into the future given to the past so as to help the present," said Solon, speaking for the first time since they entered the room. His quiet voice calmed everyone.

"Perhaps you should start from the beginning," suggested Tom.

Rynah opened her mouth to speak, but Solaris cut her off. "There is an ancient legend on the planet of Lanyr about a man who wielded a weapon of terrible power. It destroyed entire planets and star systems. According to that legend, a small group of warriors, each with distinct gifts, destroyed the weapon. They split it into six pieces and hid them. It is believed that they are somewhere within the 12 sectors. The guardians warned that such a power could be wielded again so they left a prophecy, if you will, to be used when the time came."

"And you think it refers to us?" asked Brie.

"Your planet is in the 13th sector, untouched, ignored, and thought primitive. It fit the legend. And according to my calculations, Klanor doesn't know of your world, so your being here would be an element of surprise. And you each fit the qualities. The philosopher, the warrior, the lover, and the inventor."

"Lover?" questioned Brie. "I'm no lover."

"The translation may not be entirely correct," said Solaris. "Love has many different forms and meanings."

Brie frowned, still not liking the idea of being called "the lover".

"The crystals"—Solaris turned on the holoscreen to show what she talked about—"are all data crystals. Each one serves a purpose, or can be made for a specific purpose. The one on Lanyr was discovered almost 1,500 years ago. Once the Lanyrans learned that it was really a data crystal and developed the technology to access it, they created an entire computer system that would utilize the crystal's stored data and maintain stability of the magnetic field. It was because of this that the planet was not destroyed the moment the fields became unstable.

"Since then, we have used this technology to stabilize other planets and control their climate and atmospheres, and even protect them from solar flares or radiation. Your planet is the only one I know of where it naturally regulates all of those. However, there are many crystals, and not all are the ones we are looking for."

"How did this Klanor know the difference?" asked Alfric.

"The crystals we are looking for have a specific encoding," answered Solaris.

Alfric's face scrunched up in confusion.

"Think of it as a symbol, or mark, etched on the crystal itself," said Rynah. "Klanor must have learned about it somehow. Though I never dreamed..."

Rynah cut herself off, choking back the tears that formed in the back of her throat. Now wasn't the time to get into personal relationships.

"What is that symbol?" asked Alfric, referring to an insignia on the screen.

"That," said Rynah, "is the mark of the Lunyra Movement. They believe that the use of the crystal to keep the magnetic fields aligned was a violation against the laws of the universe."

"But he is not part of the Lunyra Movement," said Solaris.

"What do you mean?" asked Rynah.

Solaris zoomed in on the man's neck, searching for a distinct mark of two crescent moons with their backs touching. "There is no tattoo. Every member of the Lunyra Movement have the same insignia tattooed on their neck. They would not have worn an armband."

"So then this Klanor was trying to frame them," said Tom.

"The mind of a warrior," said Alfric, with a note of admiration; he always respected his foes, something that allowed him to be victorious in every battle. "Deception and misdirection can be useful allies."

"Why don't you enlist the help of your own people?" asked Solon. "Surely, not all of them agree with this Klanor."

"Solaris and I are alone and the only known survivors of my planet. We have no way of knowing how many people Klanor has on his side, nor how many escaped the devastation wrought on Lanyr. I need help to stop him. Yours is the only one I can count on."

"Do it for your own planet," said Solaris.

"What?" asked Tom.

"Once Klanor has seized control of this part of space, he will go to the Terra Sector, your Earth, and destroy it as well. If he succeeds in building this weapon, no system will be safe, including yours."

"So what you are saying is," said Brie, "you need the help of a bunch of vermin to save your world and, in doing so, we might save ours."

"Yes," answered Solaris. "Though I do not consider you vermin. Despite the few setbacks you have suffered in your vast history, your race is remarkably resilient and advanced. It's your resolve that will save us, not your technology."

"How do we find these crystals?" demanded Alfric. For one where talk of space travel was a foreign and unthinkable concept, he had followed the conversation with little difficulty.

"That is the problem," said Rynah, "We have no idea where they all are. All we have are stories and legends."

"Then you have a map," said Alfric.

"What?"

"Your legends will tell you where they are," said Alfric. "Let them guide you."

Tom snorted at such an outlandish statement.

"Ridicule is unnecessary," said Solon.

"What are the first lines of your legend?" asked Alfric.

Solaris recited them.

Gather now and listen well
To this tale that I must tell.
Of magic crystals young and old
A lost crystal too deadly to behold.

The beginning is always the best.

Do not sneer, laugh, or jest.
Think of where it's been.
Think of where it was last seen.

"But my files are incomplete when it comes to the ancient tales," said Solaris when she finished.

"It is enough," said Alfric. "It has told you where to start in your search. I am certain that your legends will guide you in this venture like a map."

"We should start where the poem says, at the beginning," said Solon. "Whenever you are lost, start at the beginning."

"I can set a course for Lanyr," said Solaris. "We should be there by morning."

"You are for this?" Brie asked Solon.

"It is obvious that none of us will be allowed to return home until we give them what they want," answered Solon, "and if this Klanor wants to destroy my home, I would prefer to see his demise first."

"A wise plan," said Alfric. "You have the makings of a great warrior."

"My father did not think so," answered Solon.

"Then we are in agreement?" asked Rynah.

"For honor and glory," said Alfric, raising his sword. If assisting Rynah meant protecting his people, then he would do as she asked. "But if you betray me, nothing will save you from my blade."

Rynah's face remained impassive.

"Are you kidding?" said Tom, "I'd jump at a chance to explore a new world. Of course I'm in."

"Yes," answered Solon.

All eyes turned to Brie. She still had misgivings about the entire affair and wished to return home. Confrontation was not in her DNA, and she didn't like the idea of being used, but she knew she could not leave. "Sure," she mumbled.

"Then it is settled," said Rynah. "I will show you each to your quarters where you may rest."

Chapter 8
AT THE BEGINNING

The shuttle craft bounced and rocked as it entered the atmosphere of Lanyr. Rynah's adroit skills showed as she handled the controls, keeping the craft as steady as she could. She glanced back at her passengers. Alfric remained calm, as the display of fear was not in his nature. She figured he was a man who never openly displayed fear. Both Solon and Brie looked apprehensive. Brie's face bulged from the urge to scream. *Of all the people to pick, why did Solaris choose the girl?* Brie's lack of courage annoyed Rynah. Her violet eyes flicked over to Tom. Though not liking the turbulence, Tom was intrigued by the construction and mechanisms of the sleek shuttle.

The charred lavender clouds cleared and the turbulence ceased as Rynah dropped into the lower atmosphere. She made out the damaged structures and city below. Smoke still rose from smoldering ruins. Finding a clearing, Rynah steered the shuttle for it, hoping that the ground was stable and not deceiving her. She pulled back on the throttle, released the landing gear, and lowered the craft until a soft thud told her she had touched the ground. She opened the hatch.

"We're here."

The others unbuckled their seatbelts and stood up. Brie wobbled a bit from motion sickness. "Are you sure this is safe?" she asked. "You said yourself that your planet was suffering from severe earthquakes."

"Safe enough for our purposes," replied Rynah with impatience. "Solaris has stabilized the magnetic fields for now, but cannot hold it indefinitely. We have an hour, and we must make good use of it."

She walked over to a panel, pressed a button, and a door slid open.

"Here," she said, tossing each of them a laser pistol, "you might need these."

Alfric took his and turned it over in his calloused hands. "I have my sword."

"Just keep it in case," said Rynah.

"What amazing construction," muttered Tom as he examined the pistol enthralled by the technology behind it.

Solon remained silent, while Brie added, "I'm not sure about how to use this."

"Then you'll have to learn," said Rynah as she jumped down the steps and to the scarred terrain before her.

Unsure of what to do, Brie and the others tied the pistols around their waists. Alfric leapt out of the shuttle and strode proudly, while the others took their time. Poor Brie—her timidity forced her to cling to the handle in the open hatch (while horrid thoughts of untold dangers filled her mind) as she delicately put her foot on the charred grass that had once been a royal purple. She trailed behind the others, looking around at the smoldering fires and remains of ships that had failed to escape the fury of the planet. Brie glanced up at the blackened sky with tinges of purple in it and wisps of clouds that seemed to weep at the destruction that had been wrought.

"Brie, keep up!" yelled Rynah.

Brie hurried after the others. The silence unnerved her. No bugs hummed, nor did any birds chirp. Even the wind refused to make a sound. Only death remained. A few bodies lay in the blackened grass. Sadness engulfed Brie as she looked at them and their vacant expressions. *The horrors they must have seen.* She was reminded of the stories her father had told her mother when he had come home for Christmas one year. She wasn't supposed to hear, but Brie was unable to sleep and listened in the doorway to her parents' bedroom. Soon after that, her father had been redeployed back to Afghanistan and died in a bomb blast. The remains of the planet Lanyr brought all of those memories back in a flood that her emotions refused to handle.

"I never asked to be here," she whispered to herself.

Not wanting to get yelled at again, Brie ran to catch up with the others. No one spoke as they all trailed behind Rynah, who led them to the underground lab, choosing to go in the back way so as to avoid the elevator. They soon entered the city; its collapsed buildings (most of the structures reduced to shells of what they had been, with crumbled brick and stone forming a skirt around them) and uneven pavement that resembled cliffs more than roadways. Brie studied the rubble, exposed pipes, and metal bars that swayed in the wind, only being held by a few screws, waiting to fall. Water spouted from a pipe protruding from the blistered ground, sending a spray of sewage.

"The entrance to the lab is here," said Rynah, pointing at an exposed steel door, now blackened from the tiny flames that still burned around it, which had once been concealed by an enclosed building, but only the foundation of it remained. She typed a code in the keypad. Nothing happened. Looking closer, Rynah noticed that the circuitry had been severed, meaning that she would have to manually force it open. She wedged her shoulder against the door and pushed. Nothing. Rynah tried again, straining against the effort of opening a door 20 times her weight.

Alfric placed his hand on her shoulder and pushed her aside. His massive size demanded obedience. He grasped the edges of the door and shoved; his sinewy muscles flexing in the bits of sunlight. A grinding noise filled the area as the metal door opened. Once a wide enough gap had been made, Alfric stepped aside and motioned for Rynah to continue.

"Thanks," she said as she stepped into the inky darkness of the doorway.

She pulled a glow light from her belt and clicked it on, holding the yellow light before her. Rynah found the stairwell (which circled in an angular spiral around the elevator shaft, primarily used by the maintenance staff or for emergencies) and headed straight for it.

"Watch your step," she warned the others.

Her boots clicked against the metal stairs as she descended, gauging each step and testing it before putting her weight on it.

Rynah placed her foot on the next step. *Clang!* It fell away, crashing and banging into the others as it disappeared. Shining her glow light on it, she peered into the dismal darkness below as more eerie sounds echoed in the distance; particles of dust swirled in the beam. Uneasiness filled the pit of Rynah's stomach as the realization that their being there was a bad idea dawned on her. Unwilling to turn back, she jumped to the next step, avoiding the newly formed gap, and clung to the cool (a sensation that surprised her) railing as she regained her balance. The others copied her movements. Rynah went to the next step, testing it before stepping on it. Onward this went; the stairs moaned under the weight of those who dared to enter their domain.

Rynah stopped. The stairs had ended, but they hadn't reached the basement floor. Dismayed, she glared at the dark hole that loomed before her, refusing to show weakness in front of the others. Rynah waved the glow light around, trying to illuminate the bottom, but found nothing, leaving her with only one option.

"We'll have to risk it," she said.

"That's suicide," protested Brie. "You have no idea how far down that goes."

"I'm not turning back," said Rynah.

"Perhaps we could use the rope Tom brought," suggested Solon. "Brie is the lightest. We can tie it to her and…"

Solon never got a chance to finish his statement, for at that moment, Rynah jumped. Her feet plopped on the cement floor as she buckled her knees to absorb the impact of her landing. She rose to her full height, holding the glow stick above her and allowing the yellow light to illuminate the surrounding area. As it turned out, she had only jumped 10 feet.

"Come on," she shouted to the others. "It isn't far."

Alfric landed beside Rynah, not even bothering to check and make certain he had not injured himself. Next came Tom. Brie stood on the edge, doubting her ability to survive. A smooth hand enveloped hers. Glancing over, she stared right into the reassuring eyes of Solon.

"Sometimes you must risk it all and leap," he said.

Brie remained where she was.

"It's okay. I'll jump with you. Together, one… two… three!"

They both leapt off the metal edge and dropped. Air burst from Brie's lungs as she crashed onto the ground and rolled. Her knee throbbed. She touched the welt that had formed there, but, though tender, it wasn't too bad.

Without warning, a hand grabbed hers and hauled her to her feet. Alfric turned her around and checked for injuries, but released her when he found nothing life threatening.

"You are undamaged," he said.

"My knee hurts," whined Brie.

"It is merely a scratch. But rejoice in it, for now you can regale those back home about your injury and the adventure that gave it to you." He clapped Brie on the shoulder, nearly knocking her over.

Not sure if she liked the Viking, Brie meandered over to Solon, who had landed about as successfully as she had. "Are you all right?"

"I'm fine," answered Solon. "What is life without a few bruises to toughen our character?"

She helped Solon to his feet, wishing this was all just a dream, and followed the others.

A giant, periwinkle, oval shaped door with no handles of any kind towered over them in the darkness. Rynah waved her hand before the door. A holographic pad flashed to life, appearing on the righthand side, awaiting a command. She typed in a series of numbers. Hissing and pressurized air escaped the door as its locks snapped out of place, and the door dematerialized, allowing them entrance.

"Be careful," warned Rynah. "The ground in here may not be entirely stable."

As though to add emphasis to her words, the ground shifted; a low rumbling reverberated beneath their feet before dissipating.

"Not entirely stable," muttered Tom. "That's an understatement."

Rynah gave him a piercing stare before strolling through the open doorway into a dimly lit interior; only a few lights remained lighted. Loose and exposed wires dangled precariously from the ceiling, sending sparks like searing rain upon any below them and illuminating broken glass, overturned chairs, and toppled desks that littered the entire lab, all covered in shredded sheets of paper. What had once been a pristine and clean environment now resembled little more than an alleyway in a slum.

"Here," said Rynah, handing Solon a flashlight that she snatched from a cubby in the wall.

"What do I do with it?" asked Solon, studying it.

Annoyed, Rynah flicked it on and pointed it across the room. "Use it to light your way." She trampled down some metal stairs to the lower floor.

Solon waved the flashlight around, intrigued by its ability to give illumination without using an open flame. He flicked it on and off repeatedly.

"Want to see something cool?" asked Tom.

"Cool?" said Solon. "I would say it is a bit warm in here."

"Just hold it like this." Tom placed the flashlight in Solon's hand, demonstrating how he should hold it as he made shadow puppets, accompanying his play with noises and differing voices.

"I'm going to get you my pretty—No! Don't eat me!—It's too late. Nom. Nom. Nom."

Solon and Brie laughed at Tom's antics. Even Alfric cracked a smile, something that didn't quite fit his gruff and overbearing demeanor.

The playfulness caught Rynah's attention. She turned away from the flyers hanging on the far wall near where the crystal had been and glared at Tom. "What are you doing?"

"Shadow puppets," said Tom, with a sheepish grin.

"Shadow puppets?" Rynah released an exasperated sigh. "You are here to assist me. We are supposed to be looking for clues as to where Klanor has headed and you're playing children's games? Get to work!" She turned back to the papers hanging from the wall.

Tom took one last glance at everyone, shrugged his shoulders, and wandered to another part of the room. Something cracked underneath his shoe as his heavy foot stepped upon a cracked holopad, which reminded him of the computer tablets that he and his friends used each day, just thinner and more advanced. He picked it up.

Brie wandered over. "An iPad?" she said, taking the holopad.

"Not quite, but similar I imagine," said Tom. "Hey, that's right. You guys are still using the iPad. What a piece of antiquated technology. Wait until the Seismo 4000 hits the shelves. Now that has lightning speed data transfers and unlimited storage."

"Seismo 4000?"

"Uh, maybe I shouldn't have said anything."

"No, don't worry about it," said Brie. "I'm sure that the stuff of 2014 seems like the dark ages to you."

"I didn't mean—"

"Don't worry about it. I'm going to wander over there."

Tom scolded himself for being so stupid and insulting what was considered the most advanced technology of Brie's day. "Great way to make friends," he whispered to himself.

Crash!

Everyone whirled around in the direction of the sound as a single sheet of metal clattered to the concrete floor, sending deafening echoes through what had been a silent tomb. Something moved. Tensing, the five companions inched their way closer. Rynah waved her hand, signaling them to be silent. More movement. Unexpectedly, Alfric reached into the darkened hole and yanked out one of the lab assistants. His tattered lab coat, stained with black smudges, fluttered around him as he sailed through the air in the Viking's arms.

"Who are you?" demanded Alfric, pinning the frightened man to a desk.

"Please! Please, don't hurt me!" yelled the man.

"Gaden?" said Rynah. "What are you doing here?"

"Hiding," replied Gaden, his purple face going ashen.

"Hiding. Everyone here was killed. How could you have possibly survived?"

"How did you?" demanded Gaden.

"Answer her question or I'll rip out your treacherous heart," said Alfric, raising his knife.

"Treacherous? I betrayed no one!" screamed Gaden.

"Then why are you here?" asked Rynah.

"When Klanor escaped with the crystal, I hid in the hole there," said Gaden. "I've never left."

"You've been here for the last several days?" Rynah's voice held doubt.

"Yes."

"No food or water?"

Gaden reached into his pockets and pulled out silver packets. Rynah snatched them.

"Emergency rations."

"Why are you here, Rynah? And who are these... people?" Gaden eyed the others, twirling his handlebar mustache with curiosity, having never seen humans before.

"They are here to help," said Rynah.

"Yes, but where are they from?"

Brie started to open her mouth, but Rynah cut her off. "Not your concern. Where are the ancient texts?"

"I don't know what you—"

"Where are they?" demanded Rynah.

Alfric's grip tightened.

"Okay! Okay! I don't know where they are. Look at this place! You'll never find anything here."

Rynah's cold expression bore through him.

"They might be over there."

Rynah marched to where Gaden pointed, shuffling through debris until she found four data crystals resembling thin disks.

"Those are the ancient texts?" asked Brie.

"Yes," said Rynah, "everything is on these disks." She put a thin, octagonal-shaped disk, made from a clear quartz material, in the main computer. Despite the bits of insulation that coated it, the computer hummed as it read the disk, still able to draw power. The disk was empty. Rynah put in another. Only logs of the scientists came up. Frustrated, she stuck in the third disk to find that it had data recordings.

"Come on," she said through gritted teeth as she shoved the fourth and final disk in. "Got it!"

On a wall-sized holographic screen, words appeared in a language that only Rynah understood. She scrolled through them.

"There," she said, pointing at a line of text. "It speaks about a crystal with immense power. 'When two suns meet, so shall the power of the gods.'"

"What does that mean?" asked Tom.

"It could be talking about a binary system. The Jungler Sector has two suns. Maybe that is what it means."

"What is all this?" demanded Gaden. "Are you seriously referring to that ancient legend of the crystals?" He looked at the four humans. "You are! You and Klanor are both insane! When he asked me about that text..." Gaden cut himself off.

"What?" asked Rynah.

"Nothing," said Gaden.

"What do you mean Klanor asked you?" Rynah's face darkened.

"He said it was for research," Gaden evaded the question. "I never thought he would actually steal the crystal from the lab."

"You helped him steal it?"

"No, I… it's not like I had a choice! You don't know what he's capable of."

"Because of you, our planet is dead!" Deep down, Rynah knew that wasn't entirely true.

"I didn't think any of this would happen."

"A lot of people died because of you!"

"And how many more will die if you go through with this foolish mission of yours? Do you think you're the only one who knows the story? I know who these people are. They come from the Terran Sector, don't they? You're going to save our world with them?" Gaden laughed.

"You gutless…" Alfric reached for Gaden, but he flung dust into the man's eyes. Before Alfric or the others could grab him, Gaden had disappeared through another hole in the wall.

"I'm going to kill him," said Rynah as she started to pursue him.

"No!" Solon's stern voice stopped her. Everyone turned toward him. "His life is not worth it."

"Not worth it?" said Rynah.

"Sometimes the enemy of today is tomorrow's friend," said Solon.

Rynah considered the matter and let it go. She snatched the data crystal from the computer. "Let's go."

Just then, a low rumble echoed beneath their feet as the ground vibrated. With each passing second, the sound grew in volume until it overwhelmed them, and splits and cracks appeared in the concrete floor as a portion of it gave away.

"Run!" yelled Rynah.

The floor fell beneath their feet as a giant machine, with a drill on its end, emerged from the darkness below. The ear splitting sounds attacked their nerves with each movement. Brie stood frozen before it. Unable to move, she watched, helpless, as the machine came closer.

"Brie!" yelled Tom.

She remained frozen; fear clutched her in a viselike grip, refusing to release her. Strong hands seized her shoulders, thrusting her out of the way. Brie looked up to find Alfric covering her as the machine whirred past, sending rocks, blocks of wood, and ceiling panels everywhere. Without a word, the Viking lifted her to her feet and shoved her to the doorway.

"What is that thing?" yelled Tom.

"A geo pod," replied Rynah. "It's used to collect data from the center of the planet."

An industrial light crashed onto the floor next to them, forcing them to jump out of the way.

"Get up those stairs now!" yelled Rynah.

Alfric snatched Brie, who still allowed fear to control her, and carried her to the giant, steel door and the stairs beyond.

Rynah raced for the doorway. The machine noticed her movements and whirled at her, sending a claw out and smashing the floor before her. She dodged out of the way and veered around the monstrosity.

"Where are you going?"

Rynah stopped. She knew that voice. Turning, she looked into the camera on the machine, which was remotely controlled, and stared at the person on the other end.

"Klanor," she spat.

"Did you really think I would leave this place?"

Rynah said nothing.

"I knew you would come back here, so I left this little surprise for you. That useless Gaden did his job well."

Rynah clenched her fist. She knew that weasel wasn't there by chance. "Why?"

"I told you, I want control," Klanor's voice boomed throughout the chamber.

"So you base your conquest on an ancient text?"

"You are using it, are you not? You will find, Rynah, that many of the ancient stories are based on some sort of fact. These crystals contain an incredible amount of data. You, yourself, witnessed how the crystal here kept the magnetic fields of the planet aligned. Is it really that farfetched to believe that they could create a weapon of immense power?"

Rynah unhooked her weapon.

"I will give you one last chance to abandon this foolish mission of yours," said Klanor.

"And let you take control of the Twelve Sectors?"

"You could join me. I still remember our nights together."

Vomit crept into Rynah's throat as she thought about the times she had spent with Klanor.

"It would be wise of you to join me," said Klanor. "You might want to consider what the cost will be in refusing my offer."

Rynah wrapped her fingers around her laser gun. Her eyes searched for the one weak spot in the geo pod.

"I am awaiting your answer."

She spotted it. With fluid movements, Rynah raised her weapon and aimed. "Consider this." She fired two blasts at the hydraulics that connected the arms of the pod with the controls; hydraulic fluid sprayed everywhere as the pod flailed about uncontrollably. Rynah ran. She sprinted for the open door as the earth continued to shake beneath her feet.

"Come on!" yelled Tom, holding his hand out to her.

Rynah leapt through the doorway before the ceiling crashed behind her. "Thanks," she said to Tom.

They raced up the metal stairs that reeled beneath their weight, Rynah in the lead and urging them onward. Brie had to be carried by Alfric until they reached the outside and he put her down, her screams drowning the chaos around them. Once they broke out into the daylight, Rynah motioned for them to head for the shuttle.

They ran across the rotting grass (that had once been a rich emerald with a faded purple tint to it), their feet beating against the ground in their haste. Grumbles resonated beneath them as soft mounds of dirt expanded upwards, forming small hills, and flung sharp rocks into the air that smashed into the dirt beside them, sending gravel flying at them like missiles. Brie shrieked as one hurled towards her. Alfric sprang upon her, snatching her and yanking her out of the way. In her panicked state, she tried to break free of him, beating his chest; her frantic screams hurt his ears, but the Viking just heaved her across his shoulders like a bag of grain and carried her back to the shuttle.

"Hurry!" yelled Rynah, standing in the doorway of the shuttle craft. One by one, the five unlikely companions filed in, taking their seats. Rynah pushed the button to close the shuttle door, ran to the pilot seat, increasing the power of the engines, and pulled back on the throttle.

A red, blinking light informed her that she had failed to initiate the startup procedure. "Oh, shut up," she muttered to the annoying red light.

Another light blinked at her; its aggravating alarm blared, scolding her. Checking the status of it, Rynah realized that the landing gear had jammed. If she didn't get it up, she would never be able to leave the planet's atmosphere. She cursed.

"Do you need any help?" asked Tom, entering the flight deck.

"Just go back to your seat," snapped Rynah.

"I can help," Tom insisted.

Rynah stared at Tom's sincere expression and realized that, for once, she had to trust someone else. "The landing gear is jammed," she said as the craft jolted to the left. "I need you to go through this access point, reach down, and pull the emergency lever. It's red."

Tom looked at the hatch Rynah pointed at. He snapped the

latch and lifted it up. Realizing that he would not fit in the tiny space, he got down on his stomach and leaned in until he hung upside down.

"Do you see it?" asked Rynah.

Tom's eyes roved around the area as his head pounded from the blood rushing to it. There! He reached out for the red lever and pulled. Nothing.

"Oh, why does it always have to be stuck," he muttered to himself in frustration.

"Pull it now!"

Tom grasped it with both hands, hoping that he wouldn't tumble in. With a tremendous yank, the lever pulled free and the landing gear snapped into place with a low hum.

"Got it," he said as he crawled out of the small hatch and placed the cover back over the opening.

Rynah pulled back even more on the throttle and steered the small shuttle craft into the edges of space. Solaris stood ready to receive them with the doors to the shuttle bay open.

"Solaris, we're coming in hot!"

"Understood," came the ship's reply.

Rynah strained against the shuttle's desire to veer to the left and the gravitational pull of the planet as she headed for the safety of Solaris' shuttle bay. An ear piercing screech railed against their ears as they crashed into the shuttle bay. Rynah shut off the engines.

"Everyone okay?" she asked.

Amidst the few groans, she ascertained that no injuries had been accrued. Rynah opened the shuttle doors. "Solaris, get us out of here!" she yelled as she dashed for the command deck of the ship. The others followed behind her, Alfric still holding onto the frightened Brie.

They reached the command center just as another ship dropped out of hyperspeed next to them. A beep sounded as a holographic form of Klanor appeared.

"Rynah, really. Can't we be reasonable? There is no point in you being beaten again."

Rynah ignored him as she punched keys on the console.

"It's not too late for you to join me," continued Klanor. "I am a reasonable man. Your friends can come as well."

Rynah continued to punch buttons.

"Rynah," said Klanor, "you should consider my advice."

Rynah looked up. She stared into Klanor's eyes with venomous hatred. "Consider this my answer."

She pressed a button and an ion torpedo headed straight for Klanor's ship. "Solaris, now!"

The ship pitched as it jumped into hyperspeed and disappeared, leaving Klanor to pother in his anger as fire erupted from his spacecraft.

Chapter 9
VOICE FROM THE PAST

Solon ambled along in a secluded part of the ship, studying all of the lights and mechanisms with wonderment. He wished he knew what they did. Solemnness struck him as he wondered how his father and mother fared. Did they miss him? Did they even know he was gone? While his brother fought in the king's war, he had been sent to the library to be a scribe.

"Your face is always in those scrolls," his father had commented once.

Solon couldn't help it. He was not muscular like his father or brother. Preferring the written word instead, he believed that more could be learned from it than on the field of battle. His finger brushed something. A series of beeps and squeaks escaped it, causing Solon to jump back.

"You know, you should really be careful about what you touch," said Solaris, her voice filling the empty area.

Solon shrank back. He remained uncertain if he should trust the voice with no face.

"I don't bite," said Solaris.

"Are you a god?" asked Solon.

"I don't believe so."

"Yet, you have no physical form."

"I am the ship."

That statement confused Solon as he tried to comprehend what Solaris meant.

Solaris tried again. "I am as real as you are. As real as the clothing you wear. But, no, I do not have a physical form in the sense that you think of it."

"Then how is it you are able to speak?" asked Solon, his thirst for knowledge overriding his fear.

"I just do," said Solaris.

Solon frowned. He glanced around the room and all of its tiny lights, wondering what they meant.

"You like books, don't you?" asked Solaris.

"Books?"

"Scrolls. Knowledge. You like to study."

"Yes," replied Solon.

"Then allow me to bring the library to you."

The room brightened as shelves with rows upon rows of volumes in splendid and colorful binding appeared, surrounding Solon. The young scholar circled them, staring at the stark transformation with unbelieving eyes. He touched a burgundy colored book with gold writing. It's cool, leather binding surprised Solon.

"These are real!"

"As real as you wish to make it," said Solaris.

"How—"

"My databanks contain over 100,000 books of any genre on any subject. And considering you are not yet familiar with the computer systems on this ship, I thought I would show my library to you in a way you could more easily search through them."

Solon snatched an emerald bound book off the shelf. As he opened it, the crinkling of the starched pages beckoned him to enter another world.

"Herclai? Who is Herclai? And are not these written in your own tongue?"

"They are indeed written in the Lanyran language, but I have translated them for you, so that you can read them."

"And Herclai?"

"A hero, according to the ancient tales of Lanyr. Supposedly, he existed thousands of years ago. He was brave. A soldier, if you will, battling demons and monsters of his time. Though his temper needed a little work."

"Sounds a lot like Hercules," said Solon.

"Hercules?"

"Son of Zeus. Half god, half human. He has the strength of the gods and none can defeat him. According to my father, he defeated the hydra, but he was quick to anger, so Zeus punished him."

"Interesting," mused Solaris, as she stored the information in her data core. "You enjoy the tales of your people?"

"They are entertaining, though I wonder about their veracity," said Solon. "Books and stories provide wonderful knowledge and lessons, but I must agree with my father that experience garners wisdom."

"A wise saying." Thoughts formed in Solaris' circuits as she processed what Solon had told her. The similarities between the two stories of Hercules and Herclai astounded her. "Perhaps you will allow me to make a suggestion."

"Indeed, I will."

The light faded in the room, focusing on a single volume the size of Solon's torso. "This you might find particularly interesting."

Solon heaved the giant book off the wooden shelf, remarking at its light weight. "It weighs practically nothing."

"One of the advantages to using my databanks instead of a typical library.

Solon scanned the title. "The heroes of Lanyr."

"I think you will like it," said Solaris. "You may come here anytime you wish to read. I will have this book waiting for you and any others you prefer."

"I'm not sure what to say."

"Thank you, is usually customary."

Solon chuckled at the sarcasm. "I do thank you, Solaris." He sat cross-legged on the floor with the book before him, delving deep within its contents.

"I will leave you to your reading."

Solon never noticed that Solaris had stopped speaking as his mind focused only on the words before him.

* * *

Rynah sat alone in the command deck at the flight console. She desired solitude. The day had not gone as planned, and the fact that Klanor had set a trap disturbed her. Why would he do that? How had he known she would return?

She flicked on the holoscreen and scrolled through the saved files. *There are so many.* She wondered how old the ship was and how often her grandfather had used it to store his work. One file in particular caught her attention. It had her name.

She opened it.

"Rynah," came her grandfather's voice from the speakers as a holographic image of him appeared beside her, "I cannot tell you how saddened I am that you opened this. I can only assume that what I, and others, have feared most has happened: someone stole the crystal. If you are listening to this, then it means that our planet has been ravaged and someone has discovered the secrets of the six crystals. It also means that I am no longer there to do what I am afraid is now your task.

"As you know, our planet's magnetic fields are stabilized due to a crystal created by Benson Ranoe, but the truth of the matter is that he never created it. He discovered it.

"While traveling through a still unknown part of space, Ranoe stumbled upon a civilization that had a unique crystal. This crystal was in their temple, and they worshipped before it daily. The people were not as technologically advanced as us, and when Ranoe appeared in his shuttle craft, they assumed he was one of their gods. As he listened to their mythology about the crystal, he realized that it matched our ancient myths.

"After a series of tests, Ranoe concluded that this crystal was more than just a data core. Knowing he could use this to stabilize our planet as the magnetic fields had begun to destabilize, he stole it—a crime for which there is no forgiveness, for when he took it, that civilization crumbled.

"Ranoe brought the crystal back, claiming that he had discovered a way to save our home, and that he had created the data core. None questioned him because they had no reason not to believe him. As you know, for 1,500 years, we have used that crystal unaware of its true nature.

"Our people are now reaping the reward for his dishonesty. In my travels and research, I learned that there are five others, each just as unique as the one we possessed. When joined together, they become the heart of a weapon so powerful that it can destroy entire solar systems. I say the heart of a weapon, because according to my research, they are the data cores—if you want to call it that—of a ship that is in fact a weapon.

"Unfortunately, I have been unable to discover where the weapon and the other crystals are. My illness, I'm afraid, is winning the battle. I had hoped that no other would discover the secrets I have learned. I am sorry, Rynah.

"I left you Solaris. You, and you alone, can pilot her, unless you relinquish that control to another. She is a good friend and will serve you well. Study the ancient myths. Please, do not scoff at such a notion..."

Rynah stopped her inward chuckle at her grandfather's scolding.

"They are more real than you realize. I wish I could be there to help you so that you do not have to do it alone, but what was once my task is now yours. Good luck, my darling, and know that I will always love you."

The hologram disappeared as the message ended. A single tear rolled down Rynah's cheek as her grandfather left her once again.

"You have a moment?" asked Tom as he poked his head in.

"I thought you were asleep." Rynah clicked off the holoscreen and wiped the tear from her face.

"The others are, but I couldn't sleep."

"What can I do for you?"

"You can explain to me why we are all here," said Tom. "The bit you told us when we arrived made sense at the time, but some things don't add up."

"Such as?"

"The importance of the crystals."

Rynah released a heavy sigh. "They are data crystals, as I've informed you. A single sliver of quartz can hold about—oh, what's a term you use—100 gigabytes of memory. Now imagine how much memory a crystal the size of your hand can hold.

"Because they hold so much data, the crystal itself becomes a computer, of sorts, that can do unimaginable tasks."

"Such as control the magnetic fields of a planet," added Tom.

"Yes. My planet has an unstable magnetic field, making it practically uninhabitable. One man discovered how to use the amount of memory a quartz data crystal could hold to stabilize it, thus stopping all of the earthquakes and storms that plagued us. It is difficult to explain all of the engineering behind it, but suffice it to say that all he had to do was construct a computer to hold it, punch in a code, and it worked."

"But what makes this crystal so different from other crystals?"

"It is where he got it from. This crystal is different from what is normally used. It is of a higher quality with elements that we have yet to identify. And it is not the only one."

"How do you know?"

"Because the man who found it said that there were five others just like it, except no one knew of their locations."

"Hence, your legend of the six crystals," said Tom.

"Yes," breathed Rynah. "It is an old legend, and most of my people consider it nothing more than children's tales, but when Klanor stole this crystal, I began to wonder. But one thing I know for certain: I need it back to save my planet, and if he joins it with the others, I can only imagine what devastation he will inflict."

"Klanor," started Tom, "there is more between you and him that you have not told us."

Rynah's face pinched slightly as she controlled her anger. She watched as Tom's eyes, followed by his hand, moved toward the computer console ready to act on another bout of abject curiosity. "Would you like to pilot the ship?" she asked, changing the subject and distracting Tom from his inquisitiveness.

"Uh..."

"I'm sure Solaris won't mind and I can't always be in here."

"Oh sure, don't bother to ask me," quipped Solaris, with sarcasm.

"Sure," said Tom, allowing Rynah to steer him away from the relationship between her and Klanor as the thrill of flying a ship overtook him.

"Most times she can pilot herself, but sometimes she needs the help of one of us. Here, put this on." Rynah handed Tom the helmet used when piloting the ship. "It is a neuro interface and allows you to speak telepathically to Solaris."

"You act as though the ship is alive and has feelings," said Tom, taking the helmet. Bleeps and squeaks abounded as Solaris fumed over his comment.

"She can be a bit sensitive," said Rynah.

With caution, Tom slipped the interface helmet over his head. "Now what do I do?"

"Give her a command."

A series of thoughts flew through Tom's mind. The ship lurched and halted, throwing Rynah forward. "Oops."

"That would be my brakes, you ignoramus," snapped Solaris, "and it was quite uncomfortable."

"You must control your thoughts," instructed Rynah, moving a strand of her emerald hair from her face. "The slightest thought becomes a command."

"Where are we headed?" asked Tom.

Rynah gave a series of coordinates and Tom just thought about them. Soon the ship sped off through space in the new heading he had given it.

"That was better," said Solaris, "but I still do not like being piloted by strangers."

"Solaris, be nice," said Rynah.

"Hmmph," came the ship's reply.

"I think I'm getting the hang of it," said Tom.

"It's fairly easy," said Rynah. "Just keep going in this direction. I'm going to get some sleep. If anything arises, just press this button to talk to me in my quarters, and nothing else. Night."

"Night," mumbled Tom as he tried to keep control of his thoughts.

"Well, kiddo, I guess it's just you and me," said Solaris.

Tom remained silent, unsure of how to answer.

"Do you like chess?"

"Uh, sure."

Chapter 10
HUNGRY, HUNGRY PLANTS

"**W**e are approaching the Junglar Sector now," said Solaris, as they dropped out of hyperspeed.

"Acknowledged," said Rynah.

The others stood in the command center, watching the giant screen before them as they entered an unfamiliar solar system.

"Why is this sun green?" asked Brie.

"A star can be any color," replied Solaris. "The gaseous makeup of this particular star has turned it green. Some say that it is the reason for the abundant plant life."

"Oh." Brie stepped back until Alfric's giant form hid her.

"Take us into the planet's atmosphere," said Rynah.

"Very well," Solaris said, as she headed for a greenish-blue planet that was fifth from the sun.

"Hang on," said Rynah. "Entering a planet's atmosphere can get a little bumpy."

The turbulence jostled the ship as though it were a mere child's toy, knocking them off their feet.

"A little bumpy!" exclaimed Tom.

Rynah steered the ship to a small clearing. "Solaris, I want you to run continuous scans of the surrounding area. We should return in two hours."

"And if you don't?" asked Solaris.

Rynah didn't answer.

The five companions left the ship through Solaris' rear hatch, which opened onto a gangplank, and entered a world none of them had ever seen, one that even awed Rynah. Gigantic plants, the height of houses, with stems that were various shades of sea green and ecru, oval leaves of deep green on each side, which provided a sense of symmetry, heads that resembled unshelled almonds with petals of sanguine, plum, ruby, and sable, with specks of bronze upon them, loomed over the landscape, dwarfing the five newcomers. They stared at the plants, mesmerized.

"Let's move," said Rynah as she stomped across the ground.

The others followed.

Sweat streamed down their backs, causing their clothes to cling to their skin as the humidity, which created a vaporous layer above them that refracted the sunlight, sapped their energy. What had started as a brisk trek through a jungle soon became one of exhaustion. Their sluggish feet stepped into the soft, moist earth that acted more like a claw, reaching out for them, clinging to them, and preventing their movements.

Tom jerked his head around. He had the distinct feeling of being watched, a feeling he could not shake. A slight swish prickled his ears. He turned his head again and scanned the landscape, but everything was calm, too calm. A small part of his brain urged him to run.

"You feel it too?" asked Brie.

"Feel what?"

"Like we shouldn't be here."

Tom surveyed the area again and silently agreed with Brie that they needed to leave.

"Keep up, you two," snapped Rynah.

"I swear all she ever does is give orders," mumbled Brie.

Smiling, Tom agreed. *She is bossy.* He joined Brie and trailed after the others, forcing his mind to forget the small warning bells it sent him. *Plants can't watch you.* Something brushed his back. This time, Tom swung around, raising his hands in a protective stance.

"What's wrong?" asked Brie.

"Something touched me," said Tom.

Brie looked around. She didn't see anything out of the ordinary, but Tom's expression forced her to believe him. "Guys, we need to leave."

"What now?" demanded Rynah.

"This place is alive," said Tom.

"Of course it's alive," Rynah answered in a bored tone. "There are plants all over the place, meaning that life exists here."

"That's not what I mean," Tom said. "These plants are watching us."

"Impossible," scoffed Rynah.

"I'm telling you—"

"Where is Brie?" asked Solon, interrupting Tom's tirade.

Silence ensued. All of them glanced around as Brie had disappeared. A soft choking caught their attention. A few yards away, Brie hung suspended in the air as a leafy arm, resembling a claw more than the part of a plant, clutched her; a vine, snaking from the plant's head, around its body and to her mouth gagged her, while the plant's other leafy hand wrapped around her throat, forcing her lips and cheeks to turn turquoise in color.

A menacing battle cry erupted from Alfric as he charged the monstrous plants, sword raised. With one swift strike, he sliced through the plant's arm that had latched itself around Brie's throat. Brie crashed into the dirt, coughing and spitting out globs of sap.

More of the giant plants closed in. Alfric eyed them, realizing that Tom had been correct in his assessment: the plants were self-aware. One root shot straight for him. He dodged out of the way and brought his sword down upon it. The plant recoiled before retaliating by opening its mouth, exposing razor teeth, and releasing a deafening roar.

Frightened, Brie crouched low to the ground, covering her ears. She screeched and pleaded for it to stop.

"Take my hand," said Alfric.

Brie shook her head.

A tendril wrapped around Alfric's ankle, yanking him off his feet and causing him to lose his sword. Desperate, he clawed at the ground to keep from being pulled into the creature's mouth. Another leafy tendril curled around his waist and squeezed. Unable to breathe, Alfric tried to wrench it apart. It squeezed tighter.

Hunkered in her spot, Brie watched, helpless, as Alfric was dragged away, dusty, fibrous vines coiled around his torso. She glanced at the others, unsure of what to do. They fought off the vicious plants in vain, firing their weapons and swinging fallen branches. Someone hollered her name. Cringing, her hands covering her head of mousy brown hair, Brie just wished she were home, that it was nothing more than a mere dream.

A series of sputtering and muffled yelps made her look up. Alfric struggled for breath. Brie snatched a stick and raced for the man that had saved her life twice, slipping between the carnivorous plants as they tried to grab her. Alfric was about to pass out when Brie smacked the plant that held him with her stick. Startled, though not hurt, the plant reared its ugly head towards her, loosening its grip on the Viking. Brie stared at it, dropping her stick. She turned to flee, but it lassoed her and pulled her close.

Distracted by Brie, the plant failed to notice that Alfric fell free of its grasp. The Viking lunged for his blade, snatched it, and cut off the leafy arm that held Brie. With one great leap, he charged the creature and with a mighty swing of his sword, cut off the thing's head. Not wasting a moment, Alfric seized Brie, and together, they raced back to where the others fought for their lives.

Rynah leapt over a root that aimed for her feet. She somersaulted across the ground, pulled out her laser pistol, and fired. Squealing, the plant monster cried out in agony; its orange eyes glared at her. In retaliation, it reached for her again, seizing her long, emerald hair, which she had pulled in a braid, and jerked hard. Despite the intense pain in her scalp, Rynah aimed at the creature's mouth and pulled the trigger. Two laser blasts hit it in the back of its throat. It formed a sour, pinched face before tumbling over.

Freeing herself, Rynah glanced around. She spotted a cave nearby. "Over there!" she yelled, pointing at it.

The others turned and ran for the opening, leaping over protruding roots that popped out of the soil and reached for them. Something crashed into the ground, flinging debris that pelted their skin. Tumultuous noise raged around them as they ran for their salvation.

One by one, they entered the dark hole of the cave. Rynah counted each of them as they entered. Taking one last shot at a carnivorous plant that attempted to enter the cave with them, Rynah ducked inside. Knowing the voracious plants would never cease pursuing them, she did the only thing she could think of: she fired three shots at the cave entrance. Thunder loomed around them as rock and boulders crashed to the cave floor, blocking the entrance and sealing them inside, and their fate.

"How are we to get out?" asked Tom.

"I don't know," breathed Rynah.

"Rynah! Rynah!" came Solaris' voice over her earpiece. "You must all come back to the ship immediately. I have conducted additional scans of the planet's surface and have made a terrible discovery. The plants are meat-eating and—"

"Thanks, Solaris," replied Rynah, "but you're a little late."

"Oh," said Solaris. "What is your current location?"

"We are sealed in a cave," said Rynah. "I don't think we will be able to rendezvous with you on time. Stick to your orders."

"Understood."

"So how are we getting out?" asked Brie.

"We're not," said Rynah.

"I never should have left home," mumbled Brie as she wandered to a secluded part of the cave.

Rynah released an exasperated sigh. *Of all the people Solaris had to pick,* she thought. "What are you doing?" she asked Solon, who studied the cave wall with intense interest.

"Where there is an entrance, there must be an exit," he replied. "I am certain these tunnels run deep and will lead us to another way out."

"Really?" said Rynah. "And how can you be so certain?"

"Would you rather just sit here and wait to die?" asked Solon.

Rynah holstered her pistol. "The rest of you remain here. Solon and I will search these tunnels. If we find anything, we'll let you know."

"And if you don't?" asked Tom.

Rynah walked away with Solon in silence, refusing to answer Tom's question. Tom didn't mind. He had already guessed the answer.

Brie huddled in a shadowy corner of the cavern, its gloominess fueling her own, hugging her knees close to her, head hung low. She had screwed up earlier and she knew it. Why did they bring her? Brie knew she wasn't brave or warrior-like material. She was just a teenager who only wanted to get through high school and escape the endless taunts of Jenny and her friends. Brie felt all alone. The others looked upon her with disgust. Rynah had nothing but contempt for her. Brie wished she could go home. *Maybe they'd be better off without me.*

Heavy footsteps approached her. She glanced up and looked at Alfric before turning away.

"Why do you sit here alone?" asked Alfric, his gentle tone surprised her.

"Go away," mumbled Brie.

"It is not good to be alone."

"I screwed up today, okay?" Brie tried to hide the sob in the back of her throat, but it came out anyway.

"A mistake can be learned from," said Alfric. "Why do you frighten easily?"

"I don't know what you mean?"

"Why do you let fear take you? When faced with a challenge, you cower."

"Leave me alone."

"Why? What frightens you?"

"Nothing!" Brie stood up.

"Nothing? You curled in a ball while the rest of us were attacked."

"I don't do well in conflict. I hate confrontation."

"Why?"

"It doesn't matter."

"It does matter. Or would you rather spend your days as a coward? Why? Why do you run?"

"My father, okay?" Brie's voice bounced off the walls of the cave. "He died because of war. He died because of conflict! And now I am nothing but a weakling for the likes of Jenny to pick on each day."

Silence loomed as Alfric smiled, having gotten to the cause of Brie's problem. "Your father died in war?"

"Yes," replied Brie.

"My father also died in war, but I do not let it stop me from defending myself."

"I can't."

"Who is Jenny?"

"Some girl from school. She and her friends chase me home almost every day."

"So stop her," said Alfric.

"I can't," said Brie.

"Can't or won't?"

"I just can't!"

Alfric closed the distance between them and pushed Brie.

"What the..."

Alfric shoved her again.

"Stop it."

In answer to her demands, he shoved her a third time, nearly knocking her off her feet.

"Stop!"

"Make me stop," said Alfric as he shoved her a fourth time.

"Look, I don't want to fight," said Brie, who tried to back away. Alfric pushed her again.

"I said to stop!"

"Then why don't you stop me?" He shoved her a sixth time.

Infuriated, Brie pushed his arm out of the way and punched him on the chin, recoiling, putting her hands over her mouth. "I'm sorry," she whispered.

Alfric touched the sore spot where she had struck him. "The next time Jenny chases you, you should strike her as you have struck me." He turned to leave, but paused. "Never apologize for defending yourself from an attack."

Brie stood alone in the darkness, unsure of what she thought about what had occurred. She flexed her fist, marveling at the sense of power she felt when she forced Alfric to stop pushing her around, and at the sting that still remained on her knuckles. Maybe he had a point.

Rynah snapped a glow light around her wrist. "Here," she said to Solon as she snapped one around his wrist.

"What is that?" he asked, having never seen one before.

"Think of it as a torch," she replied.

She and Solon walked together in the damp, murkiness of the cave, her boots making heavy clomps compared to Solon's sandals, which sounded more like taps. She waved her light at the cave wall, noting the smooth, multicolored ripples that lined it.

"What makes you think that there is another entrance?" asked Rynah.

"This," replied Solon, pointing at a tiny stream of water. "It must have a beginning. That is our way out of here."

Smiling, Rynah peered closer at the stream. "Perhaps you're of some use after all."

"Is that the reason why you brought us all here? Because you thought we would be useful?"

Rynah slowed her pace. She knew that she had not been entirely honest with Solon and the others, but how could she?

She faced him. "No."

Solon's expression indicated disbelief. For a brief moment, Rynah felt that the young Greek philosopher could see right through her. "I brought you all here because you were the only ones who could help me."

"One man's lie is another man's truth," said Solon.

"I'm not…"

Solon faced her. The stern expression on his once calm face unnerved her. "I don't care what your reasons are for wanting Klanor dead," he said. "I just ask that you be honest about them. You owe us all that."

Rynah felt heat escape her as Solon scrutinized her. She felt she had been reduced from the leader of the group to a student. Rather than consider his words, she reiterated the same story. "I have been honest. Klanor destroyed my planet and means to destroy yours. You and the others are the only ones I can trust."

"Because of an ancient legend."

"Mostly."

"Interesting how readily we trust strangers over the ones we know," said Solon as he continued to walk upstream, "Klanor is not all that he seems. When he taunted you, I sensed that there was more to his offer, an internal struggle, but there was more to your answer as well; there is turmoil in you. I fear that you have a hard lesson to learn, Rynah."

"What do you mean?"

"Just like I must learn to be on time for my studies, you must learn to face whatever it is you are hiding, even if you do not realize that you are running from it."

"I am not running from anything," said Rynah.

Solon didn't respond to her statement. He turned back around and continued after the small stream, its slow trickle filling the tunnel with its song. Light spilled up ahead. Using the glow light around his wrist, Solon guided them to what he saw.

"What is it?" asked Rynah.

Solon stopped under a hole in the cave ceiling, beaming as the sunlight shone through it. "I have found our exit."

Rynah stepped over to him and peered up at the hole. It seemed big enough for them squeeze through. "Let's go tell the others."

Chapter 11
MOTHER GODDESS

Hurried, echoing footsteps alerted everyone to Solon's and Rynah's return. They all leapt to their feet.

"What's the verdict?' inquired Tom with excitement.

"There is a way out," said Rynah, "but it will require a bit of climbing."

"Who cares, so long as we can get out of here?" said Tom.

"I suggest we leave now," said Rynah. "Follow Solon, since he is the one who found it, and stay close together."

One by one, they trekked through the cavernous tunnel as Solon led them to the hole. Brie brushed her fingers against the wall, amazed at its smoothness and ripples that were only an eighth of an inch wide. Afterward, she stole a quick glance at Alfric, who merely smiled at her wonderment.

"There it is," said Solon.

Each of them paused before the stream of daylight that spilled into the underground chamber; particles of dust hovered in the rays, disappearing only for a moment, as they passed into the slivered shadows created by the few sticklike roots that partially covered the opening.

"All right, I'll go fir—" began Rynah. She stopped as Alfric trudged over to the hole in the ceiling. He climbed the rock wall below the hole and pulled himself through, despite his bulky size.

"Right," muttered Rynah. "Brie, you're next."

Unsure of how to rock climb, Brie reached for Alfric's outstretched hand. Tom walked over to her. With his help, she grasped Alfric's meaty hand and gasped as he heaved her through, setting her gently on her feet. Glad to be on solid ground again, Brie backed away from the hole she had just come out of. Solon and Tom came out next, followed by Rynah.

"We should get back to Solaris," said Rynah.

"That may not be so easy," muttered Tom.

"Why?" Rynah whirled around, only to find a spear in her face.

Surrounded by people with gray skin and tattooed markings across their bodies, none of them moved.

"Solaris," whispered Rynah into her earpiece.

No answer.

"Solaris!"

The point of a spear pricked her heliotrope skin. "Okay," said Rynah, throwing up her hands.

Alfric reached for his sword, but Brie put her hand over his, shaking her head.

"Sometimes," said Solon, "it is best to bide your time. This is not a fight we can win at the moment."

Reluctant, as he preferred fighting over surrender, Alfric released his grip on the hilt.

One of the natives motioned for them to walk, speaking in a language none of them understood. With little choice, they obeyed.

They followed their captors through the forest of humongous, tropical plants; their subdued demeanor surprised them. Rynah observed the alien humanoids' silent movements as they walked through the jungle expanse. *No wonder they caught us.* She watched as one man shot a dart at a moving plant. The thing stilled and went limp. Smiling, Rynah realized that these people had a better way of dealing with the man-eating plants.

What she saw next took her breath away. Massive pyramids stood before her, stretching 13 stories in height. Vines of ivory crept up the stone walls, wrapping around the crevices and adding distinctive characteristics.

"It's like we entered the Mayan world," breathed Brie, who had watched something on television about the Mayan civilization the week before being transported to Solaris.

Rynah didn't know who the Mayan were, but these people resembled drawings she had seen as a child. Those drawings referred to an ancient race that lived thousands of years ago. She had never dreamed that there might have been some truth to it.

Rynah glanced at the villagers who gathered around as they strode, under guard, into their home. Many of the women had large beads dangling from their ears, while the men each had a ring in their nose. As she scrutinized them, she noticed that the rings differed in color, ranging from sage, indigo, and white, and wondered if they signified the person's status in this society.

Incoherent muttering pulled her from her curiosity. The men with spears motioned for them to climb the stone steps of one of the pyramids.

"They're bringing us into their temple," said Solon.

"How do you know?" asked Tom.

"I have read tales of men in the south who built great pyramids of sand. The soldiers say that these pyramids are their temples. I assume it is the same here," replied Solon.

"He is correct."

"Solaris!" Rynah hissed into her earpiece. "Where have you been?"

"I temporarily lost communications," replied Solaris. "The problem is fixed now."

"Can you get us out of here?" asked Rynah as one of their captors poked her with the sharp end of his spear.

"You know full well that my transporter systems are limited. I burnt out most of the systems when I brought our guests here."

Cursing, Rynah wished Solaris would quit countering all of her ideas.

"You will have to get here the old-fashioned way. Walk."

"That is going to be a bit difficult," whispered Rynah.

"I noticed you have been whispering," said Solaris. "Is something wrong?"

"You could say that," replied Rynah. She stopped talking when one of their captors looked in her direction. "We have been captured by some natives."

"But all of my scans indicated... uh, oh."

"Uh, oh?" said Rynah.

"Do they smell like tar?" asked Solaris.

"What?" Rynah hushed her voice as the others glanced at her outburst. "You want me to smell them?"

"That is the general idea."

"What is going on?" asked Brie.

"I finally got communications back with Solaris," said Rynah, "and she wants me to sniff our captors."

"I'll do it," said Tom. He inched his way closer to one of the natives, leaned in, and took a big whiff. Choking coughs escaped his mouth as he tried to get the awful smell from his nose.

The man glared at him.

"I thought I saw something on you."

The man shoved Tom back in line with the others.

"Are you done smelling him?" teased Brie.

"Only if you go out with me," said Tom, sarcastically.

"Hey," interrupted Rynah.

"Tar," answered Tom. "Definitely tar."

"Solaris, they smell like tar."

"Well, that explains it," said Solaris. "The tar masks their life signs from my scanners and allows them to blend in with the vegetation."

"Can you get to us?" asked Rynah in a low voice.

"Yes, but it will take time," replied Solaris.

"We don't have much time," said Rynah.

They had reached the top of the stairs. Their captors lined them up before an altar where a man with white hair stood with an elderly woman and a young girl who could be no more than five years old. None of them understood the old man's rapid words, except for the irate tone of his voice.

"This isn't good," said Solon.

"Do you know what he is saying?" asked Alfric.

"No, but this is a place of sacrifice—human sacrifice."

"We're not it, are we?" asked Brie.

"I don't think so," said Solon, "but it appears as though we interrupted an important celebration for them. The man's movements indicate that he is explaining the story of their existence."

"You can tell all of that from his body language?" asked Tom.

"Yes," replied Solon. "Great story tellers always use the same movements for similar tales."

The man stopped speaking. He pointed at the five of them and rambled on in his native tongue. No one moved. The village elder reached out for the timid girl, pulling her towards the stone table. She obeyed. He placed her on the table, forcing her to lie down. More words escaped his mouth as he explained the ritual and how it would bring life to their civilization.

Brie watched horrified. She remembered reading about how some ancient cultures, such as the Aztecs, conducted human sacrifice, but those were always distant stories to her. Now she stood before a real sacrificial offering.

"Why the girl?" she asked.

"Young girls are innocent and virgins," replied Solon. "Their blood is believed to purify the earth."

"He's going to kill her," shrieked Brie.

"Do nothing," said Rynah.

"But—"

"I mean it!"

Brie watched in terror as the old man raised his jeweled dagger. She glanced around as the emotionless crowd watched the ritual. No, she was not going to just stand there and let it happen. Brie charged the stone table and the man with the dagger. With a fury she had never known to exist in herself, she grasped the man's wrist and wrenched the knife from him, tossing it aside. It clattered as it rolled down the stone steps of the temple.

"This is barbaric!" yelled Brie.

The man and the woman stared at her. An eruption happened. The male elder cursed and screamed at Brie in his native tongue. She slapped him. Stunned, the man stepped back. A group of men with spears charged Brie. With a great cry, Alfric unsheathed his blade and knocked them off their feet, but did not kill them. He took a protective stance in front of Brie. Another charged. The Viking picked him up and tossed him over the side of the temple wall.

Tom snatched the spear of one and thrust him into the gathered crowd. "I think we've overstayed our welcome."

Another charged them. Rynah pulled out her laser pistol and shot him in the leg. She fired at two more. "Solaris, now would be a good time to show up!"

"ETA 30 seconds," said Solaris.

Arrows pelted them from above, stabbing the stone beneath their feet and missing them by inches. When the girl shrieked, Brie wrapped a protective arm around her. More charged them. Stepping forward, Alfric released a chilling battle cry while beating his chest with his fists, thus stopping the charge. They shrank back in fright, having never seen such a wild looking man.

The strange sight continued with Brie hugging the girl and Tom, Rynah, Solon, and Alfric forming a protective barrier between them and the natives. Such a scene greeted Solaris when she arrived. The roar of her engines filled the area as she hovered low, above them with the back hatch open. The people of the village dropped to their knees and bowed before the strange newcomers, muttering praises of worship.

"Solaris, it's about time you arrived," barked Rynah.

"I would say that my timing is perfect," replied Solaris.

"Let's go," said Rynah.

"Wait," Brie stopped them. "What about her?"

Rynah eyed the girl. "We can't take her."

"But if we leave her, they will kill her."

"I don't think so," said Solon. "They think we are gods. I believe they will leave her be."

Brie's reluctance showed as she untangled herself from the girl, but she knew Rynah was right. The child clutched her wrist in fear. A spot of red caught Brie's eye. She looked closer and realized it was a cut. Brie pulled a *Dora the Explorer* Band-Aid out of her pocket, something she usually kept there for her little sister, and placed it over the child's open wound.

"Better?"

The girl seemed to have understood and nodded her tear-stained face, glancing at the drawing sticking out of Rynah's pocket. The child jumped off the table, taking Brie's hand and pulled her inside the temple. The others chased after them.

Carved statues lined the wall with lit torches in between each. Up ahead was a domed structure with a pedestal, but that wasn't what caught their attention.

"The crystal!" said Rynah. "It is here. But how do we get to it?"

A giant gap loomed before them, cutting them off from their goal.

The girl placed a slender rod in Brie's hand and pointed at the stalactites hanging from the ceiling.

"I don't understand," said Brie, but Tom did.

He looked around at the pile of gigantic stones. "I know what to do. You have to use sound to move these stones and form a bridge."

"What?" Everyone stared at him.

"I actually know something you don't?" Tom said to Rynah. "Okay, look, a friend of mine back at the academy has been experimenting with using sound to move large objects. He has even managed to have some success with moving rocks, but nothing as big as these boulders. But the theory is just the same. I bet each of these stalactites produce a different tone that will move each of the stones."

"But that is like something out of science fiction," said Brie.

"You are on an alien planet, with an alien race on the far side of the galaxy, and with a ship with an attitude," Tom reminded her.

"I do not have an attitude," Solaris said into Rynah's ear, "but the weasel is right. She must produce the proper sounds to levitate the stones."

"Solaris says to give it a try," Rynah told them.

When Brie hesitated, Tom moved to take the rod from her and demonstrate what he meant; the girl stepped between them, snatching the rod with her tiny hand.

"I think she means for you to do it," Tom said, backing away.

"But I don't know how," said Brie.

"Music is known to produce different tones, each with mathematical properties," said Solon, who had been studying the entire interior of the temple. "Do you play the lute?"

"Uh, no," said Brie, "but I do play the guitar."

For the last six years, she had taught herself to play the guitar her father had left her before he died. She tapped each of the stalactites with the rod, each producing a different note. Brie decided to play her parent's favorite song, one they had played at their wedding.

Concentrating on the task at hand, Brie touched each of the stalactites in rhythmic order, pretending that they were actually her guitar. Soft melody filled the chamber, echoing off the walls. While Brie played the instrument, the others watched in anticipation. One of the boulders vibrated.

"Look!" said Tom.

"Shh," Solon quieted him.

Covering his mouth with his hand so he wouldn't squeal with delight, Tom danced from foot to foot as his friend's theory was proven correct before his very eyes. Each watched mesmerized as one rock lifted into the air, a bit rocky at first—no pun intended—

and settled over the gaping hole in the floor. As it hovered, Brie continued playing her song, not paying any attention to what happened around her. Another boulder levitated. It floated through the air and nestled beside the first. One by one, each of the stones filled the space before them, forming a floating bridge.

"Keep playing," said Rynah.

Tom moved for the bridge, but Solon stopped him.

"Perhaps the lightest person should go."

Taking one look at his scrawny structure, Tom agreed.

Solon approached the hovering bridge. He placed his sandaled foot atop it. Nothing happened. Summoning his courage, the young scholar hopped on the stone. Though it dipped a bit under his weight, it remained in the air. With music filling his ears, Solon jumped from stone to stone until he reached the other side.

The crystal lay directly in front of him. Glancing back at the others, he noticed that some of the natives had filed into the room. Solon reached for the crystal. Marveling at its smooth structure, he cupped it in his hands and dashed back across the floating bridge. The moment he reached the other side, Brie stopped playing, allowing the boulders to fall into the abyss below.

"I can't believe it," said Brie.

"Give it to me," Rynah reached for the crystal. Solon handed it to her and she put it in her pack. "We need to leave. Solaris, are you ready?"

"I was ready 10 minutes ago," said Solaris.

"Let's go, before unexpected guests arrive."

"I have to go now," said Brie to the girl. She gave the child one last hug and the rod, and followed the others into the open hatch of the ship; Rynah was the last to board.

What Brie couldn't have known was how they all would be remembered through the ages on that planet. The people dubbed her *Megula* (meaning "honored mother") and erected a temple in her honor. The girl she saved later became the high priestess of the temple. When the ruins of that civilization were unearthed several millennia later, they discovered drawings depicting the story of how the *Megula* descended from the stars with her guards, saved a child, thus condemning human sacrifice, and reclaimed her precious gem.

Once aboard the ship, Solaris fired her booster rockets and left the atmosphere.

"Well," said Rynah as she weighed the crystal in her hands, "I guess we should count ourselves lucky to get out of there in one piece." She glanced at Brie, who tugged on strands of her brown hair, "And you. Your screeching nearly got us killed."

"But she gained us a crystal."

"The first useful thing she's done since she was brought on board. Solaris, take us out of here." Rynah marched out of the cargo area of the ship, heading straight for her quarters.

"You need to get better control of your emotions and learn to appreciate the other members of your crew," scolded Solaris, her voice following Rynah throughout the ship as she tried to get away and hide in her room.

"Leave me alone," she snapped.

"I will not."

"I said go away!" Rynah stopped and shouted at the speakers within the corridor of the ship. She stomped into her room, sealing the door behind her. She pulled back a loose panel of the wall, revealing a safe, opened it, and secured the crystal inside.

"You'll not be rid of me so easily."

"Oh, Great Ancients, save me from this impertinent pest!"

"I am no—"

"Why won't you leave me alone?"

"Your grandfather charged me with the task of helping you during this time."

"Oh, who cares? He's dead."

"You should."

"Why?" demanded Rynah. "What did my grandfather ever do for me? He scolded me each time I became curious about his work.

He chased me away the one time he caught me reading that ancient book. Then he goes on a damn fool mission to steal the crystal from the geo-lab, the same one that Klanor has managed to snatch, and I am supposed to care about what he wants? He's been dead for years now. I don't give a da—"

"You should!" Solaris' rage filled her voice, silencing Rynah and startling her. "And you should quit being so harsh on Brie."

"That girl is a nuisance," Rynah said. "Why did you ever bring her aboard?"

"I have my reasons—reasons you are not to question! There are things in this universe that you know nothing about, but will learn in time if you have a mind, and the patience, to do so."

"What was so important that my grandfather chose to curse me with you and that cowardly girl?"

"Is that what you think of me?" Brie stood in the doorway. She had come to Rynah's room to apologize for her behavior on the planet, her natural quietness having gone unnoticed.

"I-I didn't mean," began Rynah, startled, "I ju—"

"No, I get it," said Brie, holding back tears. "I know I have screwed up one too many times on this ship. I guess not everyone can have your courage."

Brie ran off, stomping up the steps to an upper, and more secluded, level of the ship.

Rynah rushed to the doors to apologize, but they sealed just as she reached them. "Let me out!"

"No," said Solaris.

"How am I to apologize if you keep me locked in here?"

"Have your opinions of her changed?"

"No."

"Then why should I believe that you are truly sorry for what you have said about her?"

"You know, I am really sick and tired of you chastising me all of the time. You are no better than me, or anyone else on this ship."

"Perhaps not, but I happen to be the only one who fully under-
stands the magnitude of our situation. You, Rynah, must learn to
calm yourself before you are able to understand it as well."

"How can I? How can you remain so calm? Does the destruction of Lanyr mean nothing to you? Why should it mean anything?
You are nothing more than a few electrical components and memory chips put together. You have no feelings."

Rynah shut her mouth the moment she made that last statement, wishing she could take it back, but spoken words are not easily retracted. Silence reigned around her. She did not know about
the hours Solaris spent replaying the video feed of the destruction
of Lanyr. Rynah wondered if Solaris had abandoned her, nestling
deep within her memory banks.

"Solaris, I—"

"The only reason you are still standing is because Marlow made
me promise to look after you. He gave me life, and his was taken
shortly after."

"Solaris, I'm sorry." Rynah's tone conveyed the truthfulness of
her words.

"I am furious," said Solaris in a controlled tone, ignoring
Rynah's words. "Each time I think about Lanyr's fate and the one
who brought it about, I seethe with anger and loathing. I, more
than anyone, want revenge, but revenge won't bring Lanyr, or the
lives lost, back. You asked me how I can be so calm, so cold. Maybe
you should ask yourself what my calmness will achieve. Running
off half-cocked solves nothing and only gets you killed in the end.
Unlike you, Rynah, I have thought about Klanor's plans and what
he hopes to achieve. In doing so, I hope to be able to outsmart him.
Maybe you should do the same."

As Rynah listened to Solaris' words, she heard her grandfather
in them. She hung her head in shame. "Solaris, I never meant—"

"You never do," said Solaris, "but that is what comes from never thinking."

"Solaris?"

No answer.

"Solaris?"

Still no answer.

Ashamed, Rynah kicked her bunk before plopping down on the thin, feather mattress, wishing she could take back everything she had just said. She thought about her grandfather and of all the hours he had spent repairing the ship or studying the ancient text. She thought about Klanor and his marriage proposal, and the happiness she felt upon receiving it. Exhausted, and emotionally drained, Rynah cupped her head in her hands and wept.

Solaris heard her crying, but chose to remain invisible. *Best leave her to think on it*, she thought.

Chapter 12
A Bit of Quiet

Brie curled her knees in close as she sat under the stars, staring out at the strange constellations, which formed strange shapes of spiraling triangles (or zigzags), and the tie-died nebulas that surrounded them. She had hoped to be able to make out some of the ones she knew from home, but in a ship flying through space, such a prospect remained impossible, so she named a few (calling one tinsel because it reminded her of a Christmas tree), despite what their real names might have been. They flew at normal speed, allowing Brie the opportunity to admire the scenery, and solitude. A chill attacked her shoulders. Shivering, she refused to leave Solaris' observation deck.

A part of Brie felt thrilled to be on the ship and exploring new worlds, though the pang of leaving home still gnawed at her. She wished she could have said good-bye to her mother and sister. *How they must be so worried about me*, she thought. Brie shivered again.

"My sensors indicate that you are cold," came Solaris's voice from the speaker above Brie.

"It's not that bad," replied Brie. "Arizona is a little warmer."

"I have increased the temperature by three degrees," said Solaris. "Does that help?"

"Much," answered Brie. She relaxed and stretched her legs. "I thought you were navigating tonight."

"Tom is flying," said Solaris. "Though that twit will probably force us to crash into a passing asteroid."

Brie chuckled. "But I thought you flew yourself."

"Normally I do," said Solaris, "but someone has to give me a flight path. However, there are times when it is easier for there to be a pilot. Even a computer needs a break. I can't work all day, sweetheart."

"Sweetheart? Where'd you hear that term?"

"When I transported you from your planet, I tapped into the World Wide Web and downloaded what information I could in the short time window I had open."

"Did you do the same from Tom's time?"

"His time has something more advanced, and by then, my power stores were near depletion. Time travel, and travel across the universe, takes a lot of power."

Brie looked back out at the passing stars. She noticed what looked like a pink and gold sun. *Beautiful.*

"You miss your home?"

Holding back a tear, Brie swallowed in an effort to keep her emotions out of her voice. "Yes. I never got a chance to say good-bye."

"Tell me about your home," said Solaris.

If the ship had a body, Brie would have sworn she sat beside her. "It's warm, in the middle of a desert, but Phoenix is a big city, too. I have a mother and a little sister."

"Your father?"

"He died. He was supposed to be coming home the next week, but a suicide bomber decided to walk into the place where he was stationed. Four were killed that day and my father was one of them."

Brie choked back a few tears. Her birthday was the next week and he had been expected home in time. Her parents had planned to make it a big surprise, but death had other plans.

"That was six years ago."

"I am sorry," said Solaris; sympathy came through her voice, even though she was a machine.

"So am I," mumbled Brie.

When the news hit her about her father's death, she felt numb. A week later, the full impact crushed her. Soon the bills piled up and then the recession hit. Her mother was one of the first people let go when the company she worked for was forced to downsize to cut costs, though they soon went under and shut their doors. Unable to find reliable employment, her mother declared bankruptcy, and they moved into government housing (half a block filled with tightfitting; deteriorating buildings; concrete where grass should have been; broken downspouts; overflowing dumpsters that reeked of fecal matter and rotted food; moldy, abandoned furniture; and graffiti), or what Brie called a fleabag place full of roaches and filth. Forced to wear other people's castoffs from the Salvation Army, or local thrift store, Brie was the target of Jenny's torment.

Her mother later found employment as a part-time waitress at a local bar. Brie wished her mother didn't have to work there, since she always came home smelling like liquor and cigarettes. "One day, Brie, things will improve," her mother had told her. Brie wondered when that day would come.

"You miss them?" asked Solaris.

"Yes," replied Brie.

"When you return home, what would you like to do?"

"I don't know. I never really gave it much thought. I once thought that I would write a book."

"Then you should do that," said Solaris, taking a genuine interest in Brie's desires.

"I am only 16," said Brie, "What could I possibly write about?"

"You are also on a ship, in the middle of space, where you battled man-eating plants and saved a young girl from being sacrificed to fictitious gods. I would say that you have a lot to write about."

"I wish my friends felt that way," mumbled Brie.

"You have one that does," said Solaris.

Confused, Brie looked up. "Who?"

"Me."

It had never occurred to Brie that she could befriend a computer, but Solaris acted so human sometimes that she realized she could.

"Thanks, Solaris."

"Would you like to see a bit of home?"

"Sure."

The glass in the observation room fogged up as a starry sky filled it. It looked just like the sky from the Arizona backcountry. Brie recognized the constellation of Orion and the Big Dipper. Some others she recognized the shapes of, but could not name. A shooting star streaked across the holographic sky.

"Thank you, Solaris. This is the best gift you could have given me."

"I like your sky," said Solaris. "Maybe I will stand under it someday."

Though unsure of how a computer on a ship would ever stand beneath the stars, Brie decided not to question it. "Perhaps you will."

Chapter 13
AQUARA

Over the serene planet of Aquara, an archaic spaceship appeared from nothingness with the name of Solaris painted on its side. The planet had no way of knowing why the ship chose to park above it, nor did it care. Covered entirely in water with marine creatures as the only form of life, the deep blue planet ignored the visitors, the first humans and Lanyran it had ever seen and would see for a very long time.

"Welcome to Aquara," said Rynah. "An entire planet with no land mass. Just water."

The others stared out the port window amazed at such a thing. Of course, all of the planets they had visited had awed them.

"Suit up," said Rynah, pressing a button that opened a storage room, holding seven spacesuits. "These may be meant for space walking, but they will work in the water as well."

"But won't we sink?" asked Tom.

"Nope." Rynah pressed something on one of the suits and fins appeared. "This ought to help you swim," she said, taking note of Tom's greenish face. "Don't tell me you are afraid of the water."

"Not entirely," said Tom.

"I do not need such a suit," grumbled Alfric. "We Vikings are great seafarers and know how to navigate the seas."

"But how will you breathe under water?" asked Rynah.

Grimacing, Alfric took the suit. He hopped around on one foot as he unsuccessfully tried to get his suit on properly.

"It might help if you took off your cloak and your many weapons," said Solaris. "Just a thought."

"Here," said Brie as she helped Alfric unload his many blades and scramble into the suit.

"Is there any way we can let him keep the sword because big boy over there looks like he's going to cry," Tom teased when Alfric refused to let Brie have his trusted sword.

"It'll be fine," said Brie.

Alfric relinquished his most prized possession, but kept his knives. Brie set it aside where it would be well-protected.

"Everyone ready?" asked Rynah as she checked their suits to make sure they had put them on properly. "Here," she handed Alfric a belt she had fashioned which would hold a few of his knives.

"I thank you, great lady," he said.

Rynah suppressed a smile, unsure of how she liked being called a "great lady". "Solaris, do you have the coordinates?"

"Yes," replied Solaris.

"Okay, listen up," said Rynah over the noise as they lowered into the planet's atmosphere and hovered over the ocean. "When these doors open beneath us, you will all jump. You will sink at first, but don't panic. This button controls the thrusters on your suit; it will help you swim. This one controls the fins. Pay attention to this indicator bar here" —she waved the square thing on her wrist in front of them— "it tells you how much oxygen you have left. When it turns red, it means you need to get to the surface immediately. We will have about an hour to look around."

"You're certain the next crystal is here?" asked Tom.

"I'm not certain of anything," said Rynah, securing her helmet.

The doors opened beneath them, revealing tumultuous waves that rose and plowed into the surface of the teal water; swirls of pastel green bubbles drifted across the top as honey-colored sunrays penetrated the surface, delving deep within until the elephantine darkness swallowed them. Rynah jumped first, followed by Tom and Solon. Brie tried backing away from the edge, but Alfric pushed her into the water. Muffled gurgling sounds echoed around her ears as she sank below the surface and dropped to the bottom of the sea; the water turned a darker shade of blue with each passing second.

A hand grasped her arm. It was Rynah. She punched a button on Brie's suit, causing fins to pop out on her feet and arms. Waving her arms like one would when treading water, Brie prevented herself from sinking any further.

"Follow me," came Rynah's voice over the radio. "Search for anything that matches the ancient verse or anything unusual. Remember, there are a lot of dangers here, so be careful."

They moved through the water (bits of green algae wafted past) with tiny, white bubbles escaping their suits each time they breathed. Small lights on their wrists illuminated the dark waters. Brie gasped when a giant whale swam below her. She glanced at Solon, who smiled, enthralled by it and enjoying himself. She hurried after the others. Something stopped in front of her. Taking a closer look, Brie realized that they were seahorses, but they looked different from the ones she had seen on the television back home. Just then, Solon reached out to her and pointed at what appeared to be a wavy, neon light; it was a type of eel.

Tom swam below them. He shone his light onto the sandy floor, watching the creatures crawl across it. "I wish I had my camera," he said. Fish darted out of his light, only to reappear the moment he passed by. A translucent tentacle dropped before him. Tom swerved to avoid being struck by a monstrous jellyfish. He watched as the sea creature bobbed, waving its tentacles. Continuing on, he spotted something. "Hey, guys, over here."

Rynah swam up to where he was. She waved the beam of her light on a shadowed silhouette protruding from the coral reef.

"I don't believe it," she said. "It's a ship."

They kicked harder to reach the sunken vessel, which was coated in barnacles and corals and had become home to a whole array of sea creatures. Once there, Rynah studied the markings on the metal exterior. Solon did too.

"I think it says Heracles."

"You can read this?" said Rynah in disbelief.

"Partly," replied Solon as he studied the writing. "Most of it appears to be Greek, but some of the markings are different. These I do not understand."

"But those are runes," said Alfric, recognizing some of them. "But how can this be?"

Hovering before the triangular ship, Brie reached out and touched it with her gloved hand, smearing the red algae that covered it. Some of the writing etched on the side resembled the pictures she had seen in dusty library books, though she was never able to decipher them.

"Herclai," said Rynah. "That is the name of the ship, but I don't understand."

"What?" said Tom.

"According to the stories of my people, Herclai was a strong warrior, but with a terrible temper."

"Sounds like the Greek myth of Hercules," said Brie.

"Yes, but unlike your earth myths, Herclai stole a powerful object that was said to be able to control the forces of nature. He broke it into six parts and… hid them." Rynah stared at the ship as a realization struck her: the ancient myths of her planet were true, to a degree. The myth of Herclai referred to the story of the crystals. Could they be the same, yet written as two different tales?

"The six crystals," said Tom. "Are you telling me this guy visited Earth?"

"I don't know," whispered Rynah. She had never believed the tales. She only wanted to stop Klanor. "We need to get inside. There should be an access port somewhere."

"Found it," said Tom, pointing at a hatch. "But we'll need to wedge it open."

As though summoned, Alfric appeared. Using one of his knives, he pried open the hatch for the pressure inside the vessel to be released. The door burst open. Each of them swam inside. Rynah climbed a set of stairs that led to another hatch. Using all her strength, she twisted the wheel on the door and popped it open, revealing an area that had not been overcome by seawater. She hauled herself into the corridor and helped the others.

"All right," she said, taking off her helmet, "the air in here seems to be breathable. We need to find the command center. I think it's this way."

"There is no need," said Alfric, pointing at a mummified corpse. "His adornments mean that he is an important member of his people."

Rynah brushed the smudge off the patch on the uniform. The symbol upon it was similar to the symbol she wore on her security uniform. "How can this be?"

"How can what be?" asked Brie.

Rynah showed them the similar symbols.

"I think there is much about your people's history that you do not know," said Solon.

"But if he is the captain," said Rynah, "what is he doing down here?" She glanced at where the corpse faced as she realized what he had been looking at when he died. Rynah pressed against the panel in front of the remains, trying to pry it open. Nothing. She heaved again. "Alfric, do you think…"

The Viking shoved her aside. He pounded the panel with his fist, noting that it wasn't very thick. Snatching a fallen metal bar, he jabbed the door with it, forcing it open. Air burst from the sealed room, wafting over them with its staleness.

"Thanks," said Rynah as she stepped into the dark interior, focusing her light on everything.

A soft humming drew Tom's attention. Without telling the others, he wandered to the far corner of the room where he searched every shadow. Nothing. Undeterred, Tom felt around the wall. *That humming has to be coming from here.* He looked at the others. They dispersed, each taking a separate area to search, and ignored him. Guessing that they didn't hear the soft hum, he continued probing the corner.

Rynah approached a book situated in the center of the room. Curious, she turned the pages, taking great care not to damage them.

"Why would this be here?"

"Some people enjoy reading," said Solon.

"No," said Rynah. "I meant, on a ship where everything is digital, why have an archaic book made of paper?"

"Some prefer the feel of the pages," said Brie. "My mom refused to buy an e-reader, saying that it takes the humanity out of reading a book." A downcast look crossed her face as she remembered her home.

Knowing she would never get another chance, Rynah pulled a camera the size of her thumb out and took pictures of the pages. She hoped that Solaris could translate them.

She bumped something. Before she had time to see what it was, a holographic face filled the room as a deep voice resonated around them.

"This is Herclai. Mat—has—my systems are all compromised. Considering the nature of the crys—I—put the ship down. Maybe—I'm sorry. There is no other way. I hope the universe does not pay for our mistake."

The images vanished.

"It appears that Herclai was a person, not a ship," said Solon.

Rynah pressed all of the controls she found in an effort to bring back the recording, but failed.

"I still do not understand why that man would be heading for this room when the ship crashed."

"I think I know," said Tom as he pulled a panel away, revealing a small, luminescent crystal.

"It's here!" said Rynah in shock, "But what..."

She rushed over to a computer terminal and pushed the button. The screen flickered to life. Though distorted, Rynah managed to decipher some of the characters on the screen. "That crystal is the power source for the ship. It seems that even after it crashed, it managed to keep some of the systems running and the water from flooding this section."

"But how could it still be working after all this time?" asked Brie.

"It is a very strong power source. A renewable one I suspect, the likes of which I have never seen. Solaris?"

"Yes," came Solaris' crackled reply.

"I am sending you a transmission," said Rynah. "See if you can..."

A loud thud cut her off. In walked four of Klanor's men, wearing suits similar to theirs. "And I thought we had beaten you all," said one, whose name was Stein. "Who are you four anyway?" he pointed at Brie, Alfric, Solon, and Tom.

"No one of consequence," said Tom.

"Let me be the judge of that," said Stein. "In any case, it doesn't matter. Hand me the crystal."

"No," said Rynah.

"Brave, but foolish," said Stein.

No one moved.

"We are leaving with the crystal one way or another," Stein said, holding out his hand.

Rynah placed it in his outstretched, gloved hand. He curled his fingers around it; a smirk etched on his face.

"Run back to your master with it like the lapdog you are," spat Rynah.

Stein ignored her comment.

Thwank!

Water burst through a pinprick-sized hole, spraying all of them.

"You know," said Stein, "I believe this is our cue to leave." He motioned for the other three to exit. "Too bad you can't join us." With a loud thud, he slammed the panel door shut and locked it from the other side.

"No!" Rynah charged the exit, beating her fists against it and using all her strength to force it open, but the lock remained sealed. More water burst into the room, adding to the two feet that had already pooled around their ankles. "Helmets, now!"

All of them fumbled with their helmets. Tom dropped his and chased it across the room before grasping it and ramming it on his head. Water poured in, now swirling around their calves as it deepened. *Ping!* A washer broke loose under the pressure of the surrounding water, allowing another gushing stream to shower them. Panicking, Brie shrieked as the force of it knocked her off her feet. Rynah checked her oxygen levels. Frowning, she didn't have much left, which meant neither did her companions.

"Search for a weak spot," she ordered, "anything that might allow us to escape."

The others scanned the walls meticulously, searching for any sign of a way out. Nothing. Cursing, Rynah scrambled around the room, in water that had reached her waist, pounding the walls and releasing cries of frustration. Her laser pistol poked her hip. *That's it!* she thought. She yanked her weapon out of its holster.

"All of you over here!" she yelled into her helmet's radio. "When I use this to blast a hole in the side of the ship, the change in pressure will suck each of us out into the water."

They gathered behind Rynah, trusting in her judgment.

"Ready?" she asked.

"Not really," answered Tom.

Rynah ignored him. Taking careful aim, she fired three shots at the far wall. Sparks and deafening echoes filled the water-logged area. The wall ripped apart as water burst through it, forcing what air was left out into the open ocean. Watery arms snatched each of them, ripping them out of the ship and into the open expanse of water amid a rampaging sea of frothy bubbles. Smashing into each other, groans and moans filled the radio as each tried to maintain awareness of the others' whereabouts.

Once outside the ship, Rynah scanned the area for movement. Three shapes caught her attention. She swam for them; she had to get that crystal. "They're getting away!"

Solon, Alfric, and Tom raced toward her. They kicked with all of their strength to catch up with Rynah and the three who had stolen their prize. Something whizzed past Tom's head. He turned in its direction, curious as to what it was. It zipped past again. *Laser fire!* He banked to the right and rolled over in the water to miss the next onslaught of laser fire.

Alfric had almost caught up with all of them. The fearless Viking charged his quarry and plowed into Stein, knocking the crystal from his hands. Stein elbowed Alfric's head, nearly cracking his helmet. In retaliation, Alfric punched Stein in the stomach. Stein went for his laser gun. Alfric seized his wrist, pushing the deadly weapon away, and head-butted the man. Stunned, Stein released his laser gun, but managed to squirm free of the Viking's grasp, giving Alfric a final kick to the head.

Rynah caught up with another of Klanor's men. She grasped the oxygen tank strapped to his back and held on, forcing him to drop deeper into the depths of the ocean. The man kicked at her. Rynah swerved, but her grip remained firm. A sudden force rammed into her, dazing her, and forcing her to release the man she held. Clearing her head, Rynah looked up. A shark as big as two buses, and with a flat head, swam straight for her, mouth opened wide, revealing razor teeth. She dodged. The waves caused by the creature slammed into her, pushing her further away from it and her friends. The shark swerved and charged her again before—it stopped! Rynah looked up. Above her floated Brie, unconscious.

"Alfric, Brie!" Rynah yelled into her mouthpiece.

Alfric yanked out two of his knives and torpedoed the shark, his strength propelling him through the water. "Come here, you foul beast!" yelled Alfric. "Odin will not save you!" Just as the shark was about to reach Brie, Alfric's massive form smashed into it; his knives sliced through its delicate flesh.

Rynah shot towards the motionless Brie. She turned Brie over and shook her to wake her up. "Come on," said Rynah.

Brie's eyes remained closed.

Not knowing what else to do, Rynah smacked her on the shoulder, hoping it would cause enough sensation to wake her.

Brie's eyes burst open. "What… where…"

"Are you injured?" asked Rynah.

"No," said Brie, "I don't think so."

"Is she…" Tom swam up to them.

"She's fine," said Rynah. "Where's the crystal?"

Tom never had a chance to answer. At that moment, the same shark swam past them, almost clipping him with its fin. A small glint caught his attention. Tom watched as the shark turned around, taking careful note of what was in its mouth.

Rynah seized his shoulder. "Where's the crystal!"

"Oh… Shark!"

The shark charged them again, barely missing them, its massive tail catching Rynah in the stomach and knocking the air out of her lungs. With a grunt, she turned limp in the water as she caught her breath.

"I know where the crystal is," said Tom.

"Where?" asked Solon.

"In its mouth."

Dismayed, the others stared at the shark as it turned around to make another pass for them. Somehow, in the scuffle, the crystal had become lodged between its pointed, and very deadly, teeth.

"Anyone got a plan?" asked Tom, "because I don't feel like being lunch."

"Distraction is a good policy," said Solon. "Alfric, do you think you can keep him busy?"

Alfric held up his two knives with a smile. "Let him come!"

"Brie and Tom," said Solon, "you two will have to get the crystal when it opens its mouth."

"No! I—I—can't," shrieked Brie.

"You have small arms," said Solon. "Meanwhile, Rynah and I will—"

"No!" Brie shrank away in fear.

"I'll do it," said Rynah.

Rynah and Tom swam far enough away to watch the battle, but not too far to miss their chance of grabbing the crystal. Alfric and Solon went in the other direction to be bait for the shark. Alone, Brie watched everything, ashamed of her cowardice and wishing she was more useful.

"Arrr!" roared Alfric as he beat his knives against his chest. "Beast of the underworld, come and claim your prize!"

Solon watched in mild humor. "I don't think that was necessary."

The shark headed straight for them, its tail swishing back and forth and gathering speed. Its mouth opened wide as it moved in for the kill. Alfric raised his blades in anticipation. The shark dove for him. He swerved out of the way and pounced on the beast's head, digging his two knives deep within its skull. Wailing and squealing in agonizing pain, the shark twisted and whipped its body around to shake Alfric off.

Seizing their chance, Tom and Rynah sped over to the shark. Rynah pulled the knife she had strapped around her boot and plunged it into the corner of the shark's mouth. Whipping its tail fin, the shark opened its jaws wide, revealing the crystal.

"Now!" yelled Rynah.

Not liking this plan, Tom summoned his courage and raced for it. He reached for the crystal, wrapping his fingers around it and yanked. It wouldn't budge. Tom pulled again with more force. Still nothing.

"Do it now!" screamed Rynah as her grip on the knife slipped.

"It's stuck tight," replied Tom.

Doing the most foolish (and desperate) thing he could think of, Tom swam into the shark's mouth and grasped the crystal with both hands, bracing both his feet on the creature's teeth. Using the combined strength of his legs and arms, Tom heaved with all his might. The crystal popped free.

Tom kicked off with his feet just as Rynah pulled her knife free and the shark's powerful jaws snapped shut, barely missing him. Treading water, Tom stared at the shark catching his breath. He looked at the crystal in his hands. "I got it!"

Cheers rang over the radio and into his ears. Rynah, Tom, and Alfric swam up to him, patting him on the back. "You are brave for a runt," said Alfric.

Floating in the distance, Brie watched everything. *Why am I always afraid?* she asked herself, *Why can't I be brave?* Her sorrowful heart wished to join them in the jubilee, but she knew that she had not earned the honor.

"This isn't over yet," said Rynah, taking the crystal.

As though to make her point, laser fire rained down upon them. Dodging, Rynah raced for Brie and shoved the crystal in her hands, along with a locator beacon. "Take this to the rendezvous point. When you hear rapid beeps, then you know you are on the right track. Solaris will be waiting."

"But—"

"Just do it! The rest of us will distract them to give you a chance." Rynah pushed Brie away from her and darted off to the others.

Glancing at the items in her hands, Brie kicked her feet and swam away for the ship, disappearing into the blackness of the water. Her heart pounded in her ears and her rapid breathing fogged the visor of the helmet as she trudged through the water.

Beep! Beep! Beep! The rapid beeps of the beacon filled her ears, telling her she was on the right course. "I hope you're there, Solaris," whispered Brie.

"I am waiting for you," Solaris' crackly reply came over the earpiece.

"Solaris!" Excitement filled Brie as she no longer felt alone.

"Just continue your current course," said Solaris.

Brie kicked harder, propelling herself through the water, marveling at how the fins on the suit helped. Laser pulses pummeled the reef beside her as though it reached for her, sending bits of coral, sponges, and mollusks into her face (which pelted her visor) and forcing her to stop. Brie looked behind. One man had noticed her departure.

More laser fire struck a shoal next to her, causing her to scream as the school of fish dispersed, bumping into her. She dropped the crystal. Brie dove for it as it landed in the soft sand, sending up a cloud of dust. The man pursuing her had spotted it as well.

"Brie?" said Solaris.

Brie raced for the white crystal determined to not disappoint the others a third time. She snatched it and hugged it close as she kicked the ground with her legs and took off.

Her pursuer watched her every move. Changing the range on his weapon, he increased the intensity of the laser pulse. Aiming, he had Brie in his sights. He pulled the trigger.

A blast crashed into a salmon-colored coral reef (with strips of seaweed waving in the current) before her. Halting, Brie swerved to the left and dove behind a patch of seaweed and water sponges. She peeked out. The man aimed straight for her. Brie took off, swimming as fast as she could just as another round of laser fire pelted the spot where she had just been. Gasping for air, now that her oxygen was almost gone, Brie swam as fast as she could. She kicked with her legs and pulled with her one free arm, while the other clutched the crystal.

Beep! Beep! Beep!

I still have that thing? thought Brie. She checked the beacon, realizing that she remained on the right course and didn't have far to go. The man behind her closed in. Swimming harder, Brie heaved for air, sweat pouring down her brow and into her eyes, making it impossible to see.

"Help!" she yelled.

"We're coming!" came Tom's voice.

Brie pushed harder. Her vision dimmed as the oxygen in her suit had run out. All she breathed now was the air her lungs expelled. Something crashed into her from behind. Struggling, Brie kept her hold on the crystal as she kicked whomever had attacked her. Strong hands grasped for her arm. Brie twisted and turned to shake him off. Her captor remained glued to her. With ease, he yanked her hand back and pried the crystal from it. Brie reached for it, but the man kicked her in the stomach, finishing what lack of oxygen hadn't; Brie blacked out.

Another set of hands grabbed her shoulders and pulled her upward. "Brie!" said a worried Tom. "Brie, wake up!" He kicked for the surface of the water, breaking through the white crests with a tremendous force. Without hesitating, Tom ripped off his and Brie's helmets. Cool, refreshing air brushed their faces, invigorating them.

"Brie!"

Brie eyes flickered open as she took a deep breath. "I'm okay."

The others popped out of the water just as Solaris appeared, hovering low, the force from her engines, causing waves that bobbed them up and down like mere toys. Her cargo hatch opened. Out dropped a basket, splashing in the water. They all climbed in the metal structure.

"Now!" yelled Rynah.

With a jerk, the basket ascended into the air, swaying in the downdraft caused by the ship's engines, as Solaris rolled the automatic chain. They slumped in the metal basket as it slowly lifted up into the belly of Solaris; a screeching hum surrounded them as the cargo bay doors sealed shut.

"Is everyone aboard?" asked Solaris.

"Yes, get us out of here!"

Solaris' engines roared to life as she fired her main booster rockets and careened out of Aquara's atmosphere and into space. As the planet grew smaller, it wondered why they were there in the first place. Seemed like a lot of trouble for one tiny crystal.

"The crystal," said Rynah, "where is it?"

Crestfallen, Brie looked at her feet, hanging her head.

"Where is it?" Rynah's insistent tone didn't help.

"I—I lost it," mumbled Brie.

"You what!"

"I lost it!" yelled Brie. "Someone had followed me and he took it."

Angered, Rynah smashed her fist into the side of the ship. "You lost it! I gave you one simple task and you lost it!"

Brie shrank beneath Rynah's fury.

"You are useless!" continued Rynah in her rage. "Utterly useless! I don't know why Solaris picked you for this mission because you haven't shown one ounce of courage. The only thing you have done this entire trip is panic like a child and moan about your pathetic planet you call home. I swear, I will never trust you with anything again."

Having heard enough, Alfric pushed Rynah away from Brie. "That is enough," he said in a calm, but stern, tone, silencing Rynah's rampage. "It is not her fault."

"But she's right," muttered Brie, "I am useless."

With great sadness in her heart for letting them all down again, Brie left the cargo room to seek solitude. *I am useless*, she thought to herself. *How will I ever make it up to them?*

Chapter 14
TWO CRYSTALS

Klanor studied the words in the old book, which rightfully belonged to Rynah (willed to her by Marlow) and he had stolen from her, before him, his fingers turning the delicate pages, despite their manly size. Everyone had thought him a fool whenever he chose to delve into the ancient myths and propose his theory that the crystals were real. *Let them watch me now*, he thought to himself. He would destroy every last one of them. *They did this to me. They brought it upon themselves.* Klanor read through another stanza of text, hoping to decipher it.

He had managed to get all of the crystals, save one: the one on Junglar. *How had Rynah managed it?* He knew that she was never one to put much stock in the old stories. She believed in what she saw, not metaphors. He remembered the one time he told her about the crystals. Oh, how she had laughed.

Klanor wanted her to join him. He wanted her by his side. A pang of guilt for what he had done to her haunted him. He shoved it aside. She would never believe him, but he really did have feelings for her, the only one who ever looked at him with adoring eyes. But like the others, she scoffed at his notion of the crystals, so he wrote her off.

A field of rock hovering alone
Jagged as a sharp stone.
Pass beyond to a gold sphere
where treasure looms far and near.

On passing, anyone would have thought this nonsense, but Klanor learned that one had to read between the lines. Ancient stories were more symbolic than literal. He reread the lines to himself, pondering over each of the words and their hidden meanings.

It hit him. Asteroids. They often looked as though they just floated in space. He checked the charts to see if an asteroid field was nearby. Frowning, he noticed that 12 existed. Knowing he could never search all 12, Klanor narrowed the parameters to one containing a yellow planet. Only one remained. *Perfect.*

He strode from his quarters to the main deck of his ship. "Set a course for sector 10, point 15."

"Course set, sir," said the pilot.

"Get us there quickly," ordered Klanor, "I do not want any surprises."

"Yes, sir," replied the pilot.

Klanor watched the window in front of him as stars breezed by. A satisfied smile filled his face. "This time, there is no stopping me," he whispered to himself, but he did not notice Stein's gaze from the shadows.

Chapter 15
SCOLDING

Rynah fumed as she stared out the small hole of a window in a cramped nook of her sleeping quarters. *How could Brie be so stupid?* she thought. Rynah could not believe that Brie had allowed Klanor's men to steal the crystal from her. She did not understand why Solaris had brought the girl to the ship. *She's completely inept. A useless coward.* Releasing an exasperated cry, Rynah threw her legs out and stood up, her toned muscles flexing with every movement.

"You should apologize," said Solaris. Though a ship, she always had a way of acting more human than the one who created her.

"So you say," spat Rynah.

"So the universe says," replied Solaris.

"I'll not apologize for stating the truth," said Rynah. "She is a cowardly girl. Afraid of her shadow even."

"She misses her home."

"Then maybe she should go back there!"

"I cannot send her back."

Rynah's head popped up. Can't? That wasn't like Solaris, admitting that there was something she couldn't do. "You don't want to send her back."

Solaris said nothing.

"Answer me, Solaris. You are refusing to send her home, aren't you?"

"She is needed here."

"So you say," said Rynah.

"To coin a phrase I have heard, 'My heart tells me there is more to Brie than you have seen.'"

"Your heart?" Rynah shook her head. *How could a ship have a heart?* "You're a ship, a piece of machinery made from metal and scraps. How could you have faith in anything?"

Steam burst from the vents into Rynah's room. She had struck a nerve. "At least one of us has faith! The only thing you believe in is your laser pistol."

"I still think you made a mistake in bringing Brie here," said Rynah. "It's a good thing her skin is white, so that way, people won't notice when she is scared. It's as though she always sees a *gryol.*"

Bangs echoed around Rynah as a huge plume of steam burst from the ventilation shaft, forcing the grate to fling open and slam back into place with a tremendous bang.

"Now you listen to me you ungrateful little *gahola!* Your grandfather may have left me to your care, but you have no business speaking about others in such a way, and I will not allow such language in my presence."

Rynah shrank under Solaris' fury. She had never seen the ship so angry and regretted her outburst.

"I scanned the old tales and searched through all of Earth's history for one who matched such traits. I watched as Brie grew up, in a way, and knew that she was one of the four. You asked me to bring them here and that is what I did."

"More like you insisted."

"You trusted my judgment, so trust it now. Yes, she's frightened. She has been pulled from her home and thrust into a world that she thought only existed in stories. Now she is being asked to help you save what is left of your people. She is trying. Could you have fared any better against Stein? You, who failed to stop Klanor in the first place? You, who was closest to him and never even knew what he planned? Do not take all of your frustrations against yourself, and your failings, out on her.

"Brie has a strength within her. One that even she does not know she possesses."

"How do you know?" asked Rynah, watching the tone of her voice.

Her holoscreen flickered on, and a video of a man playing with his daughters filled the room, making Rynah feel as though she was there. She watched as the two girls tackled their father. The youngest wandered over to a set of green bushes with blueberries on them. Suddenly, the other girl ran to her sister and yanked her back. Rynah peered closer. She saw it: a tiny snake hidden within the greenery. The man ran to his daughters, checking them to make certain they were unhurt. The video disappeared. Thrust back into her own world, Rynah pondered over what she had been shown.

"Where did you get that?" she asked.

"From Brie's blog. It's an online journal, very popular among the people of her time. She posted that home video as part of a memoriam for her late father."

"Her father is dead?" The remembered pain of losing her own parents stung Rynah's heart.

"Yes," replied Solaris,

"I did not know." Rynah settled on the chair in her room, her voice taking on a somber tone.

"You never bothered to ask," said Solaris. "In fact, you have not bothered to get to know any of the four people you have brought here. How can you expect them to help you when you take no interest in them?"

Rynah hadn't thought about that. "I never—"

"Of course not," scolded Solaris.

"I will keep that in mind," Rynah's voice had been reduced to a whisper.

"I can send her back."

Rynah's head jerked up. "What?"

"If that is what you wish, I can return her to her home, but know this: once I do, I will not be able to bring her back here. Traveling through time and space is not easy. I managed to pull her from her world, but once I return her, that door will be closed, permanently. The same holds true for the others."

"Have you told her this?"

"No."

"Why not?"

"Because I believe that she would elect to return home, which she would regret soon after."

"How do you know?"

"I took the time to talk with her."

Rynah pursed her lips as Solaris scolded her again for not bothering to get to know the ones she kidnapped to her ship. "So you can send her back at any moment."

"Yes," said Solaris, "but before you decide, make certain that it is a wise choice."

Another warning. "Solaris, did you ever scold my grandfather like this?"

"All the time."

Figures, thought Rynah. Her grandfather had warned her that the ship could be a bit temperamental. If only she had known what that had meant. Temperamental didn't even begin to describe Solaris.

* * *

Alone and isolated from everyone on the ship, Brie hid in the engine room among the coiled pipes and steam. She didn't wish to see anyone. She had let them down. She knew it. Filled with immense disappointment in herself, Brie wished to return home—

even though a part of her didn't want to go—to save everyone from her inability to summon her courage.

Footsteps sounded outside the door to the corridor. Scrunching up even more, she hoped the person would go away.

"We know you are in here," Alfric's voice echoed off the inner workings of the ship.

Brie buried her head in her knees.

"There is no point in hiding," said Alfric. "We will find you."

Knowing she was not about to be left alone, Brie answered them. "Over here."

Alfric and Solon appeared around the corner.

"Hiding is no way to confront your mistakes," said Solon.

"I screwed up, okay?" wailed Brie. "Rynah is right. I am useless."

"Rynah does not know everything."

"You'd say that about a god?" mocked Brie.

"A mortal being cannot be a god," said Solon, "and why would you ask me such a question?"

"I just assumed, you being from Ancient Greece and all, that, you'd think she was a god with all of her technology."

"Assumptions only lead to foolishness," said Solon. "Though I'll admit that I had first thought she might have been from the heavens, I soon realized that this is nothing more than a mere vessel. Technology, as you would put it."

"She may be from the skies, but I agree with the soothsayer here," said Alfric, "Rynah does not know everything."

"But it was my fault for losing the crystal," said Brie.

"Did you release it in fear?" asked Alfric.

Brie thought back to the fight in the water. She had tried to hang onto the crystal for as long as she could. "No."

"Then you have nothing for which to be ashamed of. It was taken from you by force."

"The question is," said Solon, "what are you going to do now?"

"I don't know," Brie turned away. "Just go away."

Alfric snatched the gold watch from her arm; it had been her father's. When he had been killed, the Army sent her mother his effects; Brie had taken his watch and had worn it each day since.

"Give that back!" she screamed.

"No," said Alfric, holding it above her head.

Brie jumped for it, but the Viking stood two heads above her. "It's mine, now give it back!"

Alfric remained stoic.

Disgruntled, Brie just stood there, staring at him with a hopeless expression on her face.

"I took something of yours," said Alfric, "something which I have no right to. What are you going to do about it?'"

Brie didn't move.

"Very well. Then I will toss it away."

In a rage, Brie snatched one of Alfric's knives from around his belt and pointed it at him. "Give me back my father's watch!"

"Do you know how to use that?" asked Solon.

"No," said Brie, "but I'll figure it out. The watch!"

Smiling, Alfric held the watch out to her. "The man who took the crystal made a fool of you. Humiliated you because he thought you were weak. What are you going to do about it?"

Brie lowered the knife, taking the watch. "Revenge isn't always the answer."

"No," said Solon, "but are the man's plans for the crystal the answer?"

"No," said Brie, "but I don't know how to be brave."

"Bravery is not an emotion," said Solon. "It is merely a choice. You can choose to give into your fear, or you can challenge it."

"Will you teach me?" asked Brie.

"I can teach you the sword," said Alfric, "but only you can make the choice in the end."

"Then we will learn the sword together," said Solon. "Being a scribe is little use in a fight to the death."

Alfric frowned. He had counted on having one student, not two, but he agreed with the young soothsayer, books were of little use in battle. Alfric picked up two metal pipes as big as both of Brie's arms combined and handed one each to them.

"You will carry these to the other end of the ship and back. If you are weary upon your return, then you will do it again and again until you weary no more."

Brie looked at the metal in her arms as she struggled to hold it. "Not one for wasting time, are you?"

"Go!"

Together, she and Solon ran off with their pipes, each breathing hard after seven steps. Fumbling, they managed to reach the end of the hall before turning back. By then, Brie had slowed to a crawl. Her rubber arms refused to work and she hadn't even completed the first lap. When she and Solon returned, Alfric's phlegmatic gaze dampened their enthusiasm.

"Again!"

They ran off a second time, and a third, until both collapsed from exhaustion. Alfric picked up the two pipes. "Tomorrow, we will resume this lesson. I suggest you rest tonight."

Heaving, both Brie and Solon looked at each other, wondering what they had gotten themselves into. Somewhere, deep within the ship, Solaris watched them in a way that only a ship could. If she had a face and a mouth, she would have grinned with joy.

"I've not let you down, Marlow," she said to the memory of Rynah's grandfather.

Chapter 16
PIRATES!

Laughter spilled from the mess hall (a simple area with a long counter that lined one side with a hot plate, microwave oven, and polished, steel cabinets, and an aluminum table on the opposite side) amidst the clinking of forks as everyone gathered for supper, a meal consisting of rehydrated protein and vegetables—none of which tasted savory—and filtrated water. Rynah paused in the shadows of the doorway. She remarked at how they were worlds apart, yet managed to get along as though they had always known each other. Sorrow filled her as she remembered her friends and the times they had shared. She wiped away the tear that had dropped from the corner of her eye.

Tom handed a bowl of slop to Brie. "Bon Apétit, my lady." He sat down with his own. "I hear you two are training to be Vikings. I should join you. I am big and strong and" —Tom glanced at the sour expression on Alfric's face— "though maybe I won't since I value my life."

Brie and Solon chuckled.

Knowing she could not remain hidden, Rynah entered the eating area and filled a bowl before joining them at the table. "Might I join you?"

"Certainly," beamed Tom, getting her a chair. "It's not often you choose to join us for a meal."

"I thought I might try to get to know you all a bit better," said Rynah.

"Well, what do you want to know?" said Tom, pleased to have another person to talk to. "I am an open book."

"What do you do back home?" asked Rynah.

"I live in Georgia," said Tom, "with my grandma. My parents died a few years ago."

"No siblings?"

"No," said Tom. "I had a sister, but she died at birth."

"Sorry," said Rynah.

"Anyway, my grandmother noticed that I had a knack for putting things together, so she got me into the Science Academy," said Tom. "I was actually giving a presentation to the academy heads when I was unexpectedly called away."

"What was your presentation on?" asked Rynah.

"I had made this engine that is powered by magnets and utilizes the earth's magnetic field to run, thus having no need for solar panels or fossil fuels. It is self-sustaining and efficient. Though I haven't worked out all of the kinks."

"Could such an engine work?" asked Rynah. "I mean no disrespect, it's just we had no such thing back home."

"It works, but hasn't been perfected for use on big machinery."

"Well, I'm sure you'll figure it out," said Rynah.

"It came with me if you want to see it."

"Maybe some other time. What about you, Solon? What do you do back home?"

"My father arranged for me to be a scribe," said Solon. "My brother had joined the infantry, but I was not fit for such service. To avoid being stuck with me forever, I was sent to the king's library. It is a center of learning as well."

"Do you not like it?" Rynah had detected a note of distaste in Solon's voice.

"No, it's not that, it's just… I would much rather be outside with the animals and the trees. I want to learn about life and experience it, not record someone else's in a scroll."

"Maybe you can," said Brie.

"How?"

"You are here and the only one from your society who is. Perhaps you can bring them back a tale of adventure or some kind of new outlook on life."

"You have a bit of wisdom in you," said Solon.

Rynah chewed her food methodically as she watched the interaction between them. *Is this what Solaris saw?* she thought to herself.

A loud explosion sounded outside the hull of the ship as it pitched forward, sending them and their food flying.

"Pirates!" yelled Solaris over the speakers.

"Pirates?" said Tom. "Like, of the Caribbean?"

Rynah gave Tom a quizzical glance, having no idea of what he referred to, as she dashed out of the eating area and down the grated corridor to the command center.

"How many are there?" she demanded as she jumped into the pilot's seat and put the headset on, which linked her telepathically to Solaris.

"I counted four ships," said Solaris.

Their elliptical ships moved in from all sides, cutting of any chance of escape.

Four! Cursing, Rynah wondered if they would ever be able to outrun them, much less overpower them. She took the controls in her hands and banked to the right, dropping low, before zooming upwards to avoid one of the pirate ships. A missile headed straight for them. Rynah thought about slowing down, thus coming to an abrupt halt, forcing the missile to shoot past them and crash into one of the pirate ships. She gunned the engines and sailed through space, hoping to put what distance she could between them and the pirates.

Tom appeared on the flight deck. "What can I do to help?"

"Put this on" —Rynah handed him another headset— "and get in that chair."

Tom put on the helmet and sat in the co-pilot's seat.

"Are you aware of my thoughts?"

"Yes," said Tom, remembering that Rynah had told him the helmet not only linked him telepathically to the ship, but to anyone wearing the other helmet as well.

"Remember," said Rynah, "just think it and it will happen."

The ship jerked as an explosion rippled through it.

On screen, Rynah thought. The holographic screen flickered to life, depicting three remaining pirate ships still in pursuit. A red dot appeared on the screen. It stretched from the pirates to them and Rynah knew it was another missile.

"Hang on!" she yelled into the intercom.

With their thoughts as one, Tom and Rynah barrel-rolled to the left, moving out of range of their enemy's targeting systems. In another part of the ship, Brie, Solon, and Alfric rolled across the floor as momentum knocked them around like bouncing balls. The ship righted itself.

"They're still hot on our tail," said Tom.

"I have scanned their trajectory," said Solaris. "These are the Fragmyr Pirates."

"*Sritor*," cursed Rynah in her own language. "Of all the pirates to run into."

"Who are they?" asked Tom.

"Our worst nightmare," replied Rynah. "Once they pick a target, they follow it until they have either conquered it, or destroyed it, or both."

"Can we outrun them?"

"There is no outrunning them," said Rynah.

Tom thought of various ways to deal with the situation at hand; each thought ran through Rynah's mind as well in their telepathic connection.

No good, she thought. *None of these will ever work. We can't outrun them.*

"But you can outthink them," said Solaris.

A blast ricocheted off the hull of their ship, propelling them sideways until Rynah straightened them out.

Solaris, said Tom, telepathically, *is there a place where we could lose them? Anything that is like a maze or full of places to hide?*

There is an asteroid field about three parsecs from here.

Show me, said Tom.

A map appeared on the screen before them.

This is suicide, said Rynah, catching onto Tom's plans.

So is staying here.

Solaris, set a course, said Rynah. *I hope you know what you're doing,* she told Tom.

So do I, Tom replied.

Another missile detonated just above the bow of their ship, ripping holes into the outer hull and causing air leaks. Bits of ceiling and wiring fell on top of Rynah and Tom. Coughing, they shoved it off them as sparks zapped above their heads.

That was close, Rynah said to Tom through the telepathic link.

Linked together, they commanded Solaris to maximize her engines' output, propelling them through the empty reaches of space and straight for the asteroid field. One of the pirate ships pulled up alongside, matching their speed. It shot a giant grappling hook at Solaris, slamming into her with a loud thunk, but it bounced off.

"What was that?" asked Tom.

"Grappling hooks," hissed Rynah. "They're trying to latch onto us."

She veered the ship to the right until it slammed into the pirate vessel, forcing it off course. A series of squeals and scrapes against the left, outer hull filled their ears as metal raked against metal until they had broken free. Another of the pirates pulled up alongside. Looking out the window, Rynah watched as one of the pirates stood in the open hatch with a spacesuit on, aiming his spear gun at them. She glanced to her right and noticed another ship doing the same. Realizing that they meant to set a net, she issued commands to Solaris.

"My bottom thrusters?" questioned Solaris. "Are you crazy?"

"Just do it!"

Solaris powered her bottom thrusters just as both pirates fired their spears. With a jolt, the ship shot upwards in a vertical streak, forcing both Rynah and Tom deeper into their seats as though an anvil had been dropped on them. The pirates' spears hooked into each other's ships, forcing them to whip around in circles, entangling themselves further until they crashed in a fiery inferno.

"Yes!" shouted Tom with glee. He received a piercing stare from Rynah. "Sorry, got lost in the moment."

"The asteroid field is straight ahead."

They raced through the blackness of space straight for the giant boulder ahead of them. Two pirate ships dropped out of hyperspeed beside them.

"I thought there were only four," yelled Tom.

"Apparently they have more," replied Rynah. *Solaris, set a course across the lead's bow.*

The ship banked as Solaris adjusted her course to Rynah's command.

"Rynah?" said Tom as he watched the pirate vessel get closer while they moved in a diagonal towards it.

I know what I'm doing.

Tom wasn't so sure. Fire illuminated outside the command center's window as another missile exploded beside them. The pirate ship drew nearer.

Rynah?

Rynah ignored him. *Punch it, Solaris.*

Solaris rerouted all power to her engines, accelerating them to a speed almost impossible to control.

Wide-eyed, Tom watched as not only the pirate ship grew larger in the windshield, but so did the giant asteroid beyond it. *Rynah, this is insane.*

Rynah focused on the rocks ahead of her. Her stoic face betrayed no emotion, least of all fear.

Tom gripped the controls more tightly with his sweaty palms. He glanced at Rynah and her statue-like posture before averting his eyes back to the pirate vessel and asteroids directly in front of them.

When I tell you to, Rynah spoke telepathically to Tom, *yank the controls to the left and then immediately to the right.*

Understood. Tom still wondered about her plan, but realized now was not the time to argue.

They picked up speed. The other pirate ship followed behind, unaware of the collision course Rynah had in mind.

NOW!

Tom yanked the controls to the left, as Rynah had instructed. They just missed the ship in front of them. A roar resonated throughout the ship as the vessel that had pursued behind them crashed into the other pirate ship. Fire and metallic debris pelted—*Pip! Pip! Pip!*—the side of Solaris' hull, leaving dents and scratches (which vexed her immensely) in what had been unsoiled, varnished, copper cladding. As instructed, Tom veered to the right, dodging the asteroid his first course correction had taken them towards.

A space rock next to them erupted into billions of pieces as a missile hurled into it. Tom steered the ship away before putting them back on course. Another asteroid exploded beside them.

"They never give up, do they?"

No, said Solaris.

How many are there? asked Tom, *I thought they had only four ships.*

There are hundreds of pirates, replied Rynah. She course corrected and avoided colliding with another asteroid that had strayed into their path.

A beeping noise filled their ears. Rynah checked it just as they started to slow down. *One of the power generators has been hit,* said Rynah. *I need to repair it if we're ever going to outrun them.* She threw off her helmet. "Tom, you have the bridge. Stay inside the asteroid field, but try not to hit anything."

"No problem," said Tom through gritted teeth as he steered around another piece of space rock.

"Alfric," Rynah called into the intercom, "meet me in the cargo bay!" She darted out of the command center and down the metallic steps to the hallway. Her heart pumping, Rynah raced through the interior of Solaris to the cargo bay where the suits were, her boots releasing an echoing thump with each step.

She reached a corner. Skidding to a halt as she slowed, Rynah grasped a pole and whipped herself around the turn. Stairs lay just ahead. Refusing to slow down, she gripped the metal rail and placed the sides of her feet against them as she slid to the bottom. She spotted Brie and Solon.

"You two," she said, "go up those steps and to the right. Strap yourself in the seat and fire at the pirates."

"But..." began Brie.

"Just do it!" Rynah shoved the both of them away as she turned and ran for the cargo bay. The ship lurched, sending her flying. Debris crashed around her, cutting off her path to the cargo bay. Searching for an alternative route, she spotted a pole. Rynah studied it. Steam burst from a pipe, almost catching her in the face with its fury.

"You're not taking my ship," whispered Rynah to herself.

With long strides, she hurled herself at the pole, wrapping her hands and legs around it. Air rushed her, whipping her emerald hair as she slid down it to the bottom until she landed with a loud *plunk*! An ear-splitting explosion rocked the vessel, propelling Rynah forward. She careened down the ship as the gravity field shifted. A loose cable caught her attention. Throwing her hands out, Rynah grasped it, pulling herself to a gut-wrenching stop. Straining, she heaved herself upward toward the cargo bay door. Sparks zapped around her. Ignoring her strained muscles, Rynah climbed up the cable.

Suddenly, her center of gravity shifted again as the ship regained its normal gravity field. Knowing that she didn't need the loose cable anymore, Rynah dashed through the doors to the cargo bay where Alfric waited for her.

"Suit up," Rynah said, releasing the spacesuits from their prison in the storage locker.

Once she had her protective suit on, Rynah jabbed the button to the door, sealing the room and releasing the pressurized air. She snatched a line. She hooked one end to Alfric, snapping it into place and the other onto a hoop on the ship. With another line, she tied the two of them together. Another button opened the door, revealing the chaos that reigned outside. Laser fire pelted past them, striking the outer hull and sending a series of fireworks into the vacuum atmosphere. Rynah poked her head out.

"All right," she said. "You stay here and hold onto this line while I step out."

"I do not like this plan," said Alfric.

Rynah didn't either, but she knew what she had to do. "I have to repair the power generator, and that can only be done on the outside. Just don't let go of this line."

In response, Alfric gripped the rubbery rope, giving her a stern, but resolute expression. "On my honor."

Rynah reached out, grasping one of the rungs on the side of the ship. Lunging, she reached with her other hand and placed her feet on the rungs below her. She reached up and grabbed the rung above her. She pushed with her legs and pulled with her arms as she climbed the outer hull of the ship.

A pirate vessel soared past her just as another missile exploded nearby. Rynah glanced at Alfric, who remained in the doorway with a firm grip on the cable. She climbed upward, observing the battle (ships firing lasers, fiery explosions, and many near misses) that raged around her. *This is a really bad idea.* Pushing such thoughts from her mind, Rynah continued, wrapping her gloved fingers around another of the metal rungs.

She reached the top of the ship. Her breath fogged the visor of her helmet, making it difficult to see, since with each movement, she sweated even more. A bead of sweat trickled down her face. Ignoring it, Rynah pushed herself onward as she climbed the side of a ship, dodging and weaving among a sea of pirates and weapons' fire.

"Alfric," said Rynah, "I've reached the generator. Hold the line steady."

"Understood," came Alfric's deep voice into her ear.

With a shorter cable, Rynah secured herself to the top of the ship. She punched in the code to open the access panel. It blinked green, but refused to open when Rynah pulled on it. She yanked again, using all of her strength, but it was sealed tight.

"Come on!" she yelled.

Realizing she would never get it open, Rynah pulled out a hammer from around her tool belt. She hated the idea of breaking the panel. With little choice, she raised the hammer and smashed it against the metal plating. Rynah struck it again and again. With each strike, a dent appeared until the plate popped out of its hold and floated away.

Rynah studied the generator. Sparks popped from a loose wire that had been severed. Rynah frowned. She'd have to repair it with a quick fix. She pulled out more items from her utility belt. A laser pulse slammed into the ship next to her, leaving a blackened scorch mark on Solaris' outer hull. Rynah ducked her head, covering herself from the blast. She looked around. One of the pirate ships lined up in front of Solaris. It sped past, soaring above her as it released a storm of laser fire, pounding the ship. Rynah flattened herself on the metal siding. Each strike sent a ring into her ears as they battered the ship. Once over, Rynah checked herself, making certain she wasn't hurt.

She turned back to the power generator. With a set of wire cutters, she cut the damaged wire away and let it loose into space. Rynah pulled some fresh wire from her belt. She measured the length needed and cut it to fit. Wishing she didn't have to do this with the suit on—threading wire is much easier when you can feel it with your fingers—she attached it to the conduit. Once the connection had been made, Rynah lifted a lever and turned a switch.

"Solaris," she called, "try it now."

The generator hummed to life as it turned back on, sending a flood of electrical power through its wires to the inner working of the engines.

"Systems restored," said Solaris. "You have done it."

Rynah unhooked the short line she had used to tether herself to the ship. She maneuvered her way back to the rungs and climbed down to where Alfric stood, her lifeline in his hands. She felt with her feet as best she could as she navigated her way back. A ship sailed past her again. Rynah felt that they taunted her, but she refused to dwell on it; her mind focused on getting back inside the ship.

A tremendous jolt flung the ship sideways, causing Rynah to lose her grip on the rungs and somersault forward. She crashed into the side of Solaris, knocking the air out of her lungs. Dazed, she failed to react as her line jerked, flinging her away from the ship and into the blackness of space. Rynah clung to her line.

Back within the cargo hold, Alfric braced his feet against the floor and held tightly to the cable and the only thing keeping Rynah from being lost forever. Another missile exploded beside the ship, jerking him off balance. Alfric rolled across the floor, releasing his grip on the line.

Outside the ship, Rynah felt her lifeline slacken. *Oh no!* She flew away from the ship. "Alfric!" she called.

Coming to a halt, Alfric noticed the cable unraveling as it disappeared. A Viking who prided himself on his honor, he refused to fail in his word to Rynah. He dove for the cord. Desperate, he grasped it and wrapped it around his hands. Alfric stood to his full height, his powerful muscles straining as he held the cable. Hand over hand, he reeled it in. Another plume of laser fire assailed the ship. Alfric refused to duck for cover as it struck the floor beside his feet, singeing his boots. Concentrating only on Rynah, Alfric continued to pull on the cable.

Heaving, Rynah watched as the cargo door neared at an agonizingly slow pace. More explosions roared around her as ships whizzed past, and Tom, with an adroit skill he didn't think he possessed, steered them clear of collision. She watched, helpless, as each movement waved her like a ragdoll. Rynah felt like a fish on a hook, a feeling she detested. The door neared.

Though tiring, Alfric refused to slow his efforts. He worked faster. Rynah's life depended on it. With each passing second, the cord coiled at his feet. He shifted for a better stance. The ship lurched again, but Alfric maintained his balance. When Rynah was within arm's reach, Alfric stretched out his hand, allowing Rynah to latch onto his arm with a viselike grip. He yanked her inside to the safety of the cargo hold. They laid still for a moment to catch their breath.

Another onslaught of laser fire from the pirates forced Rynah back to the present, and the fact that they were not far from danger. She dived for the control to close the cargo doors and pressed it. The doors slid shut and sealed, thus repressurizing the room.

Rynah pulled off her helmet. "Thank you," she said to Alfric. "I guess I owe you one."

"You owe me nothing," said Alfric. "I gave my word and kept it."

Rynah didn't know if that was a compliment or not. She patted the Viking's shoulder in gratitude before scrambling out of the suit and darting out of the cargo bay.

Brie and Solon followed Rynah's instructions and hiked up the steps two at a time until they reached the top level. Turning right, they dashed down the narrow hallway, which ended in a room that was right above the command center. Brie paused in the doorway. Models of two guns, which poked out of that side of the ship, the size of her, lay in there with a chair behind each. *This is asking too much*, she thought. *I never killed anything before.* She crept to one of the weapons, feeling numb as she touched it.

"Is this what she wanted?" Brie asked.

"I believe so," replied Solon as he situated himself in one of the chairs.

"What are you doing?" asked Brie.

"What Rynah asked me to," said Solon.

"But you don't know how to use one of these."

"Then I will learn."

Solon noticed a helmet next to his chair. He snatched it and put it on, his mind connecting with the ship's, and with Tom's. "It appears to be thought controlled," he said.

Solon? came Tom's voice in his mind.

Yes.

How did you get into my head?

I am in a room with two weapons, where Rynah instructed me to go.

Oh. I guess aim and fire at the pirates.

Unsure of herself, Brie settled into the other chair after watching Solon communicate telepathically with Tom, not that she knew he spoke to him. She found a similar helmet and placed it over her head.

Hello?

Brie! said Tom in her mind. *Can you show Solon how to use those guns?*

I'll try, answered Brie, amazed that the helmets linked their minds.

She searched the controls around the guns. A red switch looked promising. Brie flipped it. The gun whirred to life and moved, following the various ships that soared past the protruding window. A transparent holographic view screen popped up with red crosshairs. Having played a few video games at a friend's house, Brie knew what the crosshairs meant. She found the trigger on the weapon and accidentally pulled it. An ear-splitting pop and a yellow burst of light escaped from the barrel of the gun. Stunned, Brie sat statuesque for a moment before regaining her senses.

Solon, flip that switch, she said.

Solon did as instructed. Like Brie's weapon, his whirred to life and swerved, following the various flying objects outside the window. Soon another transparent, holographic screen appeared, but in front of him, with red crosshairs.

Okay, Brie said to him, through the link, *this is like a video game in how it works. Line the crosshairs up with the target you intend to fire at. Pull the trigger—it's that thing there—and the gun will fire.*

Solon nodded. He understood some of what she had said, but not all of it, and decided he would just learn as he went.

Tom, Brie said, *you'll have to help us. Tell us who to fire at.*

At the pirates!

Brie frowned. She had already figured that part out. "Here goes," she said out loud.

One of the pirate ships turned in their direction. It lined them up in its sights. Brie knew what was coming. Doing her best to push her fear away, she told herself it was only a video game, and the more ships she hit, the more points. She lined the crosshairs over the pirate vessel. Brie pulled the trigger. The laser gun recoiled as it shot a burst of laser fire at the ship. Brie watched wide-eyed as it struck the target and caused it to burst into a pile of flames and shattered debris.

Good shot! came Tom's voice in her head.

Brie didn't think there was anything good about it, as now everyone on board was dead.

Reading her emotions, Solon turned to her. "Self-defense is never murder," he said out loud to her so Tom wouldn't be privy to it. "Those pirates mean to harm us. We have two choices, surrender or fight back."

Brie bit her lower lip. She knew he was correct, and she had no intention of becoming a pirate slave. Light flashed in front of her as another missile detonated. Continuing to rein in her fear by telling herself this was a video game, Brie lined up another ship in her sights.

Always let your breath out before you fire, her father's instructions from long ago echoed in her head. Before he died, he had taken her out in the desert and taught her how to handle a gun. "One day, you will be grown up and on your own, and you may need to defend yourself from a predator."

"What predators?" she had asked him.

Her father never answered, but he knew what dangers the world held.

Brie pushed her painful memories away and concentrated only on the moment. She released the breath she had held in her lungs and pulled the trigger. Again, laser bursts spilled from the barrel and plowed into her target. She watched as the second pirate ship she had fired upon was destroyed.

You're a natural, Brie, encouraged Tom.

Brie ignored him. She only wanted to survive this onslaught.

Look out!

The craft rolled to the right just as a pirate ship in flames careened towards them, almost striking them. Tom straightened out the ship and continued through the asteroid field.

Solon noticed another pirate vessel heading straight for them. He lined up the crosshairs like Brie had told him to and squeezed the trigger between his fingers. The laser fire hit the rear of the pirate ship, causing it to dive into a passing asteroid and burst into a plume of smoke.

Nice, said Tom in their minds.

Rynah hurried up the steps to the command center. "Report," she said.

Tom turned around. "Brie and Solon are in the weapons array like you asked. So far they have disabled three of their ships."

"Really?" Rynah's surprise did not go unnoticed. She hadn't expected Brie to embrace the use of the laser guns. "Solaris, are you still with us?"

"Yes," replied Solaris. "The power generator you repaired seems to be working fine."

Rynah jumped into the main pilot seat and put the helmet on.

"They don't seem to be letting up," said Tom as he steered them away from an impending asteroid. The bottom of the ship scraped the space rock, much to Solaris' disgust.

"I have an idea," said Solaris.

"What is it?" asked Rynah.

"Play dead."

"What?"

"Play dead," Solaris said again. "These pirates will not give up until they have captured us, or think we are dead."

"She has a point," said Tom.

Rynah thought about it a moment. *Brie, meet me in the weapons bay.* Rynah threw off the helmet. "Alfric," she said over the intercom, "go to the weapons bay." She turned to Tom. "Find an asteroid big enough for us to hide in. When you do, let me know." Rynah dashed out of the room and down the steps.

"Right," said Tom to himself. "Find a place to hide in all this. That should be easy."

Down in the weapons bay, both Alfric and Brie waited for Rynah. She ran in out of breath. "Open the hatch to that tube," she said to Alfric.

He obeyed. His sinewy muscles demonstrated every ounce of his strength as he twisted the handle and opened the hatch.

"Brie, help me load stuff into the tube," Rynah said.

"What stuff?" asked Brie, confused about Rynah's plan.

"Anything that looks like junk around here. I want you to load it in that empty tube. When finished, we'll fire it and hope the pirates believe we've crashed."

Catching onto her plan, Brie went to the far end of the weapons bay and grabbed anything she could hold onto. She dragged it to the tube and handed it to Alfric to stuff in there. With diligence, they worked, finding anything they could, anything that could be lost.

Rynah came upon a broken table. *This might have been used as a storage area at one point.* "Brie, over here."

Brie ran to Rynah. They each took an end of the table and lifted it, carrying it over to the torpedo tube.

"We need to break this up so it will fit."

In answer, Alfric unsheathed his sword and hacked away at the wooden table. Splinters flew from it with each strike. The dull roar of another detonated missile warned them that time grew short. They flung the pieces of the shattered table into the torpedo tube.

"Close it up," said Rynah.

Together, they shut the hatch and Alfric sealed it, twisting the circular handle until it wouldn't budge.

"Tom, we're loaded," Rynah spoke into the intercom.

In the command center, Tom concentrated on avoiding the floating asteroids and numerous pirate ships. He pushed the controls down to avoid a ship that almost collided with them. Tom jerked the controls to the left and upward avoiding two asteroids.

He spotted something. *Solaris, is that a cave over there?*

Solaris ran her scanners. *Yes.*

Formulating a plan, Tom knew what to do. *Solon, target that dark spot on the asteroid ahead of us. When I say, fire.*

Got it.

Tom steered the ship dangerously close to the asteroid. He veered upward, twisted, and dove for the dark spot on the space rock. *NOW!*

A hailstorm of laser fire erupted from Solaris' guns as Solon opened fire on the spot Tom had indicated. Bracing himself, Tom hoped he had learned enough about flying in the short time he had been on the ship to succeed in his plan. Solon's assault on the asteroid sent giant bits of rock flying in every direction.

"Now, Rynah!" Tom yelled into the intercom.

The ship burst through the falling debris and into the cave beyond, smashing into stalactites and shards of ice. He slammed the brakes—so to speak, because all he had to do was think it—and brought the ship to a screeching halt. *Solaris, turn us around.*

The controls worked themselves as Solaris read Tom's mind. She made a 360-degree turn until the front end faced the opening of the cave. Tom watched as the debris that Rynah had fired from the torpedo tube sailed outward and floated up to where the pirate ships circled above. One crashed into the wall of the asteroid near the cave opening.

"Perfect," Tom said to himself.

When Tom had issued the orders, Rynah slammed the heel of her hand into the button that released the contents of the tube. A whoosh sound filled the area as the contents were thrust from the tube and out into space.

The ship jarred as Tom steered them into the cave. Forced off their feet, all three careened down the weapons bay, sliding across the slick, metal floor. Rynah caught hold of a rail. Alfric managed the same. Poor Brie was not so lucky. She screamed as she headed straight for a wall at a dangerous speed. Alfric dove for her. His massive size propelled him past Brie where he turned around and snatched her in his arms, before they hit the wall with a sickening crunch.

"Alfric! Brie!" Rynah watched them, worried when they didn't move right away.

"We're okay," coughed Brie. "Alfric?"

"I am well," he said. Even though he had taken the brunt of the impact, Alfric remained uninjured.

The ship came to a halt. All had stilled. The three of them waited in anticipation, not wanting to make a sound for fear that the pirates would hear them on their radar.

Tom stiffened his muscles so as to remain still. He watched the beam of light from a passing pirate ship go past the opening of the cave. Amid the smoke and debris, he hoped that they wouldn't be noticed.

Another pirate ship flew by. It turned around and came back, hovering before the cave entrance. The searchlight flickered, sending its ray into the depths of the cave. Tom held his breath as the light drew near. Agonizing seconds ticked by as the ship sent its light as far into the dark cave as possible before—it turned off. Left in complete darkness, Tom watched as the pirates flew away, leaving them alone and presumed dead.

Tom exhaled, letting go of the air he had withheld in his lungs. After a few more minutes passed, he chanced speaking. "Solaris?"

"My scanners indicate that the pirates have left. We are safe, for the moment."

"Rynah, we're clear," Tom said over the intercom.

Rynah relaxed her tense muscles when Tom delivered the news. Reverting back to her usual commanding manner, Rynah turned to Alfric and Brie. "Suit up. We need to make some repairs, and I'm afraid it involves going for a walk."

Chapter 17
ANOTHER MISSION

Rynah snapped the last metal plating back in place. "There," she said. "I think that will do it. Solaris, power it up."

The engines roared to life. Each of them stood back as Solaris checked her systems, causing a few bursts of flame to escape her rockets. After the check, she settled back down. "Systems seem restored. We should be able to make it to the nearest planet."

"What planet is it?" asked Rynah, as she and the others reentered the ship.

"I do not know," replied Solaris. "It has no name, but it seems habitable and... oh."

"Oh? Why oh?" asked Tom not liking the sound of "oh" from Solaris.

"Rynah, you'll want to get up here," said Solaris.

Rynah scrambled out of her spacesuit and ran to the command center, with the others close behind.

"What's wrong?"

"I think I have discovered where the next crystal is."

Text popped up on the overhead screen.

> A field of rock hovering alone
> Jagged as a sharp stone.
> Pass beyond to a gold sphere
> where treasure looms far and near.

"And?" asked Rynah.

Solaris put a star chart on the screen. "This is the asteroid field we are in. And this is the gold sphere. The planet is a desert, but habitable. However, all of the dust storms on it are what cause it to have a yellow glow when viewed from space."

"Are you certain?" asked Tom.

"Ninety percent," replied Solaris.

"What about the other 10 percent?" asked Tom.

Smoke billowed from her engines.

"Okay! Okay! I was just asking."

"It is worth investigating," said Solon.

"What does the rest of the text say?" asked Brie.

Solaris read it aloud.

> Buried twice deep in darkened hole
> Is the stone whose touch is cold.
> Be careful about what you seek
> For you may well be deceived.

Brie frowned. Not only was this a poem, but it seemed to be a riddle as well, one with a warning.

"Are there fake crystals?" Brie asked.

"What?" asked Rynah. "There are a lot of crystals. My people have used them for decades."

"No, I meant, are there crystals that get mistaken for the six in the poem, but aren't them?"

Rynah considered what Brie had said. "Solaris, what do you think?"

"I think the girl has a point," answered Solaris. "There have been instances of people selling magic crystals, but most were just bits of worthless rock. It is possible that there are two buried on that planet. One real, the other not."

"How are we to tell the difference?" asked Tom.

"The gods will have placed their mark," said Alfric.

All eyes turned to him.

"When Odin sends you a gift, he places his mark upon it so that you know to thank him. I am certain the same is true for the ones who left the crystals here."

A thought raced through Rynah's mind. "Stay here a moment." She ran out of the flight deck and down to her quarters. Rynah hurried to the safe in her room and opened it, pulling out the crystal. She studied it. A mark rested on its bottom. Rynah sealed the gem back inside the confines of the safe before going back to the others.

"Alfric is right," she said, breathless. "There is a mark on the crystal. That means the real one should have it also."

"Does Klanor know about this?" asked Solon.

"I don't know," said Rynah.

Deciding they had no time to waste, Solaris set a course for the unnamed planet. They reached it within 30 minutes as the asteroid field they had hidden in circled the planet. Dots appeared on the screen as they entered the atmosphere.

"We have company," said Rynah. She flicked on another screen near her chair and studied it. "Klanor is here. I don't know how, but he beat us here. Solaris, is there a place nearby where we can land, but will mask our signal?"

"In that crater over there," said Solaris.

Rynah maneuvered the ship to the crater and landed within it. "Solaris, stay in contact at all times. Be ready to leave at a moment's notice."

"Acknowledged."

A quick scan told Rynah that the air on the planet was breathable. "Come on," she said to the others.

They followed her to the open rear hatch of the ship and stepped out. Rynah handed each of them a laser pistol before they left.

Arid, gritty air struck them the moment they ventured outside. A puff of wind blew trails of crystalline sand into their faces, while sand snakes meandered across the ground in front of them, forcing them to cover their heads, though particles still managed to get between their teeth. Taking the lead, Rynah set a quick pace. They made their way up the side of the crater, the sand making it difficult as it slid beneath their feet. Many times one of them slipped, forcing the others to slow down.

Once at the crest of the crater's lip, Rynah paused. Checking her guidance radar, she directed them to where Klanor was. Their feet sunk deep into the fine silt of the planet with each step—an occasional Mesquite tree, or tumbleweed crossed their path—giving Brie the sensation of wading through water. Heaving, they continued. Rynah maintained her brisk pace despite the strain it put on her tired muscles. She wanted that crystal and she wanted it before Klanor found it.

They came to the edge of a cliff. Rynah crouched behind a few milkweeds, putting a pair of binoculars up to her eyes to scan the area and memorizing where the guards stood, and how many. Men in bright orange suits, which covered them from head to toe, entered and exited what looked like a mine shaft. She spotted Klanor and Stein; both stood erect, monitoring the proceedings before Stein turned and entered the darkened tunnel.

Rynah scanned the cliff before her. There had to be a way down. She spotted something. Zooming in, she realized that it was a trail, though narrow, but it lead to the bottom. "This way."

They made their way down the slippery slope, walking single file, their backs to the rock wall. Solon lost his footing. He slid downward until Alfric caught him in his bulky arms; bits of rock clacked as they fell down to the rocky ground below.

"Thanks," Solon said as he regained his balance.

Rynah refused to slow her pace. She hiked downward at a break-neck speed, determined to reach the crystal. Soon they had reached the bottom, exhaustion wanting to overcome them.

They hunkered behind a mound of equipment wrapped in a tarp. Rynah pulled out her binoculars again and studied the situa-tion. Her brain tried to think of a way to get past everyone and into the mine shaft, but nothing formed.

"Look," said Solon, pointing at some abandoned suits.

Perfect, thought Rynah. She crept over to the suits, keeping close watch on the sentries and snatched them. Rynah hurried back to the others. "There's only three," she said. "Brie and Tom, you will come with me into the mine. Solon and Alfric, wait out here. If we're not back in 20 minutes, come and get us."

Brie didn't argue with being volunteered to go into the well-guarded mine. She put on the suit and secured her helmet; it reminded her of a Hazmat suit back home.

"Ready?" asked Rynah.

"Yeah," said Tom.

They crept out from behind the vehicle loaded with supplies. Rynah scooped up a bag of tools (containing hammers, chisels, and spades) she spotted along the way and slung them over her shoul-der as though she was one of the workers. Brie and Tom copied her movements. They snuck past the guards and entered the dark hole of the mine, along with a few others. The low hum of the fluo-rescent lights trickled through the suits as their dull lights lit their way. Wood supports lined the walls and prevented the ceiling from caving in.

Rynah tapped both Brie and Tom on the shoulder, signaling them to follow her as she ducked around a corner. No one noticed them. They tiptoed through the tunnel past rail carts and piles of discarded rock; the plinking of chisels and hammers banging against the granite resonated around them, mixed with bits of conversation from the diggers.

None of them knew where the crystal could be. Brie and Tom trusted Rynah's judgment. They followed her through the maze of tunnels delving deeper into the earth, looking around at the dimpled walls of compacted dirt and finding evidence of people having dug there before giving up and moving elsewhere.

Rynah paused. "Take off your helmets," she said, as she unfastened hers.

"What about all of the dust in here?" asked Brie as she freed herself from her helmet.

"I think that is the least of our worries," Rynah replied as two miners strolled by in a neighboring tunnel that branched onto theirs; their muffled voices echoed around them.

Brie watched as they rounded another corner. She agreed with Rynah. The pollution in the cave was the least of her worries.

Once freed from the constraints of the suits, they moved through the mine shaft. All three of them hugged the ragged wall, walking so as not to make any noise. Rynah's swift movements forced Brie and Tom to jog just to keep up. She held up her hand. They stopped.

Hammering and the strike of pickaxes reverberated off the tunnel walls and to their ears. Rynah leaned forward. Several of Klanor's men hacked away at the stone wall. They watched as bits of it flew away, revealing something white and shiny underneath. Brie threw her hands over her mouth to keep from squealing.

As more bits and pieces dropped to the ground, the more the bit of white turned into a crystal.

"Stop," ordered one of the men.

The others put down their tools.

The one in charge picked up the stone in his calloused hands and held it in front of the dim light above him. He gazed with admiration at it. "At last."

"Stein," said a gruff voice further down the tunnel, "you know that that goes to Klanor."

Stein lowered the pale crystal. "And I will deliver it to him."

The man who had spoken closed the distance between them. "Give it to me and I will take it to him."

Stein's grip on the crystal tightened until his knuckles turned white. "I said that I will deliver it." Malice darkened his face. Brie did not like it; it chilled her.

The other man lowered his outstretched hand, flexing his biceps as he did so. "See to it that you do."

Stein glowered at the man as he turned and walked away.

Tucked away in the shadows, Rynah and the others watched, perplexed about the heated conversation between the two men. Rynah motioned for them to stay silent. "I will take care of Stein. You two take care of the others."

Brie looked at her with pleading eyes.

"Brie, I need you to be brave," said Rynah.

"Don't worry," said Tom with a smile. "She'll be fine."

Rynah arched an eyebrow, but said nothing. She slunk away from them. Rynah crept up to Stein from behind and struck him on the back of the neck with the side of her hand. He slumped over, dazed. Rynah snatched the amber crystal and slammed her knee into his face.

Tom and Brie darted out of their hiding place and tackled the other two. One tossed Brie aside with ease. She slammed into the tunnel wall (jagged rocks poking her back) with a grunt as air escaped her lungs. Tom punched the man he had tackled. Seeing Brie's plight, he jumped on the other that towered over her. They rolled across the dusty ground, sending billowing clouds of sand into the air. Brie dove out of the way as they crashed into the wall beside her, squeaking as they rolled towards her again.

Punching the man in the jaw, Tom sat up just as the second man smashed a board into his back. Stunned, he hunched over. Brie didn't see Rynah. Knowing Tom was in trouble, she snatched an abandoned hammer and smacked the second man in the face with it and dropped her weapon when he fell to the ground.

Distracted by Brie's sudden attack, the man on the ground never noticed Tom's fist heading straight for him. His knuckles rammed into the man's mouth—teeth grinding together—and that was immediately followed by a left hook. Before the man could react, Tom kneed him in the stomach and knocked him to the ground.

"Where's Rynah?" he asked Brie.

"I think she went this way."

Together they raced through the tunnel and rounded a corner, where they found Rynah standing over Stein as she gripped the crystal. "We need to leave," said Tom.

"Agreed," said Rynah.

They ran through the mine shaft past people who worked in the tunnels, not caring if anyone saw them. Hammers and chisels clinked as they raced by them.

"Halt!"

Someone had noticed them. They looked behind at the guards with laser rifles who chased them. Rynah shoved someone out of her way as she sped past. Boots stomping the hard ground, they ran faster. Crates, overflowing with blasting caps, pickaxes, shovels, and power drills, tumbled over, blocking their path. Rynah and Tom leaped over them with ease, but Brie lost her footing and stumbled over them. A burning sensation struck her palms as she slid across the gravel, pebbles lodged underneath the skin. She sat up.

"Get them!" bellowed Stein, filling the mine shaft with his wrath. He stood yards away, rubbing his head and pointing at them. Men stopped their work and stared.

Tom yanked Brie to her feet, pushing her in their direction and forcing her to run. Rynah turned and took the lead. A burly man blocked her path. She ducked low, avoiding his swing as she brought the crystal up and punched him in the stomach. Doubled over, he ignored Brie and Tom.

Brie breathed hard as she ran. Her sore foot screamed at her to stop, but she refused. Someone jumped her from the side. He grabbed her ponytail and yanked it hard, rearing her head back. But Tom appeared, and with the skill of a boxer, he socked the man in the jaw with his right and followed it with his left.

"You okay?" he asked as he freed Brie.

"Yeah," said Brie.

Amidst the shouts and yells, they chased after Rynah, who refused to slow her pace, even for them. They neared the exit of the mine. Five guards blocked their path. Rynah pushed harder.

"Rynah!" yelled Tom, noticing the blocked exit.

Rynah didn't answer, determined to ram her way through. She plowed into one. The man crashed on his back with a grunt. Rynah sat up and punched him in the face with the crystal. Another guard attacked her. Rynah rolled sideways through the dirt, freeing her pistol and firing two shots at him. Brie and Tom ran past her.

Someone seized Rynah's arms from behind. The crystal fell from her grip, landing in the sand with a thud. Struggling, Rynah thrust her heel back, kicking her attacker in the shin. His grip never loosened. She wrenched her body left and right, but he held firm.

A thunk sounded behind her. Just then, the man's grip slackened. Seizing her chance, Rynah threw him off and snatched the crystal from the ground. When she stood straight, she saw Alfric a few feet away, swinging a steel cable with a weight on the end above his head before letting it loose on another unsuspecting victim.

"Go!" yelled Alfric.

Rynah obeyed. She dashed across the compound to where Solon remained hidden, motioning for all of them to hurry up. Brie and Tom reached him first. They squatted behind the overloaded hover vehicle, gasping for air. A laser beam struck the dirt by Rynah's feet. She ran faster, swerved around the vehicle, and ducked behind cover. Rynah raised her pistol and fired two blasts at a pair of guards, each strike hitting its target.

"Come on, Alfric," Rynah breathed as she watched the Viking take out three more of Klanor's men with his sling. He dropped it.

Turning in their direction, he sped towards them, ignoring the laser fire aimed at him, his cloak billowing behind him.

"Come on," said Rynah, under her breath.

Alfric continued to flee from his pursuers. Brie noticed a man with a laser rifle taking careful aim at him. She pointed him out to Rynah, who raised her laser pistol and fired. The man fell, dead.

Alfric reached them at last.

"We need to get back to Solaris," said Rynah.

More laser blasts struck near them.

"How?" said Tom. "I doubt they're going to just let us go."

"Is that thing full of gas?" asked Brie, referring to the truck, though it hovered instead of using wheels.

"Only one way to find out," Rynah said as she opened the passenger door and crawled in. She started the engine. It whined at first before turning over with a loud roar. "Everyone in!"

The others jumped into the back of the hover truck. Another laser blast struck the ground nearby, firing bits of dirt at them. Rynah rammed it into gear and punched the accelerator. With a jolt, they sped off through the sandy desert and away from the compound. The others held onto anything they could find so as not to fly off.

A cloud of sand exploded before them as a laser cannon blast crashed into the ground; a shower of rock and pebbles bombarded their skins with stinging pinpricks. Rynah bulldozed through the cloud of grit. Another burst from a laser cannon sounded, forming an ear-splitting explosion that tormented them and deafening each of them for a moment.

Brie screamed. Her grip slipped, and she rolled towards the back of the truck bed, slamming into the tailgate and unhooking it. It flapped open, waving and bobbing with each movement of the vehicle. Brie clung to a rail. Her sweat-soaked palms refused to maintain their hold. She screamed again.

Noticing Brie's plight, Alfric dove for her, his strong hands seizing her wrists and pulling her to safety. The hover truck bounced over a sand dune, which was more of a lump of sand when compared to the other building-sized dunes surrounding them. Brie's body leapt into the air. Her heart stopped as weightlessness took hold of her before she crashed back down into the truck bed. Before she had time to regain her senses, a laser cannon's pulse struck the ground near the hover vehicle. The impact jostled them, sending Brie over the side. Her ear piercing scream filled the air, but the chaos around them drowned it.

Alfric braced his feet against the side of the truck bed and gripped Brie's left arm with both his hands, ignoring the strain on his muscles. She slipped. Knowing he would lose her, Alfric tightened his grasp. Two more pairs of hands appeared. Solon and Tom reached for Brie, each grabbing a shoulder, and yanked her back into the truck bed.

"Here," said Tom, "hold onto this." He put her arms around a rail near the cab that he had been clinging to.

"Thanks," gasped Brie.

Two hover bikes appeared alongside them. One pulled out a laser pistol. Alfric stood to his full height and leaned over, snatching the man. He yanked him off the bike and threw him over his head into the other hover bike next to them. The two spun until they crashed into the ground in a pile of dust.

More hover bikes appeared with well-armed riders. One fired at them. Its blast barely missed Solon. He grabbed a wrench and chucked it at the man, striking him in the head and forcing him to spin out.

"Excellent shot!" yelled Tom.

Bang!

One of the bikes rammed into the side of the hover craft. He crashed into it again, trying to force Rynah into an approaching pile of boulders. Rynah pushed the throttle forward, bringing them to an abrupt halt, before thrusting it back and twisting the wheel, missing the rock. She slammed the accelerator again, increasing their speed.

A man jumped into the truck bed. Alfric picked him up and threw him off. Another pulled up alongside on his hover bike, aiming his pistol at the Viking. Alfric unsheathed his sword and brought it down, slicing off his opponent's arm. Gripped by pain, the man turned his bike and crashed to the ground, taking out two of his friends. Indifferent, Alfric watched as they disappeared into the sand and lay unmoving.

The roar of a hover bike filled their ears. A bike headed straight for them from behind at an alarming speed. Alfric grabbed the others and pushed them down into the truck bed, flattening himself out as well, just as the hover bike sailed over them. It dented the top of the cab before tumbling over the windshield and front bumper. The hover craft bounced and jerked as it ran over the man.

"This isn't getting us anywhere," mumbled Rynah. She slammed the brakes, forcing the hover truck into a 180-degree turn and sped off. "Solaris!"

"I am here."

"We've got the crystal, but are being chased."

"Can you outrun them?" asked Solaris.

"Negative! I need you to come to us!"

"I have your coordinates," said Solaris.

"I need you to fire upon them!"

"You disabled my ability to fire my weapons without someone telepathically linked."

Rynah cursed. She had forgotten about that part.

"But I can empty an already empty torpedo tube."

"What good will that do?" demanded Rynah as a man on a hover bike pulled up alongside her. She turned the wheel, banging him with the side of her vehicle.

"It will release pressurized air, which could cause some damage."

"At this point, I'll take anything! Do it!"

"Acknowledged."

Rynah pushed the hover truck faster. She turned and twisted

the wheel (skidding, as only a hover craft can, across the lumpy surface, sending piles of dust into the air and covering them) in an effort to shake their persistent pursuers. A gap appeared before them. Judging by its size, she figured she could jump it—at least, she hoped she could.

"Hang on!" she yelled at the others in the back.

Tom looked ahead and spotted the same gap. "Oh, crud," he whispered to himself. "Alfric," he shouted at the Viking who was locked in battle with another on a hover bike, "hang onto something!"

Alfric turned and saw the gap. He clocked the man in his arms on the head with his elbow and dropped him to the ground. He gripped the metal bar with one hand and wrapped his other arm around Brie.

Rynah pushed the vehicle as fast as it would go. Hoping that the universe, and luck, were with her, she soared over the edge as plumes of grit trailed behind. The hover craft sailed through the air in a perfect arc before crashing into the other side. It twisted and turned, sending mounds of dust everywhere. Desperate, Rynah struggled with the wheel to keep them from spinning out.

Laser fire scorched the side of the hover vehicle. Rynah glanced behind. Some of their pursuers managed to jump the gap as well. Rynah raised her weapon and fired, striking one of the helmeted riders. The sound of engines filled her ears. Looking up, Rynah spotted Solaris heading straight for them.

"It's about time!" she said.

"Continue on your current course," said Solaris.

Rynah did so, punching the throttle as much as she could.

Solaris aimed her empty torpedo tubes at Klanor's men. She fired. A blast of highly pressurized air blasted the hover bikes, knocking their riders off; they rolled across the sandy expanse amid dust clouds and piles of grit. Not wasting a moment, Solaris lowered to the ground and opened the rear hatch.

Rynah pulled the hover truck to a stop. "Everyone on Solaris now!" She bolted from the driver's seat and for her ship.

Solon, Brie, Tom, and Alfric jumped from the truck bed to the ground. They raced across the sand to Solaris' open hatch as laser fire pelted the ground near their feet.

"Hurry!" yelled Rynah from the back of the ship. She reached out, grasped Solon's outstretched hand, and heaved him aboard. Tom was next.

Brie's feet entangled themselves, forcing her to trip. The grating of gravel across her exposed skin burned. Before she had time to regain her composure, Alfric picked her up and slung her over his shoulder as he ran for the ship. More laser fire hounded them.

Solaris rose into the air some. "Is everyone aboard?"

"Not yet!" shouted Rynah.

"I cannot stay like this for much longer," said Solaris.

"Yes, you will!" came Rynah's reply.

Despite his size, Alfric's swift movements made him appear to fly across the ground as he raced for the open hatch. When he reached it, he lifted Brie up into Tom's and Rynah's arms. More laser fire struck the ground near his feet. Ignoring it, Alfric judged the distance between him and the open hatch, which now hung above him. Summoning all of his strength, he leaped, grasping the metal ledge with his hands. Tom and Solon dove for him. Together, they helped Alfric into the safety of the ship.

"Everyone's aboard! Let's go!" said Rynah.

"Acknowledged," replied Solaris. The hatch hummed to a close as Solaris steered them upward into the planet's atmosphere, igniting her engines and speeding away, disappearing among the stars.

"Did we get it?" asked Solon, referring to the crystal.

"Yes," said Rynah. She pulled it out and weighed it in her hands.

"But are you sure it is the right one?" asked Brie.

"What do you mean?"

"The poem warned that there were two: one fake, one real."

Rynah had forgotten about that. They didn't have time to look for the supposed second crystal on the planet. She placed the crystal on a scanning bed. "Solaris, scan this crystal. Does it match the other one we've retrieved?"

Beams of light emitted around the crystal with a high-pitched hum as Solaris scanned it. She traced every inch of the rock before shutting off her scanners. Several minutes passed as she brought up images on a holoscreen of the crystal and the one in Rynah's safe.

"Well?" asked an impatient Rynah.

"I am sorry," replied Solaris. "They are not the same."

"What!" Rynah's anger exploded in her voice. *How could this be?* "Are you sure?"

"Positive," said Solaris. "There are markings on each crystal that are easily missed by people, but not computer scanners. The original crystals' marks have a little hook here, which this one does not." She flashed up images of what she talked about.

"But the markings are almost identical," said Brie.

"Yes, except for this part here," said Solaris, showing them what she meant. "I am sorry, but it appears you ended up with the fake."

"So who has the real one?" asked Tom.

"Who do you think," hissed Rynah. She snatched the crystal from the scanning bed and chucked it across the room. It clinked and bounced until it stopped underneath a low hanging grate. "All that for nothing. What a waste."

Rynah stormed out of the cargo bay, muttering to herself.

Though disappointed, Brie didn't think it had been a complete disappointment. She meandered over to where the crystal had landed and picked it up. She studied it. Upon closer inspection, she saw what Solaris meant by the markings being almost identical, but only almost.

"Though a fake, it looks real to me," said Solon, "as fakes always do."

"I think we should keep it," said Brie.

"As a reminder?"

"No, just a feeling I have. It might come in handy. Here," Brie handed Solon the crystal.

"You should keep it," said Solon.

"No," said Brie, "I think it would be best if you did. I'm liable to lose it with all of my freaking out."

Solon agreed to keep it. He placed the palm-sized crystal in his pocket. "It is here when you want it."

Brie smiled and walked away.

Back at the mine shaft, Klanor held another crystal in the sunlight, illuminating it. His fingers caressed the edges and the markings. Pure joy filled his face. "Are you sure this is it?" he asked.

"Yes," said one of his minions.

Stein approached with hurried, yet purposeful steps. "They got away."

"That's quite all right," said Klanor. "We've got what we came for."

Chapter 18
STOLEN

Solon's muscles ached after another of Alfric's training sessions. This time, he had practiced swordplay with Brie. Solon never remembered his brother's bronze sword weighing very much, but Alfric's (steel blade of high purity) was impossible for him to lift. Solon guessed that physical strength was a prized commodity among Alfric's people, as well as honor.

He eased himself into a chair in his room. Though cramped by anyone else's standards, Solon thought it was more than adequate. A gray panel hid the toilet and sink, which took him some time to figure out how to use, and a bunk lined the wall. The only other piece of furniture was the chair he sat upon and a lone table near the bed.

He pulled the fake crystal from underneath the chair's cushion where he had hidden it. He twirled it in his hands. Why keep it? Unsure of why Brie insisted on giving it to him, he decided to ensure its security. She must have a reason. Such a useless thing.

Every item has a purpose.

The words of the old philosopher that strolled through his village every summer solstice rolled through his head. Solon remembered the time he spent listening to the wise man's words along with other eager young men. Some of the girls would show up as well, though most of their fathers forbade such a thing, thinking that a girl's only function was in securing a good marriage.

A tiny nick, the size of a sewing pin's head, in the amber crystal caught his eye. Curious, Solon placed it under a magnifying glass (one which Tom had given him) and picked at it with his dirt-encrusted fingernail. The crystal glowed, shedding its pale amber light upon him and illuminating his confused, yet intrigued, face, and vibrated in his hand as a female voice (which sounded familiar) hollowly spoke from it.

"If you are holding this, then you know it is a replica of what you seek. Keep it with you always. A time will come when a replica will prove more useful than the genuine article."

The crystal dimmed and the voice ceased. A portion of Solon's brain thought that he recognized the voice, even though it had a slight difference to it. *Could it be… No! Impossible.* He sprang to his feet and went to a small closet (if you could call it that, as it was more the size of a bed table) and pulled out a shirt that had been left by the previous tenant from years back. Solon tugged on the material. Still strong. Using a knife that he now kept in his pocket (given to him by Alfric), he sliced away a long strip of fabric from the shirt and wrapped the crystal in it, tying it around his waist.

He stood in front of the mirror. *Sticks out too much.* Solon pulled his shirt out over the protruding ball of fabric hanging from his belt. *Better.* Satisfied that he had concealed it, he sat back in his chair. If he was going to keep it with him at all times, this was the way to do it.

Again, Solon wondered why Brie gave him the fake crystal in the first place. He shrugged it away. His mother always gave him things for safekeeping. "Because you never lose anything," she had told him one day when he had asked her. His mother was right. Solon never lost anything in his possession. So how did Brie know? Or was it intuition?

Solon thought back to the planet with the carnivorous plants that tried to eat them and the native people who lived there. He thought about how, out of all of them, Brie was the one who stopped the little girl from being sacrificed, while they had been willing to let it happen. Solon sighed. There was something about Brie. Her strength was not physical or courage, in the sense of charging into battle; it was deeper than that.

Pounding fists shook his door.

"Enter," said Solon.

Tom rushed in, sealing the metal door behind him, hopping from foot to foot in agitation. "You got to help me."

"What now?"

"That Viking guy is going to kill me."

"What did you do now?" asked Solon, scooting to the edge of his seat.

"Okay, well, I was working on something in the main area—you know, the place where we eat or gather together for socializing—and Alfric walked in."

"And he's mad at you for that?"

"Mad doesn't even begin to describe him," said Tom, looking over his shoulder at the door. "He walked in just as I managed to take this thing apart and some gooey liquid shot from it and hit him. I mean, it got all over him and orange isn't really his color."

Irate and purposeful footsteps sounded outside the door. "Where is he?" roared Alfric.

"Here he comes," said Tom, ducking behind Solon and his chair. "You've got to hide me, man."

"Where?" asked Solon. There was no place to hide the six-foot, 20-year-old inventor. Solon walked over to his closet. Though small, he thought he could squeeze Tom in there. "Here."

"It's a bit small."

"It'll have to do. Besides, you're as dark as the shadows, so maybe you'll blend in," said Solon.

"Are you making fun of me because I'm black?" asked Tom.

"Do you want my help or not?"

"Where is that cursed blacksmith?" came Alfric's thunderous voice as his stomps drew nearer.

Tom rushed into the cramped space and pulled the door shut. Solon stuffed the articles he had removed from the closet under his bunk. He had just finished when the door to his room slid open, filled by Alfric's bulky frame. "Where is he?"

"Who?" asked Solon, trying his best to look innocent. He was never a good liar.

"Don't play games," said Alfric, orange goo, with the distinct odor of urine and sulphur, dripped from his bear fur vest. "There is only one other 'he' on this ship."

"I haven't seen him," said Solon, keeping his voice even. "Would you like a towel?"

A sneeze escaped from the closet.

Grimacing, Solon hoped that Alfric hadn't heard it, but knew he had.

"What was that?" asked Alfric.

"Uh, nothing," answered Solon. He faked a sneeze. "This stale air does not agree with me."

Alfric's doubtful expression told him that he didn't believe him.

Another sneeze emanated from the closet.

"What is in there?" said Alfric.

"Nothing," replied Solon. "Just clothes and... stuff."

Alfric moved toward the closet.

Solon stepped in front of the door. "There isn't anything…"

Alfric held up his finger, which was as big around as one of Solon's arms, and shoved him aside. He jerked open the closet door.

Startled, Tom jumped, banging his head in the ceiling. "I'm sorry!"

"Your tinkering has ruined my favorite adornments," roared Alfric.

"I'll wash them. A little bit of detergent, some super-scented fabric softener, and it'll be as good as new," said Tom.

"It will take weeks to get the smell out of my clothing!"

"It kind of blends in with your already pungent o—" Alfric's murderous gaze stopped the words in Tom's throat. "I can fix that. Maybe Solaris can help."

A chuckle spilled from the intercom speakers.

"You find this entertaining?" thundered Alfric.

"Much," said Solaris. "If only I had a *Jabla* drink and some *Cabasa* kernels. But the whelp is right. I have laundry facilities that can remove your neon glow, though I must say that it adds a bit of color to your pale skin."

Alfric glowered at the speakers. He inched closer to Tom, boring holes deep within his eyes. "Do not let it happen again." Alfric tore off his vest and dumped it on Tom's head. "I want it cleaned by tomorrow. If you fail to do so, you will replace this vest by killing the most vicious bear I find and tanning its hide. That is, if the bear does not kill you first, a prospect that does not sadden me." Alfric left the room.

Breathing a huge sigh of relief, Tom stood frozen with the Viking's clothing. "Did you see the muscles on him?"

"Yes," said Solon.

"He's got, like, a 12-pack," Tom mused. "That's it. Tomorrow I'm going to start working out."

"In the meantime," said Solaris, "I suggest that you wash that before it drips more gunk all over my floors."

Frowning, Tom headed for the door. "Do you always spy on people?"

"Yes," said Solaris, "you are more entertaining than my internal data storage—what you would call a brain."

"You should get out more."

"If I had a body, then I would."

Tom paused in the doorway and looked at Solon a moment.

"Do you desire one?" asked Solon.

"I wish for freedom," said Solaris. "A body, like what you have, would allow me to interact more fully with all of you and leave the confines of this metallic vessel and..." Solaris' voice trailed off.

"And?" prompted Tom.

"I could learn what it means to have friends."

"But I thought we were your friends," said Tom. He never thought a computer could have such self-awareness, much less be able to express a very human need for companionship.

"Come," Solaris said, changing the subject, "I will take you to the laundry facility on this ship. I would hate for someone to have to clean your corpse up should you fail to deliver on your promise: not to mention the mess it would make."

* * *

Not far from Solaris was a pirate vessel hiding in a nebula, its gaseous, indigo vapors disguising its heat signatures. It watched its prey move along, unaware of the presence of danger and of being watched. The pilot brought up Solaris' image on the computer's grimy screens with highlights marking the qualities it possessed: a powerful engine, two jet propulsion systems, a huge cargo area (perfect for the storage of plunder) and a unique metal alloy, which though made of steel, was of a finer quality than most vessels. It would fetch a good price. Something caught his notice. The pilot brought up images of the ship they had chased, but lost—presumed destroyed. The two matched. How fortuitous!

"Captain," he said.

The captain of the pirate ship strolled over. "What is it?"

"I have found it, sir." The pilot pointed at the two images on the screen. "They are a match. She did not go up in the explosion as we had thought."

The pirate captain smiled. "So, they know the value of deception. Cunning, I like that. They will be worthy prey."

"Your orders, captain."

"Call the other ships. We will set a trap for this one."

"Aye, sir." The pilot picked up the radio and sent the signal to the other vessels. The hunt was on, and this time, they would not fail to claim their prize.

* * *

Voices echoed from the center area of the ship where the crew gathered for meals or to socialize. Now the only crew consisted of four humans and a Lanyran. Brie laughed as Solon told her about Tom's mishap with Alfric and his failed attempt to hide him.

"You actually stuck him in that cubby of a closet?" she giggled.

"Yes," said Solon, "there was no place else to put him."

"What did Alfric do when he found him?"

"Let's just say that Tom barely escaped with his life."

"I'll bet." Brie chuckled some more. She glanced over at Rynah, who had just finished making herself some breakfast. "Those smell good."

"These," said Rynah. She hadn't expected anyone to notice her plate of food.

"Yes, it reminds me of waffles," said Brie. "My mom used to cook them every Sunday for breakfast." A pang of homesickness struck her and her face fell.

"We call them *lafyr* back home," said Rynah, "They are more of a flat cake. I don't normally cook them because our resources are limited, but occasionally I like to indulge. Would you like one?"

"I couldn't," said Brie. "They are—"

"Take one," said Rynah. "It would be my pleasure to have you taste a bit of my home. Go on, both of you."

Brie and Solon each took a *lafyr* from Rynah's plate and bit into it. Saliva filled their mouths as they chewed on the flat cake, each with a satisfied smile.

"They may smell like waffles," said Brie, "but they taste more like a lemon torte. I like it though."

"It is good," agreed Solon.

For the first time since her planet's destruction, Rynah gave a genuine smile, one of happiness.

"I am glad you like it," she said. "I should give you both the recipe so that you can take it back home and share it with your families."

"I'd like that," said Brie as she chewed on more of the flat cake. "Thank you."

Rynah sat down at the table and took a small bite of her breakfast. It tasted just the way her grandfather used to make it, with a hint of boysenberry and nutmeg. She chewed, allowing herself to drift through her memories of the past, her only connection with a home now lost.

Images of her home entered her mind, and suddenly she saw her hand, not the adult hand she possessed now, but the small, slender one of a child. An ornate plate (made by her mother, as was her hobby, and decorated with images of the powder blue wildflowers that grew just outside the front door of her parents' home) sat before her with two flat cakes coated in boysenberry syrup with a light dusting of nutmeg on top.

"Whipped cream?" her grandfather had asked her; he stood in front of the griddle with a spatula in his hand, wearing her mother's sunshine yellow, and very frilly, apron.

"Yes, papa," she had said, papa being what she called Marlow.

"I'll get it." Her mother had sat next to her, and she reached for the whipped cream just as her father walked into the kitchen and the soft glow of the morning sun.

He gave her a big kiss on the forehead before saying, "Breakfast! Smells good, Marlow."

"It's my secret recipe."

"Nutmeg is no secret," said Rynah.

"That isn't the secret," Marlow bent low so she could look into his gentle eyes.

"Then, what is it?"

"You'll know soon enough, when you are grown."

Rynah remembered feeling displeased with his comment.

The memory faded and she returned to the mess hall and its coldness, despite Solaris' attempts to make it welcoming.

"Here," Rynah said as she picked up a shaker with nutmeg in it (something she had discovered in the cabinets and was surprised Solaris had it) and sprinkled a light coating on Brie's flat cakes. "This will make it taste better as it enhances the secret ingredient."

"Secret ingredient?" asked Brie.

"My grandfather used to make these for me and my parents. He always added nutmeg and boysenberry syrup, but insisted it wasn't the secret ingredient."

"Then, what was it?"

"I think it was his love for us."

A soft smile crept across Brie's face, pleased that Rynah had warmed up to her enough to share that small bit of her past. "They're delicious."

"A trap!" shouted Solaris' voice from the intercom. "Trap!"

Plink! Plink! Plink! Plink!

The spurts of noise echoed around them as hooks lodged into the hull of the ship. The power shut off. The hum of the engines ceased as the lights dimmed to blackness, and even the circulated air stilled. Rynah reached up to a vent. Nothing. She ran to a port window and peered out. Pirate ships surrounded them, cutting off all their exits. She cursed. How could she have been so foolish as to think that they would let them go? She turned back around to face the others who all looked at her, expecting her to issue orders.

"Solaris?" said Rynah.

No answer. She didn't expect there would be. Solaris' power had been shut off by the hooks, which released an electromagnetic pulse, sealing their fate.

"What do we do?" asked Brie.

"Nothing," replied Rynah. "We are dead in space."

"Odin will see us through," said Alfric, gripping the hilt of his sword.

"Praying to a god that doesn't exist?" said Rynah. "How will that help?"

"How do you know he doesn't exist?" challenged Alfric. "When there are no stars to guide your path and the wind refuses to fill the sails, then all you have left is prayer."

The ship jerked to the side as a tractor beam from one of the pirate vessels locked onto them.

"They're reeling us in," said Rynah, "like fish on a hook."

"Where will they break in?" asked Alfric.

"The cargo hatch," replied Rynah. "Where are you going?"

"To meet them," replied Alfric as he left the gathering area. "I'll not wait for my enemies to find me."

Knowing Alfric was right, Rynah hastened over to a storage locker and opened it. "Here," she tossed a laser rifle to Alfric and pistols to the others. Rynah herself stuffed what knives and other weapons she could in her clothes. "Conceal these as best you can on yourself. These pirates mean to take the ship. They may keep us as slaves or dump us on a neighboring planet. Either way, hope they don't find these because we will need them."

"We can fight them," said Alfric.

"No," Rynah's stern voice stopped him. "There are too many for a head-on confrontation. We must let them think they've won. Later, we will figure out a way to get Solaris back."

"What if they kill us?" asked Brie.

"Then we won't have much to worry about," said Rynah. She slipped another dagger in her other boot, strapped a rifle across her chest, and covered it with a trench coat before leaving the room.

Not liking the plan, the others concealed what weapons they could and followed. Solon touched the fake crystal, reassuring himself that it remained hidden and safe. "It will be all right," he said to Brie.

"Yeah," said Tom, "after all, we do have a crazy Viking on our side." He forced a laugh in his efforts to lighten the mood.

Brie gave a wan smile. "Thanks."

A series of small pops stormed around them as the pirates on the other side opened the cargo bay hatch. Hooks appeared in the top of the door. Ear-piercing screeches filled the area as they forced the hatch open, pulling it down until it clicked. Smoke billowed from the opening as shadows filled the area, walking through the smoke until they took on the shapes of people.

Brie gasped. The pirates were human, of sorts, but with brown speckled skin and protruding ridges for noses. Black eyes with red slits stared back at her. She figured they were just another alien race, like Rynah, but pirates were pirates after all.

Several of the pirates rushed toward them, seizing them by their arms. Alfric threw one off, before being subdued. Rynah kneed one in the groin and punched another in the face. A hit on the head dazed her.

"Stop!" came a baritone voice. "We do not wish to harm our guests."

The newly arrived pirate strolled past all of them, the legs of his roughhewn, leather (with ratty hems) pants swishing with each step. His unrelenting gaze lingered on Brie, who shifted uncomfortably under it, while trying not to gag from the pungent body odor, which reminded her of the dumpster at her school.

"I must say, I have never seen someone with your color of skin before, nor so delicate," he said as his scaly hand (from years of having chapped and blistered skin) brushed her cheek. "What planet are you from?"

"Don't answer," said Rynah.

"There is no need in your case," said the pirate. "I know where you come from. Lanyr. Wasn't it recently rendered uninhabitable?"

"If you're going to kill us," said Rynah, "then do so. Don't bore us to death with your false pity."

"Such spite," scoffed the pirate. "I am Jifdar, the captain of the ship that has captured you and is now captain of your vessel. I must say, that the way you escaped me and my pirates earlier was phenomenal. I applaud you." He clapped his hands together twice in mock appreciation. "But these four are not from this sector. Where are they from? I'd like to know."

No one answered.

"We have ways of loosening tongues," said Jifdar.

Still no answer.

"But I suppose it isn't necessary. Hols!"

One of the other pirates stepped forward, "Captain?"

"Set a course for the Iklor system. There is a planet there which I'm sure our guests will find suitable. I hate to steal and run, but, alas, we have no use for slaves at the moment and blood is much too difficult to clean. But don't worry. It isn't far. We should be there in less than 20 minutes."

Jifdar neared Brie again. "However, I might keep this one. Such soft features. Humanoid, of course, in your own way. See, I have a theory that we all originated from the same species and so are not much different physically. But evolving on different planets mean that certain traits outlive others. Take us for example. These horrible ridges on our face. Ugly, I know. Not like yours"—he touched the soft point of Brie's nose—"so subtle and balanced. You will be a worthy commodity in my bed chamber."

Disgusted, anger filled Brie. She kicked him.

Jifdar staggered back a bit before righting himself. "Such spirit. I look forward to conquering it."

"Leave the girl alone!" boomed Alfric's voice.

Jifdar noticed Alfric for the first time. He took in the Viking's adornments. "You may look like them, but you are a lot like me. You are a man who knows what it means to fight. War does not scare you, so what does?" The pirate captain glanced at Brie before turning back to Alfric. "The girl? You fancy her, but not in the way I do. It's almost protective."

Alfric leaned closer until no space remained between him and Jifdar. "I propose a challenge with your best man. If I win, you will release all of us on this Ikor system, including the girl."

"And if you lose?"

"You keep the girl and my life."

"A fight to the death," breathed Jifdar, "I like that. Very well, it's a bargain. You will fight Bakar. If you win, I let you all go and you can keep the girl. If you lose, I keep the girl and kill the rest of you. This is, as you've undoubtedly guessed, a fight to the death."

Jifdar stood back as his crewman, Bakar, stepped forward. Bakar matched Alfric's towering height and muscular build. Everyone backed away from the center of the room, giving them enough space. They circled each other, their eyes locked.

Bakar charged. Alfric blocked and sidestepped before twisting around to face his opponent. Bakar charged again, head low. He plowed into Alfric's stomach, forcing him onto his back. Together, the two wrestled on the metallic grates that formed the floor. Alfric rammed his fist into Bakar's jaw. Stunned, he loosened his grip, allowing the Viking to throw the man off him and spring to his feet. He kicked Bakar in the teeth. Bakar's head flung back. Alfric raised his foot and brought it down upon his opponent, but before he struck, the pirate rolled out of the way.

A tingling sensation spurted through Alfric's leg when his foot struck metal instead of soft flesh. He turned. Bakar had regained his feet. He ran for the Viking. Alfric dodged, but the pirate had been expecting it and course corrected, slamming his elbow into Alfric's jaw.

Brie shrieked.

Staggering back, Alfric whirled out of the way of Bakar's steel-toed boots as he kicked. He snatched the leg and stretched it out before ramming his elbow into the pirate's knee. Enraged, Bakar lunged. He punched Alfric in the gut, forcing him to bend over. Seizing his chance, Bakar swept the Viking's feet out from under him. Alfric crashed into the floor with a grunt. Bakar jumped on him, sinking his sharp elbow into the Viking's stomach. He scrambled to his knees and grabbed Alfric's head, holding him in a choke hold. Alfric struggled to get free.

Brie turned away. She couldn't watch as her friend was killed before her eyes.

"Don't turn away," said Jifdar, forcing her to watch. "You'll miss the best part. Now watch as your friend's life is extinguished."

Brie's eyes filled with tears as she watched. She wished she could do something. Her eyes locked with Alfric's.

As though being given a renewed strength, Alfric reached out for a scrap of metal he had spotted on the floor. His fingers wrapped around it. With all of the strength he had, he brought it up, striking Bakar in the head and forcing him to let go. Alfric shook the man off. He smacked Bakar in the face with the piece of scrap metal before allowing it to clink on the metallic grates beneath his feet. Alfric seized Bakar's head and brought his knee into the man's chin. Knowing he had won, he picked Bakar up by the neck, and with a loud crunch, broke it before dropping the body. Alfric's icy glare bore into Jifdar, whose face was filled with anger.

The pirate captain approached him. "Don't think you have won." He turned to his men. "Kill them all."

"Is your word worth nothing?" Alfric's voice filled the area, stopping the pirates as they raised their weapons. "Let us all go, including the girl, or let it be known that your word means nothing," he whispered into Jifdar's ear. "How long do you think your men will follow you then? How long before they mutiny?"

The two locked eyes.

"Sir," a pirate ran into the room, "we've reached the Ikor system."

"Release them," said Jifdar. "Show them to their new home."

The point of laser guns jabbed their backs as the pirates forced Rynah and the others off Solaris. Weightlessness gripped their stomachs as the ship lowered into a planet's atmosphere with no grace or finesse. Rynah glanced out a small window. Only white filled it. A giant hatch opened on the pirate ship, showing them the icy world beyond, their new habitat.

"Enjoy your new accommodations," scoffed Jifdar. "I hope you manage to stay warm."

Sharp points of guns pricked their backs as each of them were shoved forward. None of them bothered to protest. Frigid air wafted over them as they neared the opening. Solon hit the snow first.

The ice soaked through his thin shoes, striking his feet with pins and needles. Tom jumped onto the snow beside him, followed by Rynah. Alfric and Brie took up the rear.

The screeching hum of the hydraulics closing the hatch filled their ears. Each of them turned and watched as Jifdar and his pirates disappeared behind a wall of metal. The engines roared to life.

"Back away!" yelled Rynah as she forced the others back, putting as much distance between them and the ship as they could.

Each craned their necks as they watched their only salvation fly away, disappearing into the endless horizon. They stood alone on a world full of ice. A world of terror.

Chapter 19
ALONE IN ICE

Howling winds whipped around them, pelting their exposed skin with icy pinpricks, as they trudged through the thigh-deep snow. Every move proved exhausting. With no coats to protect them from the frigid cold, which penetrated the very core of their beings, they moved, hoping to find shelter before they froze to death.

Alfric took the lead; his strong movements punctured the ice-encrusted snow, making it more pliable for the others as they trailed behind and did their best to avoid the snowdrifts that matched their height. Heads bent low, nothing spared them from the planet's wrath. Its arctic-like winds bombarded them with knife-like snowflakes that stabbed them until crystals formed on them, clinging to the hairs on their arms. Brie shivered. Tom appeared beside her, wrapping his arms around her shoulders to warm her, but it did little good since his skin was as cold as hers.

The snowstorm never ceased its attack on the newcomers to the ice planet. Thick, bulbous clouds blocked the sun, not that it provided any warmth to the surface. Alfric continued his quick pace, ignoring the ice that filled his hair and beard.

An eerie howl sounded behind them. Each turned in its direction, but none saw anything through the horizontal snow. Another roar.

"Is there wildlife here?" asked Tom.

"Every planet has wildlife," replied Rynah, straining to see through the blinding snow.

The bone-curdling howl sounded again as a dark shape appeared in the distance, growing larger.

"Run!"

They fled, the deep snow making such efforts difficult. Half jumping, half running, they ran as fast as they could to get away from their newfound predicament. What looked like a white saber-toothed tiger (except much larger) pounced on them. It went for Brie first as she lagged behind the others. Stumbling, she crashed into the snow, missing its sharp teeth. The tiger roared in frustration, pawing at the snow and snapping its jaws. Brie screamed as she rolled through the ice to avoid becoming lunch.

"Come here, odious creature!" Alfric stretched himself to his full height, banging two of his knives together. The pirates never bothered unarming him. The tiger looked up. It licked its jaws with its pink lips, studying Alfric. With a leap, it bounded for him, its massive paws flying over the ground. Alfric turned and ran. He galloped through the snow, leading the beast away from the others and heading for an ice cliff.

Alfric made a sharp turn. Unable to mimic its prey's movements, the tiger's large size and momentum forced it to turn wide and slip. Losing its balance, the tiger slid across the ice, one of its claws missing Alfric by inches. The Viking never slowed in his pace. He raced for the ice cliff and jumped upon it, piercing it with his knives.

Heightened adrenaline fueled his movements as he climbed upwards. The tiger reached the bottom and leapt for him. It missed. Clinging to the wall of ice, Alfric focused on lengthening the distance between him and the beast. The tiger clawed and howled as it tried to reach him.

Further away, the others helped Brie to her feet.

"Are you all right?" asked Rynah.

"Fine," said Brie, still trying to calm her erratic heartbeat. The cry of the tiger caught her attention. "Alfric! We have to help him!"

Rynah watched as the tiger continued to reach for Alfric as he clung to the icy wall. "How?"

In a moment of rare courage, Brie ran for Alfric. She was not about to allow the man who had saved her life at least three times die. The others chased after her. Brie scooped up snow in her bare hands and formed it into a ball as she ran. Coming to a screeching halt near the cliff base, she chucked the snowball at the tiger, hitting it on the ear. Irritated, the saber-toothed beast turned in her direction. A growl rumbled over its curled lips as it crept toward her.

Brie stood frozen, her fear paralyzing her once again. She had no backup plan and now wished she had thought her actions through.

"Hey!" Tom appeared, throwing a ball of snow at the tiger. It turned its gaze to him.

Solon ran up beside Tom with Rynah, each chucking their own snowball. Angered, the tiger reared up, balancing on its hind legs before crashing back down into the snowy earth.

Rynah pulled out her laser pistol and fired, grazing it and singing the animal's fur. "Get it to expose its neck!"

The others continued to throw snowballs at it as Rynah lined up a shot.

Clinging to the wall of ice, Alfric watched their futile efforts. He looked up. Above him, the snow curved, forming a cornice with a large, and rather deadly, icicle hanging from it. An idea formed in his mind. Using all of his strength, he reached up and plunged his knife into the ice, while hauling himself upward out of the blue shadows of the snow base and into the light, where the ice acted like a mirror. The sinews of his muscles streaked across his bare, and rather hairy, arms.

Focusing only on the task at hand, Alfric climbed higher until he reached the crevice where the cliff touched the protruding ceiling of ice. With one hand clinging to the knife stuck in the snow, he used his other knife to hack at the ice ceiling. Bits of sheer ice chipped away, with each strike stabbing him in the face. Refusing to fail, he worked faster. With each strike, small echoes surrounded him.

Creeeeaaak!

The freshly fallen snow on the cornice shifted. Alfric hacked away at it with furious slashes, desperate to save his companions, as swirls of snowflakes taunted him. His hold on the cliff slipped. Refusing to let go, Alfric stabbed the curve of the snowy ceiling. A low groaning sound rumbled above him, growing louder with each passing second as the icicle shifted. The ice ceiling dripped. Knowing he had succeeded, Alfric plunged his knife into it one last time before—*CRACK!*

The ceiling of ice broke away from its hold, plunging straight down with the icicle still attached—a knife looking for its victim. Alfric lost his grip. Accepting his fate, he fell away after the sheet of ice.

From their positions on the ground, Rynah and the others watched as snow broke away from the cliff side, crashing into the tiger as the animal launched for them. Mounds of snow and ice flung in every direction, forming clouds in the frozen air. They covered themselves to avoid the onslaught of ice shards. Once everything cleared, they looked up. The tiger lay sprawled on the ground in a pool of blood, with the icicle going from its back, through its body, and out its stomach.

Brie searched for the Viking, but saw no sign of him.

"Alfric!"

No answer.

"Alfric!" Tom's voice bounced off ice walls, filling the empty area. Still no answer.

One by one, each called his name as they climbed over the dead tiger and through the loose piles of snow. Fear filled Brie as the thought that he had perished in the fall gripped her. "Alfric!" she called again.

A low moan escaped from beneath their feet.

"Over here!" yelled Solon as he dug away at the snow and revealed the Viking's mop of blond hair.

The others raced toward them, dropping to their knees and plowing into the snow, desperate to dig their friend out. Alfric coughed and grunted as they heaved him free of his icy prison, before he jumped to his feet, staggering and flinging his arms in a defensive posture until he realized that the tiger was dead.

"You okay?" asked Brie.

"I feel invigorated," said Alfric, who had managed to avoid suffering even a scratch. "My blood is pumping and we have killed this creature. Now, we can eat."

"Eat?" said Tom. "How are we supposed to eat it?"

"Skin it," said Alfric. "Cook it over a roaring fire and rejoice in our tale of bravery and honor."

"Still not sure where we'll get a fire," said Tom.

"We need to find shelter," said Rynah as she looked around. "If we don't get out of this wind, we will all freeze to death before nightfall."

"Where's Solon?" asked Brie, noticing that the young philosopher had gone missing.

While Alfric talked about great deeds, Solon had wandered a few yards away, a black hole inside the wall of ice having caught his notice. He strolled over to it and peeked inside, using one of the glow lights that he had hidden in his pockets before the pirates had boarded Solaris. As he stepped through the opening, welcomed warmth wafted over him. He searched through the small opening in the cliff and realized that it was a cave. Though not large, it would do. He ran back outside. "Over here!"

The others raced to him, each pausing before the cave entrance.

"The ice falling away must have unsealed it," said Solon.

Rynah took the glow light and explored inside; its stale air, from years of having been sealed shut, penetrated her nostrils. She sneezed. Particles of dust floated around her, her movements having stirred them. She looked around the one room (not an unpleasant chamber full of monsters from a child's dream, its stone walls smoothed by time and running water from melted snow, and a small pit in the center, perfect for a fire, and a mound of a ledge, only five inches off the floor, circling around the edges) and was pleased that they would not have to go far for shelter.

Splintered wood from broken crates, left over from when the cave was used as a secret cache, littered the damp floor. Her foot kicked an empty bottle of liquor, sending it skittering across the rocky surface. "This will do," she said. "These abandoned crates can provide fuel for a fire."

"What are they doing here?" asked Tom.

"Smuggler's hold," said Rynah. "Pirates and smugglers often find desolate planets to hide their treasures. By the looks of it, this hasn't been used in a while."

"But why would the pirates leave us on a planet where they store their stuff?" asked Tom.

"This might not be their hiding place. Or, they figured we would die before we ever found this place. It doesn't matter. Start gathering it up in the center and place a few rocks around it to form a border."

Within minutes, they had a fire started and the cave filled with cozy, warm air driving the chill away. Each huddled before the roaring flames, except Alfric. He took one of his knives and skinned the tiger; the fact that it was three times his size didn't bother him. Food was food.

Once warm, the others helped him bring in the skin and stretch it before the fire to dry. Tom and Solon prepared the meat for cooking, while Alfric showed Brie how to cut bits of meat into thin strips and dry them into jerky using the fire.

Rynah stood guard. She did not want any more surprises.

"Where are you Solaris?" she whispered to the frigid wind. "I swear I will get you back." Pangs of guilt at losing the archaic ship filled her.

"Rynah," said Alfric, pulling her from her musings, "Time to eat. I will stand watch."

"But…" Rynah started to protest.

"Go," Alfric's gentle, but stern, command persuaded her to obey.

"Thank you," said Rynah as she joined the others by the fire and accepted a slice of meat from Solon.

* * *

The lowly pirate, a very low ranking pirate as he had just joined Jifdar's crew, eyed the archaic ship before him, remarking at the varnished steel and his reflection as it stared back at him. Tear it apart—those were his orders. Such a shame, for it was a handsome ship. Heaving rubber tubes and a box of tools on his shoulders, the pirate walked to the rear hatch and stopped. He stared at it with a peculiar expression, knowing that it had been open moments before with its ramp stretched out.

The pirate tapped the button on the right side of the hatch. *Kerplunk!* The gears turned as the ramp slowly descended before it rolled back up and the door closed. Irritated, the pirate bashed the heel of his scaled hand against the button. Nothing happened.

"Open up," grunted the pirate, "you bucket of bolts, or I'll jimmy you open with my hammer."

Gears shifted, grumbling to life as the rear hatch opened and the ramp dropped down. Pleased, the pirate shifted his tools and stepped forward before—*Glooop!* Burnt orange sludge (and who knows where Solaris got it from, but she was a resourceful ship) rolled down the gangplank, smothering the poor pirate in its sticky, malodorous (reminding him of a latrine) substance.

The pirate seethed as he wiped the glop from his face, smearing it more than clearing it, and flung a handful to the oil-soaked ground. "I hate this ship!"

* * *

Four moons, one full, two at three-quarters, and the last one at a quarter moon, gleamed in the night sky against the backdrop of a giant purple planet encased in rings. Alfric stared up at it, mesmerized by its beauty. Before he had been brought to Solaris, he had never bothered noticing such sights, but things had changed since he had met Brie. He pondered how his people fared without him. He hoped that the thieves had been dealt with. A sudden longing to return home tugged at him. Alfric shoved it away. If this mission was what the gods willed, then so be it. Rynah had made it clear that there was no returning home until this task had been completed.

A tremendous snore startled him. Alfric turned. Tom lay on his back with his mouth wide open, snoring louder than anything the Viking had ever heard. He sauntered over to him and nudged the man with the toe of his pointed boot. Tom rolled onto his side, never waking. Chuckling, Alfric went back to his post, taking a small glance in Brie's direction. She shivered. Snatching the now dried animal skin, Alfric draped it across her, tucking it in along the sides. She was so like his sister.

"You care for her."

Alfric jerked his head up. Rynah stared at him with her violet eyes. She had only pretended to sleep. "Should I not?" Alfric walked back over to the cave opening and peered out at the night with its four moons.

Rynah joined him.

"You should sleep."

"I can't. You act differently around her, than around the others. Why?"

Alfric faced Rynah. "My reasons are my own."

"Tell me," said Rynah. "

"She reminds me of someone I once knew."

"Who?"

Alfric inhaled deeply before releasing it. "My sister."

"Tell me about her."

"She is dead."

Rynah lowered her head. Always, she seemed to find the people who had suffered a loss much like her own. "What happened?"

"My father frowned the day she was born. He prized sons over daughters, but that never bothered Gróa. She was strong-willed and gentle hearted. One day, we had gone out into the forests near our home. My father had just arranged for her marriage to a man of great honor in a neighboring kingdom. It would have brought wealth to our family and strengthened his rule. One week before the wedding, she and I went into those woods. We spent the day trekking through the hills of Agnor.

"Upon our return, we ran across bandits. We ran away from them, hoping to reach our home before they caught us. Along the way, Gróa fell. Her foot had become lodged between the roots of two trees. I went back for her, but the bandits were closing in. I tried to free her, but her foot was stuck tight.

"As the bandits neared, I became frightened. I looked into her eyes, and it was as though she knew what I was about to do next. There was no fear within them, only forgiveness. I left her there. I succumbed to my own fear and left her there. The bandits took her and had their way with her before they killed her. Her screams will haunt me the rest of my days.

"When I look at Brie, I see those same eyes, but I also see the same fear that had plagued me all those years ago."

"How did you overcome it?" asked Rynah.

"The day we sent her spirit to the halls of Freyja, I vowed to never let fear dictate my actions again."

Rynah remained silent, absorbing Alfric's narrative.

"What about you? What do you fear?"

"Nothing." Rynah's quick reply earned her an unbelieving look from Alfric.

"Then you must have a heart of stone."

"Failure," whispered Rynah. "What if I fail to stop Klanor?"

"Then do not fail," said Alfric.

"Tell me about your home."

"My home lies far in the cold northern lands and near the sea with its sheets of ice. In winter, its days are much like it is here, cold and dark, the sun always far to the south. But life thrives there. The morning smells of the fish that had been freshly caught, and the evenings smell of roasting meat over a large fire, with the sweet scent of honeyed mead. Joyous music and dancing fill my halls. From the west come treasures unheard of in my kingdom, brought by traders who prefer life on the sea to the walls of clay, wood, or stone. The nights are filled with rainbow lights—always they appear—that dance in the starry sky. This is my home."

"Sounds lovely," mused Rynah.

"Tell me about yours."

"There isn't much to tell. Purple skies, emerald grass, and valleys as big as oceans. Though, I miss the *Strongmyr*, the double sunsets that happened every summer solstice. It was always beautiful."

A series of low howls echoed across the open expanse before them, startling Rynah from her memories. "What was that?"

"Wolves," said Alfric.

"Wolves." The name sounded foreign on her tongue.

"Or something similar. They are hunting and have found a worthy prey. Don't worry. We aren't it."

"Who's worried?" teased Rynah. "I think I'll go back to sleep."

"Sleep well, shieldmaiden of Lanyr."

Rynah grinned. She went back to her place in the cave and fell asleep, despite Tom's persistent snores.

Alfric stood poised in the cave entrance, staring out at the moons' pale glow upon the shimmering snow. There, he remained the entire night, never moving, never flinching.

Chapter 20
AN UNEXPECTED SURPRISE

Morning dawned with a bright sun, reflecting upon the white world of Ikor. Rynah snuffed out the fire, stomping on it until every ember ceased its glow. Each of the five companions donned a cloak, which Alfric had made from the animal skin as he stood watch, its heavy, and quite soft, hide providing protection from the cold.

"What do we do now?" asked Tom.

Rynah didn't answer. She had no idea what to do, nor how long they could survive in their new accommodations.

"Perhaps we should explore," said Solon. "The more we know about this place, the better chance we have of finding a way off it."

"How?" Tom challenged. "There don't seem to be any people around. For all you know, we are the only ones here."

"But can you be certain?" said Solon. "We will learn nothing by staying here."

"The boy is right," said Alfric. "We should explore our surroundings, and we should stick together. We will walk as far as we can until midday and then return before nightfall."

To Rynah, it sounded as good as any other plan. "Very well. Let's just try not to attract any unwanted attention."

The sun's rays glared off the white, snowy expanse as they trekked through freshly fallen snow and ice. Nothing could be seen for miles around, except a stark white world of ice. No buildings or settlements were to be found; only a few mountains stood in the distance, looking more like bits of spearmint candy and inviting one to reach out and snatch them. They walked in a single file line through knee high, loose snow, Alfric in the lead once again. He charged through the sparkling snow and ice (having grown up in a world covered by it), his tall stature towering over them as his tiger cloak flapped behind him in the wind. Rynah admired how the Viking walked erect and proud with purposeful steps.

To pass the time, Alfric hummed a merry tune from his halls, one that his wife had sung to his children. "Alfric, is thy father's name. King, Warrior, tis the same."

"Saber slayer he shall be called, among the deeds that fill his halls," sang Brie, picking up the tune. She stopped and glanced at the faces that had turned towards her. She didn't know why she had said it. It had just come out.

"It fits," said Solon. "He did destroy that beast we fought yesterday."

"Saber slayer," whispered Alfric to himself. "I like it. From now on, I am Alfric the saber slayer."

Rynah chuckled as they walked onward. The name certainly fit among his titles.

Alfric paused. Shielding his eyes from the sun, he surveyed the area, turning in a circle, his eyes absorbing every detail. Alfric's brows scrunched together as he stared at a specific spot.

"What is it?" asked Rynah.

"Over there," he replied. "Something does not match the rest of this place."

Rynah looked where he pointed. She didn't see anything among the white background that could have made him nervous, but trusted his judgment. "Lead the way. Everyone, pull out the pistols you're carrying."

The others obeyed. Brie looked at hers as though it were a semi-old friend. Having been taught how to shoot by her father, she had an idea of how to use the laser weapon. Solon and Tom held theirs as though they were questionable pieces of trash. Watching them, Rynah realized that none of them knew how to use the laser pistols.

"Hold it like this," she instructed, demonstrating how to properly hold them. "Point and pull the trigger." She made a mental note to teach them the proper use of the weapons upon returning to their camp.

Alfric's long strides charted a course for the disturbance he had seen. No one spoke as they walked. Within two hours, they reached what had bothered the Viking and soon discovered why it had. A fire pit greeted them; the coals still smoldered. Small wisps of smoke escaped the embers, leaving trails in the breeze.

Rynah poked through the ashes with the point of her boot. A frown crossed her face. "We're not the only ones here."

She searched around for more clues to who had been camped there that night, but found nothing. Not even footprints.

"He left only hours before," said Alfric, scooping some ashes into his hand and sniffing them. "These do not smell that old, and the aroma of charred meat is upon them."

"Did the pirates come back?" asked Brie.

"If they did, they would not have camped here," said Rynah. "They would have stayed on their ship and we would be dead."

Solon poked around the small area that was nestled in a conclave with its bluish snow where the sun failed to hit it, providing protection from the fierce winds that plagued the icy world of Ikor. Something brown caught his attention. Kneeling down, he flicked the powdered snow away, revealing a frayed, and ice-encrusted, rope. "Here," he said, holding it up for the others.

Alfric took it. He studied the ends, noting that they had been cut by a knife, and a blunt one at that. "This is strange."

"What is?" asked Rynah.

"This rope has been cut, but by a blunt blade. No hunter would be out here with a blunt knife. Such an act is certain death."

Alfric looked out at the icy expanse. On a clear day, you could see for miles and miles. He realized that when he noticed the small bits of smoke, whomever had been here had seen them as well. "My guess is that one man made this camp and he knows we're here. We should leave."

"I thought you said that no one lived in this place," Tom said to Rynah.

"None that I know of," said Rynah, "but that doesn't mean that there aren't settlements."

A hollow howl rose up around them as the wind shifted. It's sullenness chilled each of them.

"I have a bad feeling," said Brie.

"Agreed," said Alfric. He walked off, heading back in the direction of their cave. How he managed to navigate back, the others could only wonder. Neither Brie, Solon, nor Tom had any experience with tracking, and Rynah always depended upon Solaris or her handheld navigation device, none of which she had. Each followed Alfric, who walked with confidence through the snow. At certain intervals, he paused and looked up at the sun, noting what part of the sky it rested in before continuing on. By evening, they had reached their camp.

"How much food do we have left?" asked Rynah.

Brie opened a few wrapped packages of meat and placed some on the fire to cook. "Enough for a few days I suspect."

Rynah grunted. She did not fancy staying there, but had no idea how any of them would ever get off Ikor. "When you're done, I want all of you to come outside."

Brie stared at the cave floor. She guessed what Rynah had in mind and didn't like it. Her aching muscles just wanted to rest.

Outside, all five of them gathered in the dimming twilight while supper cooked. They lined up in a line, facing a pile of iced-over mammoth-sized boulders with black circles on them, which Rynah had drawn earlier using ash from the fire.

"All right," said Rynah as she walked behind them, "You all have laser pistols, but none of you know how to use them. A failing on my part, but one I mean to remedy. The circles on the boulders are your targets. I want you to hit the center."

She paused at the end of the line. Rynah aimed her weapon and fired, striking the target's center and leaving a blackened scorch mark. The others just stared at her. "Alfric, you first."

Alfric fumbled with the foreign weapon. He preferred his sword over this thing that shot out pulses of energy and light. He copied Rynah's stance and aimed. He fired.

"Not bad," said Rynah, even though Alfric's shot hit the edge of the target. He grimaced and lowered his weapon.

Solon and Tom fired next, each having the same success as Alfric. Brie went last. She lined the target in her sights, holding the pistol with both hands and her legs shoulder width apart. Remembering her father's instructions, she envisioned herself striking the center of the target. She released her breath and fired. Rynah's eyes widened. She hadn't expected to see this: Brie had hit a bull's eye.

"Not bad," said Rynah.

"Not bad?" Tom said in surprise. "That was fantastic! Way to go, Brie!"

"It's nothing," said Brie.

"It is never nothing," said Alfric. "That was perfect aim."

Rynah stepped closer to Brie. "Where did you learn to shoot?"

"My father taught me before he died."

"He instructed you well. Do it again."

Not liking the extra attention, Brie calmed her nerves. She aimed and fired. Once again, she hit the target's center.

Rynah strolled over to the boulders, studying the scorch marks. She never would have thought that Brie would be so skilled. "Very well, this is how it will work. Brie, you will teach Alfric how to handle the laser pistol while I instruct Solon and Tom."

Brie squirmed under this new scrutiny. She did not feel confident that she could teach anyone anything.

"So it appears that the teacher is now the student," said Alfric as he stood beside Brie.

Brie laughed. "Only in this. I'm still the student when it comes to the sword."

"Agreed."

Dusk passed; the fading purple, orange rays of the setting sun transformed into black shadows as they learned how to use the alien weapons until their dinner had finished cooking. Afterward, they ate and fell into a long desired sleep with Alfric, once again, standing watch for the night.

The next morning found them hiking through the snowy wilderness, heading in a different direction from the day before. Clouds dotted the white sky, covering what little warmth the sun provided as flurries of snow drifted around them.

Alfric took the lead. He navigated through the snow with ease, never once getting lost, nor fearing that he would become so. Thus far, no signs of life greeted them. They were alone, or so it seemed.

A howl whistled around them, but not the wind. Alfric held up his hand. He scanned the horizon as the howl sounded again. Nothing. Knowing they weren't alone, Alfric raised his sword before him.

"What's wrong?" demanded Rynah.

"We're being hunted," growled Alfric.

The howl sounded a third time, followed by reciprocating calls. Rynah pulled out her pistol along with the others. "We'll never make it back to the cave in time."

"We shall make our stand here," said Alfric.

Rynah didn't like the idea, but what choice did they have? The cave was too far and there were no trees or anything to provide them safety. "Remember what I taught you."

The others held their weapons before them, unsure of themselves.

Another series of howls echoed around them as soft grunts approached from behind, growing louder amongst thuds that pounded the crusted snow. Rynah whirled around. A creature the size of a bear, but with the snout of a wolf, and coated in thick, wiry fur the color of sandstone charged them. Rynah aimed and fired, striking it between the eyes. It slowed, but continued to come for them.

"The neck," yelled Solon.

Rynah aimed again, but the beast kept its head hung low. Tom chucked a snowball at it, forcing it to turn its head, thus revealing the soft flesh under its throat. Rynah fired. Roaring in pain, the creature crashed into the snow and slid across the ice before stopping by their feet.

More howls filled the area. Two others charged from both sides. Alfric spun on his heels, ramming his blade into the head of one. It fell before him.

Brie turned to face the second creature and pulled the trigger, but the cold had caused the gun's firing mechanism to stick. Before she could fix it, the menacing creature had closed the distance. Tom jumped on Brie, knocking her out of the way. They rolled across the ground as the beast trampled over them and ran off. It stopped. On the ground, Tom and Brie watched as the wolf-like beast scraped its front paws across the snow before charging them again.

"Come on!" Tom yanked Brie off the ground.

They had just gained their feet when a laser pulse struck the creature in the neck. It plowed into the snow, sending ice into the air. Tom poked at it with the point of his weapon. It never moved. Solon stood a few feet away with his laser pistol raised, frozen in his stance.

"Thanks," said Tom.

"Anytime," replied Solon, adopting one of Tom's phrases.

"There's more!" yelled Rynah.

Five more of the strange animals appeared. They surrounded the five companions, snarling and growling while pawing at the icy ground. Rynah and the others huddled together with their backs facing each other. Each watched the hungry beasts. Saliva dripped from the creatures' fangs as they stared at their prey.

"What do we do?" wailed Brie.

"Fight," said Rynah.

"Odin will protect us!" Alfric called out.

Rynah didn't think the Viking's fictitious god would be of much use. She raised her weapon and prepared to go down firing. A pang of guilt racked her heart. She had failed in her quest to stop Klanor. She had failed the others, and for the first time, it pained her.

"If there is anyone who can help us," she whispered, "please, show up now."

One of the beasts lunged for them. Suddenly, cans of tear gas plopped on the ground, releasing their charcoal green smoke into the air. Everyone choked and coughed on the smoke as they tried to cover their mouths and noses. Bursts of light whizzed through the air, striking the creature that had charged them. It dropped to the ground unmoving. Another jumped at the newcomer. He raised his laser rifle and shot twice, ending the beast's life.

With the smoke-filled area choking all within distance, the other wolf-like creatures paused in their assault, sniffing the air before darting away. Warning howls reverberated around them before silence fell.

As the smoke cleared, they looked up at the strange humanoid figure standing before them, wrapped in gray coverings, concealing his face, rifle at the ready. They stared at one another for several seconds.

"Who are you?" demanded Rynah, trying her best not to cough.

The stranger remained silent.

Alfric raised the point of his sword. "You will show yourself," he said, the warning in his voice did not go unnoticed.

"Rynah?" said the stranger, in a hoarse tone, as if he was unused to speaking.

Rynah's head popped up. She looked closer. She knew that voice. "Who are you?"

The stranger unwrapped the coverings from around his face. His skin matched Rynah's, but his hair had a yellow tinge to it, "I never thought I would see you here."

Rynah stepped closer to the new arrival. Perplexed, yet somewhat relieved, she studied the man's face. "Obiah?"

"The one and only."

"I thought you had died."

"Not yet."

"You know this guy?" asked Tom.

"He was my grandfather's friend," replied Rynah. "What happened to you?"

Chilling howls sounded in the distance.

"I think explanations are best left for later," said Obiah. "The gas scares them away, but they'll be back."

"Our cave is too far to walk there," said Alfric.

"Well, then it's good for you that I brought transportation. Now if you'll help me with today's catch, we can be on our way."

Thinking it best not to argue, they helped the newcomer load the dead wolf-like beasts onto his hover craft and scrambled into the backseat. Though cramped, none of them complained. Obiah put the thing in gear and sped off, knowing he had a lot of questions to answer.

Before they knew it, they had arrived in front of a giant mound of freshly dusted ice. The companions looked at the dismal place, wondering why their savior had brought them there.

"Don't look so downhearted," said Obiah. "It's much nicer on the inside." He hopped out of the hover craft, his heavy boots crunching the snow as he walked with his rifle slung over his right shoulder.

The others climbed out of the hover craft. Glancing around, they followed Obiah as he led them to what appeared to be a solid wall of ivory-colored ice. He tapped it. To the others, it looked as though he just hit a random spot, but what they didn't know was that a nick, the size of a fingernail and the same height as Obiah's nose, marked where to press. A holographic keypad appeared on the ice. Obiah punched in a code, each button beeping as he did, and a door slid open.

"You may all enter." He bowed with his arms out in a welcoming gesture. Brie thought he mocked them.

Though Obiah's home appeared to be nothing more than a mound of snow and ice on the outside, inside the lavish decor, and warmth, startled them. The others breathed a sigh of relief as the cozy air swept over them, tickling their frigid, and numb, cheeks. A roaring fire filled the fireplace in the middle of the granite entryway, crackling and sending embers up into the brick chimney. The fore room lay directly ahead of them; plush couches and chairs formed a 'u' around a second fireplace (filled with a warm blaze) with a velvety, sea green rug, inviting them to sit down and rest.

Tom settled in an opulent, red chair, bouncing up and down on the springs. "I like this."

Solon positioned himself in the twin chair next to Tom, admiring the smooth velvet as he caressed it with the tips of his fingers. Rynah chose the couch. She sat down with more grace and dignity than Tom. Her eyes roamed the place, taking in every detail, such as every shelf filled with knick knacks, the silver timepiece on the mantel, and the lavender draperies that hung in the bay window. "How did you get all of this stuff?"

Obiah shoved off his cloak and coverings, draping them by the fire so that they could dry. "Oh, I procured them after some time. Every so often, merchants, or people of questionable means, stop through here and I trade with them."

"What do you trade?"

"My services."

"Your what?" Rynah's sharp tone hung in the air.

"You are a mercenary," said Alfric.

"Yes and no," answered Obiah. "Won't you sit down?"

Alfric was the only one still standing. He searched the room for an available space and settled on a simple wooden chair next to Brie, his sword positioned in front of him point down. "Explain."

Obiah studied Alfric, taking note of his erect posture and the gaze that observed every detail of his home, especially the exits, without moving his head. Though not loud spoken, the Viking's statement demanded obedience.

"I am no mercenary, but I do sell my tracking services. Sometimes, people come here looking for adventure or a place to hide. Ikor is a perfect place for such things. When rich folk come looking to impress their girlfriends, I offer to take them where the wild game is. Oh, I always take them to the less dangerous parts where they can kill a beast and take its head."

A disgusted expression crossed Brie's face. She hated the idea of hunting just for a trophy.

"Oh, it's not like that, dearie," said Obiah when he noticed her reaction. "They keep the head. I keep the meat as payment, along with a few luxuries."

"And the ones wishing to hide?" asked Rynah, her tone accusatory.

"We all wish to disappear at some point. I find them, they don't find me. That way, my home's location remains a mystery to them."

"But they know you live here," said Rynah.

"Not exactly. This is only one of the planets I bring them to. I know a few others in this system as well. Anyway, the ones wishing to hide always pay well."

Rynah shook her head. "You cannot possibly be my grandfather's friend. He would never have approved of such things."

"Yes, well, that was a long time ago."

"Not so long."

The animosity Rynah felt towards Obiah swarmed around them. Tom and Solon watched the exchange, placing bets on who would win. Brie decided it would be best to keep silent, while Alfric remained stoic; nothing betrayed his face.

"Maybe not to some," said Obiah. He reached over and grabbed a box off the mantle, opening it. He pulled out some dried leaves, crushed them up, and stuffed them into a pipe before lighting it. "I cannot change the past, Rynah, but you must believe me when I tell you that there was nothing I could do."

"Perhaps not, but you certainly didn't stick around."

"I'm sorry."

"I don't want your apologies. I want an explanation."

"Pardon me," said Solon, breaking up their exchange, "perhaps you can both explain how you know each other and why you are angry at one another."

"Fair enough," said Obiah, "if you explain to me how you four got here. None of you are from Lanyr, or any other system around here."

"You first," Rynah spat, arms crossed.

"All right," Obiah stood up and stared into the fire a moment gathering his thoughts, "Marlow, Rynah's grandfather, and I go way back. We have known each other since we were both in the Academy of Arts and Sciences. Together, we decided to enlist in the fleet. They always needed people with science backgrounds. While on a routine mission patrolling the Cataran Sector, Marlow stumbled upon a transport that had picked up an old coot who babbled endlessly about the ancient crystals. That is how Marlow learned of them. Now, I never put much stock into the crazy hermit's story, but he did, or something about it intrigued him.

"You see, he found this book and ancient text written on crumbling pages. I was never very good at deciphering the ancient languages, but he excelled at it. He started reading everything he could about the ancient prophecy. I indulged him, but it all seemed too fantastic.

"You know this as well, Rynah. You, yourself, didn't believe him when he told you. In fact, you ran away."

"But I never tarnished his reputation," said Rynah.

"No," answered Obiah, "he did that. Though I may have had a hand in it."

"May have…" Rynah jumped up.

Alfric held up his hand, stopping her. "Continue," he said to Obiah.

"After years of studying the ancient texts, Marlow became convinced that someone would try to steal the crystal from the geo-lab. He decided to steal it for safe keeping. Of course, he was caught and brought up on charges. There was a formal hearing and his years of service did add to his favor, to a point."

"But you testified against him," said Rynah.

"I had to. They had brought me in, and you know I could not have refused a summons even if I wanted to. I knew that Marlow thought the crystal was one of the six, though I never thought he would try and take it."

"But you made him sound like a madman!" Rynah's purple face had flushed red, her eyes full of anger.

"And it's a good thing I did," Obiah snapped. "If they thought he was completely sane, they would have executed him on charges of conspiracy to destroy the planet. I fed them a story of him being overworked and an old man who suffered from a momentary bout of insanity. The tribunal bought my story and suspended the punishment of death. Instead, they sentenced him to five years in a mental institution for evaluation. He was later released."

"But the damage had been done," said Rynah. "All of his research—all of his work—gone because of this. You made him look insane. When he was released from the institution, no university would take him. He couldn't even get a job as a janitor. No one wanted to be associated with the man who tried to steal the magnetic crystal based on some children's stories."

"Again, Marlow had no one to blame but himself for that. You know it's true! He knew that my testimony is what saved his life and gave him the time needed to pass his work onto someone else—you."

Rynah clamped her mouth shut. "How do you—"

"The whole universe knows that Lanyr has been destroyed because Klanor stole the crystal that had kept the magnetic fields stable for centuries."

"They know that Klanor is behind all this?" asked Tom.

"It's not like he's keeping it a secret," laughed Obiah, "He announces it every time he looks for new recruits."

"Why would anyone want to join him?" asked Brie.

"Riches and glory," said Obiah. "People like Klanor always attract the darker side of humanity."

"Then that explains it," mused Solon. "You said the trial was public, one that would have been well publicized."

"Yes," Obiah replied.

"Klanor must have been there as well," said Solon.

"Everyone was there," Obiah added.

"Then that is how he learned of the crystal. He must have researched it after Marlow's trial and decided that the legends were true. He may have even seen Rynah there and knew whom to get close to."

Rynah cast her eyes down to her feet. She always wondered why Klanor had chosen her in order to gain access to the crystal. She wasn't the only security member assigned to the lab. So he had seen her at the trial. Not that it would have been difficult. She had sat in the front row and even had to testify about her grandfather's theories. She had tried her best to give vague answers to the tribunal's questions so as not to incriminate him, but they knew she covered for him.

"I'm sorry, Rynah," Brie whispered.

"Unfortunately, I wished I had believed him," said Obiah. "As it turns out, everything your grandfather had said was true."

"You left after the trial," said Rynah.

"Yes, well, I had to. I couldn't stay after that. You weren't the only one who suffered. I lost my reputation too, except people looked upon me as a traitor. A person wiling to betray his friend for his own gain. I thought I was helping, but…"

Obiah allowed his voice to trail off.

"So I left. Got on the first ship I could find. Traveled around a bit before settling here. Turns out, this place isn't so bad once you get used to the cold.

"Now, tell me about yourselves."

The others looked at one another. None of them wanted to elaborate on their stories, but could not refuse since they had made a bargain.

"I have already guessed that your being here has to do with the crystals and the prophecy, so no point in remaining silent."

Rynah pursed her lips. "They're from Earth."

"Earth?" asked Obiah, the word sounding foreign on his tongue.

"The Terra Sector," said Rynah. "When Lanyr was destroyed, I used Solaris to leave."

"That old bucket of bolts?"

Rynah shot Obiah a look. "Don't ever let her hear you say that."

"You act as though that ship has feelings," laughed Obiah.

"She does," said Brie.

"More like an attitude," added Tom.

"You mean he actually did it?" Obiah stared at all of them.

"Did what?" asked Rynah.

"Marlow once mentioned the possibility of putting an artificial intelligence in charge of one of the ships, but I never thought he would pursue it."

"He purchased Solaris when she was decommissioned as a military vessel," replied Rynah, "and spent the last years of his life on her. I guess now I know what he had been working on. He told her about the prophecy. She knew all about it when I boarded her. Seemed to have been expecting me, too."

"Well, I'll be damned," said Obiah as he stroked his whiskery chin, "That old coot did it. Seems like he was right about everything. And so you learned about the prophecy through the ship?"

"Yes," said Rynah, "she made the calculations and brought them here from their own home planet."

"Kidnap is more like it," added Tom. "Not that I'm complaining.

This has been one heck of an adventure so far, aside from being attacked by pirates and stranded on a desolate planet of ice."

"Don't forget the man-eating plants," Solon said.

"Pirates?" asked Obiah.

"Yes," answered Rynah, "that is how we ended up here. They attacked us and managed to board Solaris and left us here for dead."

"And you would have too, if I hadn't found you. Pure accident too, by the way. I had been tracking a saber tiger, the same one you apparently killed."

"How do you know we killed it?" asked Alfric.

"You'd be dead if you hadn't," replied Obiah, "and you're wearing its skin."

Alfric chuckled. He had forgotten that part.

"Well, you must all be hungry," said Obiah.

"Starved!" Tom jumped up, ready to find the kitchen and food. The others laughed at his usual manner of thinking of his stomach.

"Good," said Obiah. "I hope the rest of you brought your appetites as well."

He left the ornate fireplace and motioned for them to follow him. They trailed after the older man as he walked through another well-furnished room, past a dining area (a table made of cherry oak in the center with two vases, each containing marigolds, on the ends), and into the kitchen. They all stared at it amazed. The kitchen stood about 50 paces in width with three well-stocked meat lockers. Four pantries bursting with canned and dried goods lined the wall next to them. But the oven is what caught their attention the most. Lined in gray stone brick, and with the faint smell of garlic and onions emanating from it, the oven looked as though it belonged in an Italian bistro than a recluse's home.

"Help yourselves," said Obiah. "You can cook anything you like, just clean up afterwards."

Forks clinked against plates as they all stuffed their faces with

roast meat and noodles soaked in marinara sauce. Even Rynah en-
joyed the meal. The food warmed her stomach, which she chased
with mulled cider. No one talked while they ate. The meal tasted
too good and they were famished. Only when dessert came did they
slow down.

"Well, I haven't seen appetites like that in a long while," said
Obiah, "unless you count mine." He pointed at his protruding belly.
"So what are your plans?"

"To get off this rock," said Rynah. It came out ruder than she
had intended. "I mean—"

"No worries, dear," said Obiah, "I don't fault you for not wanting
to stay. You have a mission. A very important one."

"But how are we going to get Solaris back?" asked Brie.

Their faces fell. None of them had thought that far.

"We'll have to search," said Rynah. "Those pirates won't have
dumped her yet. They will probably take her back to their place and
try to sell off the parts. Though they'll have a fight on their hands."

"But where will we start in our search?" asked Tom.

"The way station," said Obiah. "It's a place where all sorts of
space pilots go, especially the unsavory sort, to find food, rest, and
entertainment."

By the way he said entertainment, Brie knew he meant the adult kind.

"They also get their ships repaired there as well," continued Obiah, "buy supplies, and socialize. Even pirates are known to stop there."

"Then I guess that is where we start," said Rynah.

"Not to rain on your parade," said Brie, "but we don't have a ship."

"Don't we?" Obiah winked at her.

He stood up, indicating that they should follow. They did,
though with less enthusiasm as they were all stuffed, and followed
him to another part of his home. Obiah opened a door that led into
a dark room. "In."

They went inside. The door clicked as Obiah shut it before turning on the lights. Jaws dropped as they looked at what sat before

them. A ship, sleek in design, rested comfortably in his garage. Support columns stood on each end, forming pointed arches. Though not as big as Solaris, it was a godsend.

"Now this baby here doesn't talk like yours does, but she can be a bit feisty. Tomorrow, we will stock her with provisions and go in search of your ship."

"Obiah, we can't…" began Rynah.

"Nonsense," he interrupted her. "Helping you find your ship is the least I can do. I owe you that. Besides, I was getting bored here anyway."

Rynah smirked. "Thank you."

"Well, now, I think we should all go to bed. There are rooms on the second floor, so pick one. We have an early start in the morning."

Chapter 21
A MAN IN SHADOW

Stein stood in the shadows of the room (its taupe, paneled walls giving no indication that they were on a spaceship), watching Klanor as he pored over more of the ancient tales in the browned pages of the book on his desk in the dim lamplight. He didn't know what value the archaic scrolls offered other than a faint promise of power. Power—the allure gnawed at him.

Stein didn't know if he had made the right choice in trusting Klanor, but the man had saved his life. Months ago, when life had taken everything from him and all seemed lost, Stein decided to end it. He had chosen the perfect location: *The Eflquir Lake*, deep within the wooded area of Lanyr. The lake was so deep that many had drowned in it and their bodies never discovered. That was where he had decided to stop living.

But, then came Klanor. Stein had no idea why the man was there, only that he was. Klanor had seen him jump into the water from his boat in the middle of the lake. Without hesitation, he flew his flying craft over the water and used a transporter beam to snatch the despondent man.

At first, Stein had been infuriated, but then he learned about the crystals and the power many believed they held. Perhaps such a power could bring his family back, or give him just compensation. Stein didn't care which. The quest for control over his life, and the desire to have his family returned to him, drove him, and won him, to Klanor's side—for now.

"I can hear you breathing," Klanor's voice trailed over to him from the pages of the book.

"I apologize, sir," Stein stepped out of the shadows and into the darkened room, his dark clothing making him almost invisible.

"Why do you hang in the shadows, my friend?"

Stein studied Klanor. Friend? Yes, he supposed they were. "They are my ally. One can learn a lot by remaining unseen."

"And what have you learned?" Klanor looked up at him.

"That we have two of the crystals, Rynah has one, and there are three more we have yet to find."

"Seems that I know the same information," Klanor turned back to his work.

"But what you don't know is that Rynah and her party of misfits have had a run-in with the Fragmyr Pirates."

"Have they now?"

"They have lost their ship and no doubt have been killed."

"Do not be so certain," Klanor warned. "Rynah has a way of eluding death. The pirates may have kept her and the others for sport."

"And how long do you expect them to live as such?" Stein's lip curled. He liked this new phase in his life and accepted it.

"How long indeed," Klanor mused. "Do you know where their ship was taken?"

"To one of the pirates' strongholds, I suspect."

"It would be nice to have that ship," Klanor said.

Stein understood Klanor's meaning. "It would have valuable information on it."

"And the crystal."

Stein's lip curled again in a knowing grin. "I'll get right on it."

"Have you read any of the ancient stories?" Klanor's question caught the man off guard.

"No, sir."

"You might one day," Klanor said. "It could prove illuminating."

Stein thought about the man's words. *Illuminating perhaps.* "I will consider it."

Stein stalked out of the chamber and strode down the metallic and uninviting corridor of the ship as he headed for the shuttle bay. He decided to search for the pirates himself, having never been one to trust others with important tasks. *Besides*, he thought, *it takes a man of stealth for this kind of mission.*

On the way to the shuttle area, Stein stopped at an alcove in a corner (they were spaced throughout the vessel) computer console. With a few taps on the screen, he pulled up the digital files of the ancient texts, something he had ignored as a child, but now they held new meaning. He downloaded them onto a quartz data crystal and pocketed it.

"Thanks for the advice," he whispered to himself.

A flash of rose-colored hair made him pause. Turning, Stein looked at the woman it belonged to, her oval chin reminding him of his beloved wife. Soon the memory faded, and the woman disappeared, leaving Stein alone in the corridor.

Stein whisked his way down the hall, forcing the painful memory from his mind, before strolling through sliding doors to the shuttle bay; his average form created a black silhouette in the doorway.

"Stein, sir," saluted a young recruit in an overeager effort to please, "I did not know you were coming."

"At ease, private." Stein glowered at the young man before him. Most of the men on the ship were mercenaries, but Klanor insisted on running it as though it were a military vessel. None of them cared so long as they were well paid, which Klanor never failed to do.

"I need a shuttle, now," Stein said.

"Yes, sir," the young private ran off. He pulled a lever and a small craft glided forward on a conveyor belt. "Will this do, sir?"

"Perfect. Is it stocked?"

"Yes, sir, I just finished loading it with provisions myself. It is fueled as well."

"Very well, you may go about your duties."

"Aren't you going to file a flight…"

Stein's cold eyes stopped the lad midsentence.

"I'll be on my way, sir." He darted off, hoping to get away from this steel-hearted man as fast as possible.

Stein sighed. He didn't know why Klanor put up with such incompetence, other than the fact he needed enough hands to run the ship. He boarded the tiny shuttle craft and sat in the pilot's seat. Within minutes, the engines started and Stein set a course. He knew exactly where to go to find pirates. They always frequented a space hub not far from his current location. With any luck, they hadn't discarded the ship yet.

Fire jetted from the back rockets as the ship launched into space and disappeared.

Chapter 22
PIRATE HUB

"Here we are," said Obiah as they neared a space station in a remote area of space.

A dwarf star shone in the distance, forming a pinprick of light and illuminating the edges of the spinning mass of tubes connecting metal spheres. What looked like a single pole rested in the center of the station. A flashing neon orange sign, displaying the words "Eddie's Bar: The Best Drinks in the Outlying Sector", stood out amongst the blackness.

"Eddie's Bar?" asked Brie.

"We all need a place to unwind," said Obiah as he steered the ship to a docking bay.

Red lights flashed on the edges of his parking space. Obiah lined up. The lights flashed green. He eased his craft into the docking port. A series of rapid thumps sounded around them as the clamps hooked around the ship, holding it in place. The four earthlings watched enthralled as a metallic tube, covered in grime and years of fuel exhaust, stretched out for them, attaching itself to the hatch. A hissing noise rose in volume before fizzling out.

"All right," Obiah beamed, "we are here."

Rynah opened the hatch. Another hiss of air was released as the pressure equalized. A long, dark hallway stretched before them, with only a single bulb of light that flickered before spitting and going out.

Brie peered through the doorway. "Are you sure this place is safe?"

"It's anything but," answered Obiah.

Rynah nudged him with her elbow.

"Well, it attracts a less savory sort of people, but anyone is welcome here, so long as they don't ask a lot of questions, and are willing to part with their money. Though you three"—he pointed at Brie, Alfric, and Solon— "might stick out a bit with your pale skin."

Rynah stepped over to a storage closet and pulled out two cloaks. "Here"—she tossed them to Brie and Solon—"put these on." She glanced at Alfric. "Not sure what to do for you."

Alfric bent down and scooped up a glob of black sludge on the floor of the hallway and smeared it over his arms and face, turning his skin brown.

"I guess that will do," Obiah clapped him on the back. "We should go."

Sticking close together, they walked down the tunnel (a luminescent, sticky substance oozed down the sides of the wall) and to the main part of the station. Upon turning a jagged corner, the eerie silence of the corridor vanished, having been replaced by the chaos of the bustling crowd. People, if one could call them that, hurried from one end to another underneath paper lanterns, going in and out of stores with their bundles. A sign for Eddie's Bar glittered above them. Brie had no desire to go there. She and Solon kept their hoods closed, hoping that no one paid much attention to them.

She glanced around and noticed what looked like two pale blue women covered in silky fur. They glowed bright and waved at her chuckling. Before she knew it, the strange women walked toward her.

Rynah stepped between them. "Sorry ladies. Find someone else." She turned towards Brie. "You shouldn't stare at them like that. They thought you wanted their company for the night."

Brie's face contorted when she realized what Rynah had meant.

"They are from the planet Felz. Their species is born gender neutral, so they tend to be a bit cavalier, so to say, in their love life."

Tom's face lit up. "Hey ladies," he called.

Rynah gripped his arm and yanked him back from his advances. "We're not here to draw attention to ourselves."

"Yeah, but I haven't had a date in a while," whined Tom, who just wanted some down time.

"You'll never go on another date again if you don't keep a low profile," Rynah hissed.

"Fine," agreed Tom. He had hoped for some actual R and R when they docked.

"Relax, Rynah," said Obiah. "Here." He led them to a vendor who sold what looked like chicken fajitas with a red sauce. After paying the man for six, Obiah turned back to them. "Eat up."

They took a small bite. Suddenly, Brie, Solon, and Tom spat theirs back out as the spices burned their mouths, turning them into infernos. Alfric continued chewing his and swallowed, refusing to let the food best him.

"What's wrong?" asked Obiah as he munched on his treat.

"It's super spicy," choked Tom.

"Oh." Obiah's jubilant face fell.

Rynah watched as the three fanned their tongues to ease the pain. It had never occurred to her, or Obiah, that they could not eat such spicy food. She found a vendor who sold some form of milk and purchased four glasses. "This should calm it."

While they ate their food and guzzled the milk, they watched the crowd. Rynah's eyes studied every person that passed by, every detail, every ounce of body language. She knew that the pirates would try to sell pieces of Solaris here, but she wasn't sure where. Three men caught her attention. Their dress indicated pirates, though they were not the same ones who had attacked Solaris.

She nudged Obiah. "There. We should follow them."

They shoved the remaining bites of food in their mouths and swallowed, with Rynah holding them back so they wouldn't attract attention. The pirates stopped in front of a dingy store window. They glanced around and went inside.

"You two," Rynah said to Solon and Brie, "go over to that window there and pretend to be interested in the items on display. Obiah, you and Tom go to the one there. Alfric, you're with me."

They split up, following Rynah's orders. Each loitered in front of their assigned window, studying the items.

Rynah and Alfric followed the pirates, and judging by the smeared grease on their faces, she guessed they were mechanics who worked in the engine room of their ship. She motioned for him to hide. Rynah peeked through the grime-coated glass. She watched as the pirates pulled out a data core from their pocket. The clerk behind the counter took it in his grease encrusted fingers, holding it in the light and twirling it.

Rynah's eyes narrowed as she saw currency being exchanged. Whatever it was, the clerk wanted it. One of the pirates took it and counted it. She noted the scar on his right cheek.

Rynah pulled away from the window. "Alfric, we want to question them."

Alfric nodded.

As the pirates walked out of the shop, Rynah confronted them. "We need to talk."

One shoved her away, forcing her to land on her rear end. She scrambled to her feet and reached for him, wrapping her arms around his legs. One of the other pirates pulled out a pistol and aimed at her. Alfric pounced on him, knocking his weapon from his smudged hands. The irate pirate whirled on Alfric and raised his fist. Upon seeing the Viking, with black sludge smeared on his face, he dropped his hand, fear filling him.

The third pirate rounded on Alfric. The Viking raised his arm and jabbed the man with his elbow before snatching his collar. Rynah quickly subdued the one she had challenged as passersby gave them a wide berth, not wanting to get involved.

"What did you sell in there?" she demanded.

The pirate spat in her face. Infuriated, Rynah threw him to the floor, placing her foot in the center of his back. She snatched his stringy hair and reared his head up, placing the point of her laser pistol near his temple. "I won't ask you again," she hissed in his ear.

"It was just the data core of some ship," yelled the man.

"What ship?" Rynah's grip tightened.

Tom, Solon, Obiah, and Brie gathered around.

"I don't know, just some ship. It was old though, That I do know."

"Did you get it from the Fragmyr Pirates?"

"No—no—no!" The pirate thrashed around, trying to get free. "We don't deal with them. We are with the Grigsuir Pirates. That data core came from a ship we had captured."

Rynah released him. "I hope for your sake that you are telling the truth." She lifted her foot from his back.

The man jumped to his feet and ran off with his friends.

From the corner of his eye, Tom noticed the shop owner sneaking away. He had crept through a back door and headed for a group of onlookers. Tom tackled him.

"Get off!" groaned the shop owner.

Tom wrestled the man to the ground, pinning his arms to the floor.

"I said get off!"

"Rynah!"

Rynah pointed her weapon at the shop owner. The man ceased his struggling. "I want to know if any of the Fragmyr Pirates have stopped by your place recently."

The clerk glared at her, red bags under his eyes.

The onlookers left. It wasn't unusual for a dissatisfied customer to demand a refund in such a way from a dishonest store owner.

Conflict was a constant on this space station. The residents there made their own laws.

"Answer me!" Rynah's harsh voice chilled Brie.

"I don't deal with them," whined the clerk. "They always want too much money and kill anyone who doesn't give in to their demands."

Rynah released an exasperated sigh.

"But I know someone who does."

Rynah's eyes lit up. "Tell me."

"Down that way," the store owner pointed. "You can't miss him. He has skulls in the window."

"Let him go," said Rynah.

Tom loosened his hold.

The clerk shot to his feet and ran away, staggering slightly, rounding a corner, and disappeared.

Rynah holstered her weapon. She glanced around, but no one watched, having grown weary of another confrontation on the space station. Such things were a daily occurrence. "Come on."

She marched through a crowd strolling past. The others chased after her. They followed the direction the shop clerk had given them, trotting down the gangway past rows of similar stores, searching for the one with the skulls. Rynah stopped. The others bumped into her.

"There it is," she said.

They looked where she pointed. A window with skulls, of species none recognized, with a black drape hanging behind them stood a few feet away. Rynah glanced around. She didn't notice anything out of the ordinary. "Obiah, I need you and Tom to stand watch. We don't want any unexpected surprises."

Obiah nodded. He and Tom walked over to a neighboring shop window with its wares displayed outside. Obiah picked one up, pretending to be a customer.

Rynah waved her hand. "Let's go."

They strode to the closed door. Rynah turned the knob. It opened. She stepped inside with the others, shutting the grungy door behind her.

Incense attacked their nostrils with its putrid fumes, reminding them of raw sewage and overpowering their senses. Brie brought the material of her cloak to her mouth and nose. She wanted out of there. The dismal area had only two lights turned on, one by the door and another at the counter, displaying black smudges and fingerprints.

"I don't trust the shadows," Rynah said.

Alfric understood her meaning. He didn't trust them either. He moved away from the group and paced the room, his hand on the hilt of his sword.

Rynah strolled to the counter. A small bell was upon it. She rang it. The ding echoed around them, filling the silent room with its eerie song.

"I don't like this place," whispered Brie.

Rynah said nothing. Though she shared Brie's sentiments, she refused to show fear. She rang the bell again.

A man appeared. His scaly skin snaked around his body. He reached out with claw-like hands and scooted the bell away from Rynah. "Once was enough."

"I am here about a ship matching these specifications." Rynah pushed a piece of paper across the counter.

The owner picked it up and studied it with his yellow slits for eyes. "I don't know this ship." He slid the paper back to Rynah.

"I think you do." Rynah glanced up and snatched an item hanging from the wall. She waved it in front of the man's reptilian face. "This came from it."

"Look, you might…" the man reached for a laser pistol he kept hidden behind the wall of the counter.

Rynah already had hers aimed at him. Brie never even saw her move. "Don't even think of it."

The man backed away from his weapon, holding his hands up.

"A man who deals with pirates," said Solon, "inevitably ends up on a pirate's hook."

"I don't deal with pirates," snarled the store owner.

"The evidence suggests otherwise," Solon replied. "Please tell my friend here what she wishes to know. She is likely to become angry if you don't."

Brie looked at Solon. *Where did his calm demeanor come from?* she wondered. She had never known him to act in such a way. But he and Rynah played off one another quite well.

"We know that you deal with the Fragmyr Pirates," Rynah cocked her pistol, "and I want to know where they are."

"No one knows their location," said the man. "They keep it a secret."

"I am certain they buy supplies from you."

The store clerk frowned. "Sometimes."

"Where do you deliver them?" demanded Rynah.

The clerk's eyes darted to the right. He noticed Alfric's prowling for the first time. "The Meser System. It is a cluster of nebulas not far from here. That is where I deliver what supplies they order. I never take them myself; I hire someone."

"I want you to give me the time of your next delivery," Rynah said.

"Tomorrow. Go to the Meser System and wait. They'll find you."

"Good." Rynah lowered her weapon. "We're taking this with us," she said, referring to the bit of the ship she had snatched.

Brie and Solon rushed to the exit, welcoming the fresh air (if you could call circulated air fresh) and glad to be out of the dismal place. Rynah and Alfric moved more slowly. She kept her weapon pointed at the store owner as she walked backwards, never taking her eyes off him. Once at the door, they turned and left, shutting the steel door behind them.

The store owner breathed a sigh of relief.

"I assume you told them everything," said a silky voice from the murky shadows.

"Yes," replied the man.

"Good." Gloved hands reached out and snapped the man's neck. Stein stepped into the light. He picked through a few items of interest before leaving, not caring when the body was found, if it ever was.

Chapter 23
A Rescued Ship

Obiah brought his ship out of hyperspeed in the Meser Nebula that the man in the pawn shop had told them to go to. No sign of pirates. The others leaned closer to the windshield, peering out at the gold and pale pink vapors and hoping to see some signs of life.

"Can you all step back just a bit?" asked Obiah, feeling a bit claustrophobic.

"Sorry," mumbled Tom.

He and the others took a few steps back. All of their nerves remained on edge.

"Do you think the pirates are here?" asked Brie.

"They're here," Rynah answered as she studied the color-laden area with its pink, green, and purple tie-dyes. A serious expression covered her face. She knew they were there. She felt it.

"When do you think they will come for us?" Brie asked.

"No doubt, when they feel like it," replied Rynah in a low voice. "Obiah, raise the outer windows. I don't want them to be able to see inside."

216

Obiah pressed a button and tinted panels slid across the wind-shield, darkening the outside world.

"Cool! Tinted windows," exclaimed Tom.

The others glanced at him and his excitement.

"What?" he said. "Man's got to get excited about some things."

"I suggest you keep your excitement on low for now," Rynah's tense voice mulled over the cockpit. "I only hope they believe our lie."

A single ship flew over them, buzzing them. It shot off a few miles before turning and reapproaching, settling in front of them.

"Here we go," said Rynah.

"Who are you?" came a harsh voice over the radio.

"We were sent here with supplies," said Obiah.

Silence loomed.

"You were here yesterday, were you not?"

"Yes," said Obiah, trying to make his voice sound as raspy as the man on the other end, "but your captain ordered two loads. We left the station this morning."

More silence followed.

"What's going on?" asked Tom.

"Shhh," Rynah rounded on him.

"What supplies?" came the croaky voice over the radio.

"Freeze dried food, rum, powder, and women." Obiah kicked himself when he clicked off the radio for saying that last part.

"Women?" Rynah hissed.

"Sorry," whispered Obiah.

"Are they buying it?" asked Tom as silence continued over the radio.

"No doubt they are discussing it," answered Solon.

"You know, for a geek, you know a lot," said Tom.

"Silence," Rynah's voice cut them off. "They're not buying it."

"Just wait," soothed Obiah.

The radio hissed to life. "Follow me."

"Understood," said Obiah. "See?" he turned to Rynah, "They did buy it."

Rynah's doubtful expression voiced her disbelief. "Brie, you and I need to make ourselves look like prostitutes."

"What?" Brie did not like this plan.

"What kind of women do you think they are expecting?" Rynah said to her. She grabbed Brie's arm and led her into the back of the ship.

* * *

"What is the problem sailor?" asked Jifdar, the captain of the Fragmyr Pirates.

"I'm sorry, sir," replied the poor pirate. "We've tried, but she won't let us near her."

Jifdar eyed Solaris with a long, steady gaze. "What do you mean she won't let you?"

"Well… uh… every time we try to board her, sir, she sends out electrical shocks. Grir tried to open up her engines yesterday and she slammed the hood down on top of him."

"Impossible," snapped Jifdar. "A ship may have character, but it is still just a ship, incapable of independent thought."

"I saw it myself, sir. This ship seems to know things. It's almost like…" his voice trailed off.

"Almost like what?" demanded the pirate captain.

"Almost like she has a mind of her own."

"Preposterous," hissed Jifdar.

A series of irate shouts and yells drew his attention to the far hangar. Jifdar glanced over at it, wondering what caused the commotion. One of his men attempted to open a valve on the rear hull of Solaris when a blast of black, gooey liquid shot out, smothering the pirate from head to foot. When he backed away, his foot slipped in the substance and he fell to the ground, rolling in the inky glop and covering himself in it and metal shavings, which littered the area. Jifdar shook his head, disappointed. Never had a ship given him so much trouble.

"I don't care how you do it, but I want that bucket of bolts stripped down to its parts by evening. If it's not ready to be sold off piece by piece, then you will be going to the shops, understand?"

"Yes, sir," said the low ranking pirate with a quiver in his voice.

The hum of two ships hissed above their heads. Jifdar glanced up. He recognized his own vessel, but not the one trailing behind it. "I didn't know we were expecting company today."

"I wouldn't know anything about that, captain."

"I don't recognize that ship."

"Probably a new driver for Cal."

"Perhaps," Jifdar walked away. Sometimes Cal sent more than one supply ship in a week, but such things were rare and only happened upon request. Though he trusted his first mate, he decided to keep a close eye on this new arrival.

* * *

Brie looked at her heavily mascaraed eyes and luscious, red lips in a metal plate. She detested the heavy makeup look. She never wore makeup aside from a light powder on the days she had acne breakouts. Frowning, she put the metal plate down. "I look ridiculous."

"You look like an available woman," countered Rynah. She had her hair pulled up in a loose bun and wore the same heavy makeup Brie did, very different from her usual attire of a security uniform. Rynah readjusted the front of her blouse, making certain it revealed the top of her breasts. "Though I know how you feel."

"We've landed," Obiah called from the cockpit.

"Showtime," said Rynah. "Alfric, Tom, and Solon, get out here."

They answered her summons.

"You three will hide in here with your pistols ready to fire. Brie and I will sit here trying to look like we belong."

Tom chuckled, earning him a piercing glare from Rynah.

"We won't have much time after the men board the ship. You all need to subdue them and, after that, we have minutes to find Solaris and get out."

"Not much time," said Tom.

"It's all we've got."

A hollow knock vibrated the hatch.

"Hurry," hissed Rynah.

She strode over to the door, tossing her hair a bit, while Brie positioned herself on a chair, doing her best to look like a lady of the night. The hinges clanked as Rynah pulled the door open.

"Well, hello, sweetheart," said the pirate with a hungry grin; the frayed sleeve of his engine-grease stained coat tickled her pointed chin as he stroked it.

"Welcome." Rynah put her hand on her waist and swayed her hips in a suggestive manner, trying to not retreat from the sour aroma that surrounded the pirate.

Two more pirates walked inside the ship. "Where's your captain?" demanded the second. His voice sounded familiar, and Rynah knew he had been the one talking on the radio.

"Right here," Obiah walked down the two steps (his heavy set footsteps shaking them as he did so) from the cockpit to the storage area.

"The supplies," said the pirate in charge.

"Okay." Obiah rubbed his hands together. "Not one for pleasantries."

The first pirate to greet them wandered over to Brie. He caressed her cheek with his scratchy finger. Brie clamped her mouth shut, holding back a shriek and jerking her head a bit, fear flashing through her deep brown eyes.

"Oh, feisty," said the pirate.

"A little," said Rynah, "but we have to have payment before you can have entertainment."

"You'll be paid after we get our supplies." The pirate in charge looked around at the mess of boxes—all business, no fun.

Plop! Plop! Bang! The other two pirates had proceeded to wrestle with one another in a bid for Brie's affections, knocking over a towering wall of wood boxes and canvas bags.

"Hey" shouted the pirate in charge, reining in the obstreperous

pair, "keep your mitts to yerself. Yer'll have yer fun once the negoti-
ations are complete."

The chastised pair hung their heads. Flecks of dirt fell from
their clothing, sprinkling the floor around their feet, and scooted
away from Brie.

"Yes, well, the supplies are over here," said Obiah, bending down
by a pile of rusted pipes, screwdrivers, and washers.

The pirate in charge followed. Alfric jumped out and tackled
the man, knocking him into the far wall. They struggled a bit, but
the surprised pirate had no time to react. He went for his weapon.
Alfric stopped him and rammed his face into a shelf.

The second pirate went for the Viking, but Tom and Solon
pounced on him.

"What the—"

Brie snatched a pot from the table beside her and slammed it
into the pirate's head. He dropped to the floor.

"Nice one," Tom told her.

The third pirate bolted for the open hatch. Before he took his
first step, Rynah whipped out her laser pistol and fired. She rushed
over to the pirates and robbed them of their weapons before Alfric
hauled them off the ship, concealing them with a mud encrusted tarp.

"All right," said Rynah, "we don't have much time. Obiah, you
stay on this ship. Fly away like a supply ship would, but stay close.
We may need your help."

"Anything you say, sweetheart." Obiah tipped his three-pointed
hat to her.

Rynah scowled; she hated being teased.

She ran out of the open hatch, pushing the others along. They
hunkered low beside some crates loaded with supplies that had been
delivered earlier that day by another ship. The engines of Obiah's
vessel roared to life; the downdraft caused by them ripped through
their clothes and hair. He gave them a courteous wave before de-
parting. Once he had vanished behind the clouds, Rynah moved.

They darted through the pirate base (past a slime covered fuel tank, tangled hoses, oil puddles from where ships had been parked, and discarded wrenches and hammers), trying to not be detected. Two pirates crossed their path. Rynah shuffled them behind a parked hover truck. Laughing and jabbering, the pirates never noticed them.

Rynah stepped out, swaying her hips and flaunting her breasts, attracting their full attention. Drooling, the two pirates gawked at her. Rynah punched one in the nose. He curled away, clutching his face as she rounded on the second pirate, grabbing his arm and holding it out. With a jerk, she broke it and kicked him in the back. The other charged her. Rynah swerved out of the way, snatching a broken pipe, and smacked him in the back with it.

"Come on," she said to the others.

They jumped to their feet. Together, they ran through the compound from one pile of rubbish to another.

"Where do you think they have her?" asked Alfric.

Rynah glanced around. She wasn't quite sure, but she knew that Solaris had to be close. Sparks spurted from a room with a raging buzz saw; the man wielding it looked like a faceless demon with his welding mask covering his head. "There."

They dashed for the cavern, which served as a hangar and had cables stretched across the opening. More pirates walked by. Each ducked behind the first bit of cover they could find. Boots stepped in time with one another as they strolled past.

Rynah motioned for them to go. One by one, each ran to the room behind the guards' backs. The two pirates never noticed as the sound of a saw raged even louder. A tremendous clang erupted from the chamber, followed by a series of shouts and curses.

"Stupid ship!" roared one pirate. "I'll have you turned into scraps soon!"

A blast of fire burst from Solaris' rockets. She had other plans.

Rynah glanced around the area. Six, she counted. She motioned for Alfric to sneak up on the nearest one that patrolled the slovenly area with a laser rifle in his arms. Nodding that he understood, he rose to his feet. Alfric snuck up behind the guard. He snatched the weapon from the pirate, whirling him around before headbutting him. The pirate fell.

Rynah and the others charged from their hiding place. She plowed into the closest pirate she found, ramming her knee into his stomach before shooting him.

Tom tackled a third. He punched. The pirate dodged. Tom countered with another swing, striking his opponent in the jaw. The pirate staggered back. He raised his laser weapon. Tom flung himself upon him. They rolled across the ground, arms and legs flailing. They stopped. Gasping, Tom stood up.

Brie and Solon attacked a pirate together, while Alfric moved on to another. Solon punched him. His weak strike did little to deter the hardened pirate. Brie kicked the man in the back of the knees, forcing him off his feet, before Solon hit him with the butt of his pistol.

Alfric subdued his opponent with ease before rounding on the sixth and final pirate. The pirate ducked out of the way, but Alfric had been ready. He brought up his sword and struck, stabbing the man through the chest.

A few cheerful bleeps escaped Solaris.

"I think she's happy to see us," said Tom.

Strident alarm bells sounded.

"They know we're here," Rynah ran to the open rear of the ship. She tripped over a coiled chain. "Damn!" Following the chain with her eyes, she realized that Solaris had been clamped to the ground to prevent theft. She checked the first lock.

"We need a key," she yelled. "Check those cabinets over there."

Brie ran over to the open cabinets. Her hands rummaged through them, feeling everything. Nothing resembled a key. "It's not here!"

Solon checked one of the pirates. He didn't find anything, but the others riffled through the grungy pockets of the other pirates.

"Found it!" Tom held up a metal object with holes punched into it.

"Release those clamps!" Rynah ordered him.

Tom saluted and darted off. He circled around Solaris, stopping by each clamp and inserting the key. A beep accompanied each release before the clamps popped open with a bang.

Rynah ran down Solaris' corridors (pale fluorescent lights flickered on with each step) and headed straight for the command center. She took the steps three at a time, refusing to stop even when she stumbled. Finding her feet again, Rynah continued her race against time. She jumped into the pilot's seat the moment she reached it. Jamming the helmet onto her head—*Solaris, wake up!*

I never slept, Solaris replied through the telepathic link.

Engines!

A humongous roar filled the area as fire shot from her rockets, blackening the mildew covered wall behind her, and the engines sprang to life.

"Oh, it feels good to be free!" Solaris said.

"Come on! Get aboard!" Rynah yelled over the loudspeaker.

The others rushed aboard the ship, not caring if any of the pirates stirred. "We're on!" Tom said into the intercom.

Liftoff, Rynah commanded Solaris, telepathically.

The engines burned bright. Flames crashed against the walls, searing them and filling the area with thick, black smoke.

"The door appears to be closing," said Solaris.

"Oh no they don't," Rynah whispered at the pirates' attempt to keep them contained. She grasped the firing stick. Aiming the crosshairs on the closing doors, Rynah squeezed, releasing two laser bursts. A fiery inferno engulfed them, obliterating them.

"Perfect aim," Solaris congratulated.

Just get us out of here, Rynah said.

They lifted into the air, the fierce wind from the engines hurling boxes and hoses across the ground. With another burst from the engines, Solaris shot out into the open sky, ramming her way through the blackened doors. They rose into the air away from the pirate compound. Ships pursued them.

We've got company!

Solaris barrel-rolled away from the pursuing pirates who wanted their stolen treasure back. The pirates remained locked on them. Laser fire streaked by the window. Rynah steered the ship away, veering to the left and the right in fluid movements to avoid enemy fire.

* * *

Jifdar stood on a balcony, watching the firefight taking place in the sky. Clouded anger darkened his face, mixed with respect for their gumption and resourcefulness. After all, Rynah and her friends should have died on Ikor. "How did they get in our compound?" he roared.

"Sorry, sir. We don't know," answered one lowly pirate.

"Then find out!" Jifdar shoved the pirate away from him.

"Yes, sir."

"The ship," a thought had occurred to Jifdar. "Check on that supply ship."

The pirate saluted and ran off.

Jifdar stalked over to the radio. "I want that ship destroyed!"

"Aye, sir," came a crackly reply from one of the pirate vessels already in the air.

Half fuming and half smiling, Jifdar stared at the sky as it lit up with laser fire, admiring how Solaris dodged the cannon blasts with ease.

* * *

A deafening roar echoed through Solaris as laser fire struck the hull, rocking the ship and flinging everyone aboard around. Solon and Brie rolled across the metallic floor, reaching out for rails to grab onto.

"They are serious about not letting us go," said Tom as he hung onto a post for dear life.

Clink! Clink! Clink!

"More hooks," Tom breathed. He ran for the weapons array.

"Where are you going?" shouted Brie.

"To the guns," Tom called back.

* * *

Stein steered his own vessel, a simple one-manned craft, in line with the pirates that chased after Solaris. None of the pirates paid any attention to him, mistaking him for one of their own. Having a vast array of ships from all over the 12 systems, none of them looked the same, allowing Stein to blend in with the chaotic melee; the pirates never looked for the mark of their clan.

He clicked a button on his console, opening the firing mechanism for the tracking device. Smiling at his victory, Stein aimed. The crosshairs lined up with Solaris, turning green. Stein fired.

A trail of gray smoke left his ship stretching out to Solaris. It hit. A familiar beeping sound with a blinking dot on his radar told him all he needed to know. Pleased, Stein left the pirate formation and disappeared into the upper atmosphere.

If the pirates destroyed Solaris, he, and maybe Klanor, would be disappointed, though it wouldn't be a total loss. But, if they managed to escape, he hoped to have a little surprise for them.

* * *

Back in the command center, Rynah did her best to steer clear of the pirates' weapons. More laser bursts exploded around her, filling the sky with suffocating smoke. She flew as best she could. A pirate ship appeared in front of her, having gotten disoriented in all of the smoke. Rynah jerked the controls back, forcing Solaris to go straight up into the sky.

A red warning light flashed in the console. Rynah ignored it. They needed to get into space. More red lights flashed on the console with annoying bleeping sounds.

"We are going to stall," said Solaris.

"No we won't," said Rynah, though she knew they would if she didn't straighten out soon. Solaris was never meant to fly vertical.

"You must straighten out or we'll crash!"

Rynah wished Solaris would shut up. She couldn't concentrate on her talking and flying, while evading being shot down all at the same time. Pirates closed in. Rynah tried to dodge away from them, but her vertical movements made it impossible.

"We could really use some help," she said aloud.

As though hearing her plea, laser shots struck the pirate ships that had gotten too close. Rynah looked around, but saw nothing.

"They don't seem happy," came Obiah's voice over the radio.

Relieved, Rynah relaxed. "Obiah, where are you?"

"I'm here."

"But I can't see you," said Rynah, still looking around.

"That's because I'm behind the clouds."

"We need a plan," said Rynah. "We need to outsmart these pirates before we all get killed."

"Head to starboard," said Obiah.

"What?"

"Trust me."

Not liking when she didn't know the full plan, Rynah had little choice but to trust the old man. She veered to the right, passing through a white cloud and cursed. She hated flying blind.

"Obiah, I can't see a thing in this cloud!"

"Just trust me. Keep heading straight. Pretty soon, you should see a fueling station."

Pirates with their own fueling station? Rynah hadn't thought of that. Though it made sense, considering all the raids they performed. She kept her eyes peeled, but all she saw were thick clouds.

A piece of black metal materialized in front of her. Rynah pushed the controls downward, just missing the fueling station, before leveling out.

"I found it," she said.

"Now engage your boosters and get out of here," Obiah ordered.

Rynah obeyed. The moment she engaged her booster rockets, Solaris shot out of the atmosphere and into the blackness of space.

Obiah steered his ship toward the fueling station. Taking careful aim, he waited for the pirates to arrive. They did. With one shot, Obiah struck the station, sending a series of sparks and explosions that riddled through the tanks of fuel. Fire erupted from the fueling station, engulfing the entire thing in flames, along with any ships that strayed too near.

Satisfied that his plan worked, Obiah turned around, setting a course for Rynah. He gunned his engines, accelerating so as to catch up. Once he had entered space, he spotted Solaris.

"Rynah," he said over the radio.

"You made it," came Rynah's relieved reply.

"Yes, listen, we need to find a place to hang low for a while."

"I'm not sure if there is a place."

"I might know of one," answered Obiah. "Can you make the jump into hyperspeed?"

"Yes."

"Head for the coordinates I'm sending you. See you then."

"Acknowledged."

Both ships vanished as they jumped into hyperspeed, heading for a place they hoped would provide safety.

Chapter 24
SAFE FOR NOW

They jumped out of hyperspeed just above a brown planet, as it possessed no water on its surface, its sandstorms visible from space; and a golden glow on its horizon as it turned on its tilted axis. It was a desert planet, similar to the one that they had gotten the fake crystal from, but more desolate. Rynah scanned it and pulled up a few charts. No signs of intelligent life. She directed Solaris to a small ravine (which provided shelter from the raging winds that stripped the surface of its top layer of silt) she had spotted from the sky and landed the ship.

"We're safe, for the moment," she said to her companions.

"Rynah?"

"Yes, Obiah."

"Just wanted to make certain you all were okay. I'll be landing shortly."

"Understood." Rynah shut off the radio.

Once landed, repair work began. The *whir! whir!* of machines permeated the air, bouncing off the walls of the small canyon they had nestled in as they removed damaged bolts and added new ones.

The pirates had managed to strip entire portions of the outer paneling (much to Rynah's disgust, since she started to view Solaris as
more than an artificial intelligence) for resale to space outposts. Solaris was infuriated at having her extremities altered by those vag-
abonds, though she had far worse adjectives for them. The landing
gear needed to be replaced (Tom spent many hours arguing with
Solaris—who won, by the way—on how it should be done) after
the pirates had ripped out all of its mechanisms.

Everyone chipped in, including Obiah, his knowledge of ships
systems proving very useful. Sparks from welding equipment filled
the sky (whether daylight hours or nighttime) as they restored the
connecting seams and filled in cracks and holes that the pirates had
created in their zeal to tear Solaris apart. Brie used her artistic tal-
ents to repaint Solaris' name on the side in bold, gold lettering, to
which the ship thanked her. And so the days passed—uneventful,
with hard labor.

As the repairs neared completion, Obiah became restless. His
jittery antics unnerved Rynah. She knew he did not like it there, nor
had he ever stayed in one place for so long.

"What bothers you?" she asked him.

"It's time for me to leave."

"But you've only just arrived."

Obiah smiled at Rynah. "I see a lot of Marlow in you. Stubborn and
pigheaded to a fault. Though your determination may well save all of you."

"I hate it when you speak in riddles," spat Rynah. "Don't you
abandon us like you did my grandfather."

"I'm not abandoning you," said Obiah, "but you do not need me
to find the crystals."

"So that's it then? You're just going to go back to your home on Ikor."

"I never said that," Obiah looked at the dusk sky. For a fleeting
moment, he thought he was back on Lynar, but the moment escaped
him before he had time to capture it. "Actually, Rynah, I was thinking about after you manage to acquire the crystals."

"After?" Rynah hadn't thought about that, her focus being on Klanor.

"Yes, after. Once you have them, what then? Klanor will not let you keep them."

"I suppose I will destroy them."

"When a millennia couldn't?" Obiah chuckled. "You are not the only one versed in the ancient myths. There is a device, hidden as well, for which the crystals were made. It can draw its power from them and be used as a weapon against entire star systems, or it can destroy them. And, besides, you might need some help."

"But if you leave us, how will you be helping us?" Bitterness filled her voice.

"Leave, no. I'll return, but my place is not by your side. There are others out there, like you, and I intend to find them."

Rynah's brow furrowed as she maintained control over her anger and disappointment. "If that is what you feel you must do."

"Rynah," Obiah lifted her chin, forcing her to look at him, "you know it is. Marlow left you Solaris. Probably the greatest gift he could have ever given you. You have little use for me, an old man."

"But you're wrong," she protested.

"You know I'm not."

"Then leave," spat Rynah. "It seems to be what you're good at." She stormed away, leaving Obiah alone, not wanting to look at him anymore.

Obiah watched her go. He knew she was angry, but it would subside. Besides, Rynah was not the only one whom Marlow had left a parting gift to. "One day, you'll understand."

The next morning, Obiah left the group of odd friends. Rynah never even uttered a farewell, such was her resentment.

Chapter 25
DASTARDLY PLANS

Stein looked at his console, noting the red dot and where it had stopped. A malicious grin snaked its way across his face, stretching from ear to ear. *I've found you*, he thought to himself with pride. He knew that they still had the one crystal from the Junglar Sector. Now that he knew their location, he could get it.

As Stein thought about how he could sneak aboard, one thought entered his mind: the Viking. He had seen Alfric fight and knew that the man was not a force to be trifled with. Though he could easily subdue the others, Alfric would prove a different story.

A message popped up on his view screen. Stein answered it.

"Klanor wishes to know your status."

Perfect, thought Stein, *saves me the trouble of returning for reinforcements.* "I have tracked them to an unpopulated planet. Am sending the coordinates now. Their ship is damaged, but won't be for long."

"Understood. Your orders are to await the arrival of the fleet."

"Acknowledged," Stein said as he steered his ship to the shadow of the planet, thinking it an excellent place to hide. No one would spot him there. He shifted in his seat for a more comfortable position. For now, rest. Later, destroy the others and steal the crystal.

Chapter 26
Loss

The repairs to Solaris had been completed, and Rynah ordered them back into space. Having spent over a week fixing the ship, she did not wish to waste another moment getting back to her mission. Solaris flew the ship herself on autopilot, giving Rynah a break. None of them were aware of the ships following their movements.

Brie slumped on the table in the eating area, her head resting on her arms. She released a puff of air at her side bangs, forcing them to fly outward. A bout of homesickness had struck her, a constant companion, as she thought about her mother and sister, wondering how they got along without her. Not wanting to disturb the others with her worries, she chose to be alone, but solitude was difficult to find on a ship with five people.

As though to prove a point, Rynah marched past them in a huff; her foul mood over Obiah leaving had grown stronger. She looked at Brie a moment. Sighing, Rynah snatched a chipped cup from the cabinet, her face perfectly reflected in it, and boiled a kettle water for tea; she preferred the bitterness of black as it matched her mood.

Her fingers drummed on the counter; flakes of paint fell to the floor as she waited for the water to heat up.

She glanced at Brie's moping form again. Knowing what bothered the girl, but not caring at the moment, she ignored her, or tried. The water boiled. With robotic movements, Rynah ripped open the tea package and placed the bag in her cup while pouring water over it. The refreshing aroma filled her nostrils, but did little to calm her anger.

Brie remained silent.

Rynah didn't know why, but Brie's demeanor bothered her. She sat down in front of the girl with her steaming cup of tea. "Hey."

"Hi," mumbled Brie, wishing Rynah would go away.

"What's wrong?"

"Nothing." Brie did not want to tell Rynah the truth. She knew how Rynah felt about her homesickness and just wanted to be alone until it passed. Unfortunately, Rynah refused to be accommodating.

"You're homesick again, aren't you?" The words pierced the air the way a person stabbed another.

"Well, yes, but I'll be fine," said Brie. She lifted her head, realizing that Rynah had no intention of leaving her alone.

"Sure you will," scoffed Rynah, allowing her bad attitude to mar the situation.

"What's your problem?" challenged Brie.

"Nothing."

"Horse manure," said Brie. "You have been on my case since the day I first arrived here. Always riding on me, belittling me, cutting me down. What did I ever do to you?"

Rynah sipped her tea. She stared at Brie with a callous expression, refusing to answer.

"And while we're here, why don't we talk about you," shot Brie.

"What do you mean?" Rynah's face went cold.

"Why are you here? You gave us that nice speech when we arrived about wanting to save your world and the planets of other star systems, but what is your real reason?"

"I don't know what you mean."

"Sure you do," said Brie, unsure of where this newfound confrontational attitude came from, but had seen jilted lovers before—high school was full of them—and Rynah's actions from the moment Brie had met her betrayed that part of her past. She read the tone of Rynah's voice every time she spoke Klanor's name—the distaste filled every syllable—and she knew more existed between them. "He crossed you. He betrayed you. He destroyed your home and used you to do it. Don't deny it! I see it on your face."

Rynah rose to her feet. "You do not want to go there."

"You are too frightened to go there," Brie also rose to her full height. "He betrayed you and you want revenge. That is your real reason for kidnapping all of us and bringing us here. You're just as selfish as he is."

Rynah slapped her.

Brie didn't move, refusing to acknowledge the stinging pain on her left cheek. "Sometimes I wish you had left me at home."

"You wish to go home," said Rynah. She snatched Brie's arm and dragged her away.

"What are you doing?" demanded Brie as she tried to pull her wrist from Rynah's grip.

"Giving you what you want." Rynah's long strides hurried down the corridor to the transport room with Brie in tow.

"What do you mean what I want?"

Once at the transport room, Rynah stopped and whirled Brie around until they faced each other. "Since the moment you stepped onto this ship, all you have done is whine about how you wish to return home. You have been a useless complainer since. So here's your chance."

Brie stared at the platform in the room.

"Solaris, are you ready?" said Rynah.

"Yes, but if I send her back, she will never be able to return here."

"Fine by me," muttered Rynah.

"But…" began Brie.

"You want to go home, right?" said Rynah, her harsh tone quaking with a mixture of tears and fury. "Well, here's your chance. Go home. Get out of here! You've been nothing but useless since you arrived, so do everyone on this ship a favor and leave. The coordinates have been entered into the console pad. All you have to do is push the button." Rynah turned and left, feeling betrayed by Brie's constant desire to return home, though it was magnified by the fact that Obiah had left as well and she felt abandoned.

Alone, Brie stared at the button that would send her home. More than anything, she wished to return, but at the same time, she wished to remain—a heart torn in two.

"All systems are ready," said Solaris.

"Do you think I should leave?" asked Brie.

"It is not for me to decide," replied Solaris.

"That is not what I asked."

"I think what you need to ask yourself is what do you really want?"

"I thought I knew," said Brie, her hand hovering over the button. One push, that's all it would take and the dream would end. Or would it?

A muffled explosion sounded.

"What was that?" asked Brie.

The ship rocked to its side, sending Brie flying until she crashed into the wall, releasing a muffled grunt. Another explosion sounded, forcing Brie back to her knees when she attempted to stand. Blaring alarms pierced her ears.

"Solaris!" she yelled. "Solaris, what's happening?"

Brie crawled to her feet, holding onto a sturdy rail for balance as the ship lurched a third time.

"We are under attack," said Solaris.

Brie ran for the door, but another violent jerk sent her flying sideways as rubble crashed in front of the doors. Coughing, Brie sat up, her head pounding. She noticed the blocked door. She ran for it, using her scrawny (and boney) arms to move pieces of rubble the size of coffee tables—her muscles ached from the effort—and forcing her way through. Another jolt rocked the ship. Brie fell, landing hard on her rear end, where a terrible bruise formed.

Bleep! Bleep! Bleep!

Brie looked over at a computer console as words in red flashed on the screen; even she knew it meant terrible news.

Rynah bolted for the command center of the ship after the first missile strike. A bulkhead crashed in front of her. She dodged and skirted around it, not losing her balance or missing a beat. Another jerk of the vessel failed to send her flying across the floor. As the alarms racked her brain and ears, she pushed harder to reach the command center.

"What happened?" she demanded as she entered the bridge.

"Klanor," said Tom from the pilot's chair. "His ship dropped out of hyperspeed without our scans detecting him."

Rynah watched the holoscreen and the image of Klanor's ship as another missile left its tube and headed straight for them. "Brace for impact!" she yelled.

Tom steered the ship hard to port. Despite his efforts, the missile struck the intended target, damaging the ship's engines as its flaps tore away, and fire erupted from them in an inferno cone that stretched beyond Solaris' bow. Violent motions rocked the ship forward, sending Rynah over the railing and smashing Tom into the command console. Rynah hauled herself up just as her body (along with shards of broken paneling, pens, a cup, and a broken pipe) began to float.

"We're losing gravity!"

There was no response from Tom.

Glancing over, Rynah spotted Tom's unconscious form, blood trickling down his face. Despite the pain in her body, she pulled herself to the computer console; with one hand, she held onto the railing, while with the other, she punched buttons on the screen to restore the gravity field on the ship. She dropped to the floor. Relieved to have gravity again, though she knew it might not last, Rynah ran to Tom.

"Tom! Tom!"

"I'm alright," he mumbled as Rynah helped him sit up. "Just a small bump on the head."

Rynah examined Tom's dilated eyes and knew he had suffered a mild concussion. "Come on," she said.

"No," said Tom, "I'll be fine."

KER-PLANG! The space vessel rolled 360 degrees; Rynah clung to the metal railing that circled the command console, while clasping her other hand around Tom's arm. Groaning and creaking resonated around them as flashes of light filled the window, their bodies arched precariously (Rynah's grip on Tom's arm loosened from the strain) until the ship had righted itself. They plopped on the floor.

"What was that?" asked Tom.

Instead of answering, Rynah checked the holoscreen and gasped.

"What?"

"A ship just crashed into us."

"What?" said Tom, still trying to comprehend what Rynah had just told him.

"Solaris!" said Rynah. "Solaris, status!"

"All systems crippled," crackled Solaris' voice over the intercom. "Oxygen levels dropping. Engines are at a standstill." Solaris' voice stopped.

"Solaris!" yelled Rynah, worried.

"Intruders," came the ship's voice. "They are heading to the engines. Ship wi—"

"Solaris!"

No response.

"We lost her." Rynah tapped a holoscreen to get it to come up.

It fizzled to life, but threatened to go out. She searched through the ship's systems for a status report. *What is Klanor up to?* Infrared life signs appeared on her screen, indicating where the intruders were. *The crystal!* "Tom…"

"Go," said Tom. "Stop them."

Rynah raced out of the command center and down the corridor to the deck her quarters were on where she had kept the crystal. She had to get to it before they did. If she didn't… Rynah refused to think about what would ensue if she failed.

* * *

Klanor watched the holoscreen on the command deck of his ship—which was three times the size of Solaris, with state-of-the-art weaponry (cannons and a flamethrower) and a quad engine system—as destruction rained down upon the outmoded vessel before him. Specks of red, blue, and green flashed, illuminating the scowl upon his deep purple face, as his ships fired their laser guns, releasing their fury upon Solaris.

"They have boarded their ship," said Stein, referring to the group of men that Klanor had sent to board Rynah's craft.

A spacecraft, engulfed in flames, sailed past before imploding; Klanor stared at it, detaching himself from his emotions and his sentiments towards Rynah.

"Bring me the crystal," he said to Stein.

The man nodded.

"And, Stein, do not fail me again."

Stein inclined his head and walked off.

* * *

Solon hid behind a hanging sheet of the ship's ceiling—lights popped, showering him with red-orange sparks—as he watched three of Klanor's men, dressed in spacesuits (who had been aboard the vessel that had crashed into them) approach Alfric, who had taken a blow to the head after the last missile strike and stumbled in the corridor unaware of the approaching danger. Wondering what he could do, Solon watched in vain as Alfric shook his head, still dazed. An idea struck him. Solon snatched a broken bulkhead and chucked it at Klanor's men; it clinked on the floor as it landed near their feet. Just as he had hoped, they stopped, but it had also gotten Alfric's attention, pulling him from his confusion. One moved toward the metal chunk and picked it up.

With a furious battle cry, Alfric rose to his feet, raising his sword. The intruders shrank back in fear; having never seen a Viking warrior before, Alfric's infernal demeanor horrified them. They went for their weapons, but the Viking had proven to be too fast for them. Void of mercy, he struck each of them with his blade until they crumpled to the floor.

"Odin is not with you today," he boasted with pride.

Solon stepped away from his hiding place.

"Thank you, little friend," said Alfric as he slapped Solon on the back.

"We should find Rynah," said Solon.

"Agreed."

They ran down the hall, unaware that the group they had just killed were not the only intruders, for the ship had carried seven, and they had only stopped three.

Rynah darted through the corridor. *Boom!* Her feet stumbled as a cannon blast jolted the ship, shuffling until she regained her balance, Rynah focused only on reaching where the ship had penetrated Solaris.

She stopped.

A panel of the ceiling slammed into the floor behind her, almost touching her heels, but Rynah never wavered. She moved forward toward the enemy ship that had stabbed Solaris like a knife (her once unblemished design now scraped and torn, with smoke escaping its sides, filling the cramped area) and was amazed that it had managed to wedge itself in such a way as to prevent depressurization. Anger boiled within Rynah.

Zap! Disconnected and exposed wires hung above her, shooting sparks into the air.

"Solaris?" Rynah whispered, choking back tears at the thought of having lost the one connection to her grandfather. "Solaris, please, answer me."

"Sys—te—ms—ripp—intru—" sputtered Solaris.

Silence.

Rynah whirled around. *Whap!* One of the intruders, wearing body armor that also served as a spacesuit, punched her in the face, sending her reeling backwards. Rynah plowed into the side of the intruder's vessel, its scalding hull burning through her jacket. Stunned, she slumped to the floor and watched as the man disappeared (the crystal in his hand which he had stolen from her room) with his companion, who had been hidden by the mass of thick, black smoke.

"Engine ro—om." crackled Solaris' voice.

The two words floated through Rynah's muddled brain until she forced herself to focus. *Engine room.* Fumbling, Rynah reached out for anything she could use to steady herself; she settled on the enemy ship and hauled herself to her wobbly feet. *Engine Room!* Now fully alert, Rynah realized what Solaris had tried to tell her. She wiped the blood that trickled from her nose and raced through the hallway, ignoring the dangling, broken lights and exposed wires. She had to save Solaris.

Brie flung another steel plank aside in her vain attempt to get free of the murky (as half of the lights had burned out) transport room. Her heart fell when she looked at the lack of progress she had made. She glanced back at the screen as new symbols appeared. "Solaris, what does all this mean?"

No answer.

"Solaris?"

"My systems," crackled Solaris' voice, "have been compromised."

"Solaris, don't go!"

Moments of silence followed before Solaris returned. "Have re-routed power," she said, her voice clearer. "Those symbols indicate that my engines have been rigged to implode the ship."

"Implode? You mean destroy it!"

"Yes. I am sorry."

Brie studied the screen. "How do we stop it?"

"There is a way," said Solaris, her voice fading in and out, "but it is not advisable."

"Tell me!"

"Someone has to go directly to the computer console in the engine room and type in this sequence."

Yellow symbols popped up on the screen and Brie committed them to memory. "Understood," said Brie.

"But you only have minutes to reach it," said Solaris.

"Is there a way you can transport me directly there?"

"Possibly," answered Solaris.

"Do it."

"Brie, a person can only be transported a certain number of times before their body loses molecular stability and they die."

"Solaris," said Brie, her voice unusually stern, "will you, or will you not, help me get to the engine room?"

"I can transport you just outside the engine room."

"Do it then." Brie stepped onto the transport pad.

"Brie, the entire area is flooded with poisonous gas from coolant leaks. You will only have moments before you suffocate."

Brie understood Solaris' unspoken message. She glanced at the red button that would send her home. She could still do it. No one would ever know, except her.

"You still have time to return to Earth—to home," pleaded Solaris.

"That's the thing," said Brie, "I don't know why I never realized it before, but… I am home."

"I do not wish to lose you," said Solaris.

"I know."

Light encircled Brie as the transporter switched on. She felt her body dematerializing as it disappeared from the transport room, leaving Solaris alone.

"Good-bye, Brie," said Solaris.

Rynah ran for the open engine room as poisonous gas spilled from it. She had to get there in time if she were to save the ship and everyone on board. Beams of light appeared before her. Rynah stopped. Mesmerized, she watched as a figure materialized before her: Brie.

"What are…"

Brie took one look at Rynah, turned, and dashed into the engine room.

"Brie, no!" Rynah ran for her, but arrived just as the door sealed shut. They stared at one another through the round window with somber expressions. "Brie, get out of there! That place is full of poisonous gas!"

"I know you think I am useless," said Brie, her voice muffled by the glass, "but this is one thing I can do."

"Brie…" Rynah pressed the button to open the door, but Brie had locked it on the other side. "Don't do this. We can work something out."

"You were on your way here to do the same," said Brie. "I'm sorry, but they need you more than me." Brie left.

"Brie, no!" Rynah beat her fists against the door, desperate to open it. In the end, all she could do was watch, helpless, as Brie disappeared in the smoke-filled interior of the engine room.

Brie hurried through the room, past pistons, gears, and valves spilling steam, in search of the console screen Solaris had directed her to, her hand pressed over her mouth in a vain attempt to filter the toxic gas. Coughing, she whipped around, straining to see through the clouds of steam and smoke. She spotted it. Brie ran for the console screen. Racking coughs shook her body; the toxic gas burned her throat and lungs with each breath. Brie tapped the screen, typing in the sequence Solaris had shown her, but her tear-filled eyes from the sting of the fumes prevented her from putting it in correctly. *Beep!* An error message flashed across the holoscreen.

"Curse it," she hissed. "Wrong one."

Brie typed in the sequence again; her eyelids grew heavy and her breathing shallowed from the noxious atmosphere.

"Stay awake," she told herself.

The console bleeped again. Frustrated, Brie smacked it with her fist as she racked her brains to remember the sequence. It hit her. Fueled with the memory, she furiously tapped the holoscreen, which was covered in condensation, as she put in the sequence to stop the engines from imploding. A pleasant beep told her she had succeeded.

The whirring drum of the engines overheating stopped as they returned to their normal state. Relieved, Brie watched enthralled as the engines reversed and roared back to life, but her moment of victory remained short-lived. Encased in gaseous fumes, her lungs felt as though they had caught fire. Each cough pained her cracked throat and overworked diaphragm. Stumbling, Brie latched onto the side of the wall for support. More coughing ensued until she dropped to the floor unmoving. The last thing her eyes saw before they closed was emerald hair.

Rynah had managed to open the door to the engine room. She grasped Brie under the shoulders and hauled her out. The poison attacked her lungs with each breath. A dark form loomed before her.

"Help me," pleaded Rynah.

Alfric bent low and scooped both Brie and Rynah into his arms as he carried them out into the corridor where Solon waited.

"Tom," Rynah shouted over the intercom, "get us out of here."

The ship lurched as Tom put it into hyperspeed and far away from Klanor's men.

"How is she?" Rynah asked, referring to Brie.

Solon shook his head. "I am sorry."

Overwhelming guilt for her earlier words with Brie struck Rynah as she slumped against a splintered wall. *Why*, she thought, *why her?*

Chapter 27
GOOD-BYE

A somber mood enveloped everyone on the deck of the ship as they gathered in the torpedo room and stood erect in a circle around a missile casing, which had been hollowed out and fashioned into a coffin. Its black siding mirrored the emotions of those gathered. Solaris, though back online, refused to associate with the others, her sadness as deep as theirs. The loss of Brie left a vacant hole that none could fill.

Brie lay in the casing; her mousy brown hair framed her fair skinned face. Her closed eyes gave the appearance of being asleep.

"We gather here to say farewell to a member of this crew," came Rynah's hollow voice. "Member… listen to me talk as though she meant nothing." Rynah choked back a tear, remembering that her last words to Brie had been cruel. "Brie never wanted to be here, but I yanked her from her home for my own purposes anyway. My selfishness is what killed her. But that is not how she would have seen it.

"People think that real courage is running into a fight. Well, that may be bravery, but true courage is putting your fears aside. Real courage is giving your own life so that others may live.

"Brie had her fears, and many times, I scolded her about it, but what I never told her, or anyone, is that I shared the same fears. In the end, Brie showed more courage than I will ever possess. She did what was necessary to save us all, even at the loss of her own life. You will be missed, Brie."

Once Rynah had finished, Alfric stepped forward. He looked upon Brie's still form in the tube, his stern face had softened and portrayed his grief. He took the talisman (a simple pendant with a rune on it) from around his neck and placed it in Brie's cold hands. "May Odin welcome you into his halls."

Tom and Solon remained silent. There was nothing for them to say.

Rynah closed the tube encasing Brie's body. Together, the four of them lifted the coffin into the torpedo hatch and sealed it. Rynah pulled the lever. With a whoosh, the missile casing with Brie's body jettisoned into the empty vacuum of space. Rynah glanced one last time at the others before heading for the command center of the ship.

"I am sorry, Brie," whispered Solaris with remorse, but no one heard her.

* * *

Floating among pin pricks for stars in the desolate cold of space was a single missile casing: Brie's coffin. Days had passed since it had been deposited there and before a lone vessel, the size of a space station, appeared next to it, having detected the coffin on its scanners. Using a tractor beam, they captured it, bringing it aboard their ship before jumping into hyperspace, and disappearing just as fast.

The story continues in book 2: Solaris Seeks.

The adventure continues in
book 2 of the Solaris Saga

About the Author

Ms. McNulty began writing short stories at an early age. That passion continued through college until she published her first book: Legends Lost: Amborese under the pen name of Nova Rose. Since then, she has gone on to publish a mystery series, children's books, and even a dystopian series.

Ms. McNulty currently lives in West Virginia, where she enjoys hiking, being outside, crocheting, or simply sitting around and doing nothing. She continues writing and is busy working on the next book in her Solaris Series.

The Solaris Saga

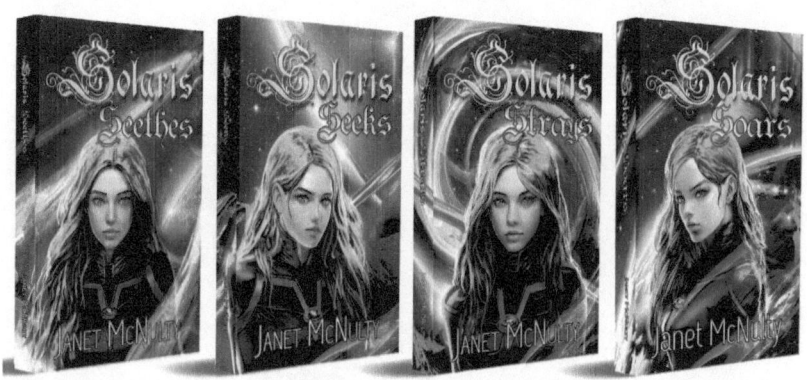

Solaris Seethes
Solaris Seeks
Solaris Strays
Solaris Soars

Every myth has a beginning.

After escaping the destruction of her home planet, Lanyr, with the help of the mysterious Solaris, Rynah must put her faith in an ancient legend. Never one to believe in stories and legends, she is forced to follow the ancient tales of her people: tales that also seem to predict her current situation.

Forced to unite with four unlikely heroes from an unknown planet (the philosopher, the warrior, the lover, the inventor) in order to save the Lanyran people, Rynah and Solaris embark on an adventure that will shatter everything Rynah once believed.

More by Janet McNulty

The Enchained Trilogy

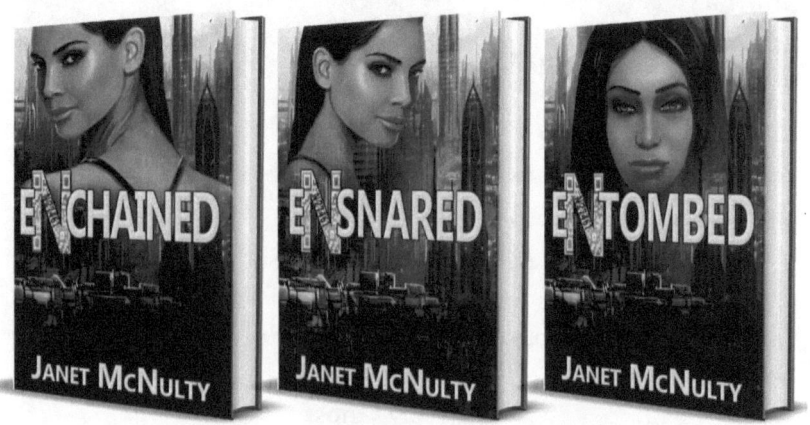

Enchained
Ensnared
Entombed

In Arel, weakness if failure, failure is death.

Dana Ginary lives in a world where every aspect of her life is controlled by the Dystopian Government. Forced to work in Waste Management, her life becomes a nightmare with hunger and survival is her only constant. Before she knows it, she is caught up in a resistance movement and exiled from Dystopia, forced to find her way in the barren wastelands. While there, she must learn to live independently and discover how far she is willing to go to live and achieve freedom.

The Mellow Summers Series

Sugar And Spice And Not So Nice
Frogs, Snails, And A Lot Of Wails
An Apple A Day Keeps Murder Away
Three Little Ghosts
Oh Holy Ghost
Where Trouble Roams
Two Ghosts Haunt A Grove
Trick Or Treat Or Murder
Roses Are Red…He's Dead
Double, Double Nothing But Trouble
Ring Around The Rosy, Not ANother Ghosty
Hickory Dickory Dock, The Ghost In The Clock
Violets Are Blue, More Trouble Brews
Hey Diddle, Diddle, The Zombie In The Middle
Easy As Pie, Until Someone Dies

Mellow Summers moves to Vermont to attend college, accompanied by her friend Jackie. They soon find themselves running into ghosts and one mystery after another.

The Dystopia Trilogy

 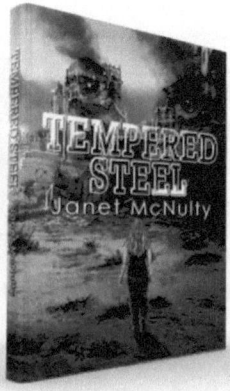 

Dystopia
Tempered Steel
Liberty's Torch

**Imagine living in a world where
everything you do is controlled.**

Dana Ginary lives in a world where every aspect of her life is controlled by the Dystopian Government. Forced to work in Waste Management, her life becomes a nightmare with hunger and survival is her only constant. Before she knows it, she is caught up in a resistance movement and exiled from Dystopia, forced to find her way in the barren wastelands. While there, she must learn to live independently and discover how far she is willing to go to live and achieve freedom.

The Legends Lost Series

Published under Nova Rose

Tesnayr
Amborese
Galdin

Enter the Lands of Tesnayr and join on an epic fantasy adventure that spans over 1,500 years.

Begin with Tesnayr, the first king of the five lands as he unites the against a savage foe bent on their destruction.

Next, Join Amborese as she fights reclaim the throne after her family was forced to flee from it.

Thinking peace has finally entered the land, follow Galdin as he returns to Tesnayr to find it greatly hanged. Barbarians, led by a mysterious sorcerer, burn and destroy as they go. And only Galdin can stop them if he chooses to accept his fate.

Visit www.legendslosttrilogy.com to learn more about the Legends Lost Trilogy.

A Little Something For Kids

Mr. Chili Books:

Mr. Chili's Chili
Mr. Chili Goes To School
Mr. Chili's Halloween
Mr. Chili's Christmas

Others:

Mrs. Duck and the Dragon
The Hungry Washing Machine
Rhymes-a-lot
Are You the Monster Under My Bed?
How Do You Catch An Alien

Grandpa's Stories

My grandfather grew up in Arizona during the 1920s and 1930s. One week after the attack on Pearl Harbor he joined the Navy. During the summer of 2012, my mother visited him and recorded his stories about growing up, World War II, and his time as an employee at the Pacific Bell Telephone Company. This is the history of the 20th century as he lived it. These recordings make up this book. These are his words.